AFRIC...

DAVID HOPKINS trained as ~~~ but went on to write an~~ ~~~~~~~ ~~~~~ in Africa, Italy and England. In between, he started and ran a small cinema and film festival, and published a magazine. Through his independent production company OCCAM he wrote and directed a four-hour adaptation of Shelley's *Zastrozzi* and wrote and produced the animation series *Sweet Disaster*, both first screened on Channel 4. He is currently producing another animation, called *Babel*, and is at work on another novel and two screenplays. He is also producer representative from the U.K. for the European Association of the Animated Cartoon. He is married to and works with Jane and has two children, Kate and Dan, who both work in the film and television industry.

AFRICAN COMEDY

DAVID HOPKINS

Flamingo
Published by Fontana Paperbacks

First published by William Collins Sons & Co. Ltd 1988
This Flamingo edition first published by Fontana Paperbacks 1989

Flamingo is an imprint of Fontana Paperbacks,
part of the Collins Publishing Group,
8 Grafton Street, London W1X 3LA

Printed and bound in Great Britain by
William Collins Sons & Co. Ltd, Glasgow

Contents

1	Loss	7
2	Brezhnev and Nixon	15
3	The Champagne Cocktail Party, Part I	20
4	Statue	26
5	The Kiss	30
6	The Champagne Cocktail Party, Part II	34
7	Revolution	42
8	The New Elizabethan Age	45
9	The Nuba Mountains	51
10	The Canals of Mars	57
11	The Red Sea	62
12	Home	64
13	The Proper Study of Mankind	70
14	The Minister of the Interior	79
15	The Sanity of Anthony Eden	89
16	Shrapnel	100
17	Lumbar Punch	107
18	Plankton	114
19	Blizzard	121
20	Annual Leave	132
21	Giant	140
22	Paradise	150
23	Spivs	160
24	Hell	168
25	Basic Design	177
26	Traitor	185
27	Empire	194
28	The Defence of the West	201
29	Theft	210
30	Optimism of the Will	217

1
LOSS

Michael lacked practical application. He was immersed in dreams; a post-war spoilt brat, fed on too much cream and bananas. He had no idea of the limitations and tragedies of life.

The gravel at the edge of the country lane crunched under his feet. Cold water ran out of the tarmac surface where springs were pushing underneath. A stream ran by the side of the lane where he, in a fury of contemplation, walked. Winter chaffinches fluttered in the cold branches along the lane.

DEAR MICHAEL, It's marvellous weather here. It hasn't rained for two years. There are grapefruits in the garden, bougainvillaea and petunias. The oranges are still green. We really do miss you. I do hope you've settled down now and it's not raining too much. Father has an equestrian bronze to do of the future Head of State. That will help, won't it? We were introduced to the Minister of the Interior yesterday at a party. He seemed interested but we didn't really know what to say to him. He had bits of white cheese round his mouth.

Our servant plucked a turkey yesterday and it walked about naked making a loud noise. Then they cut its head off and it carried on walking. It was terrible. We don't know what to do about servants. It's such a problem. Your father gets into a state about it.

We do hope you are getting on with your piano lessons. You couldn't really go to school here. Only the Americans have a school. Honestly they have frozen steaks flown in. No one really likes the Americans. They are definitely overconfident.

His feet were cold. He was alone, illegally, as Sunday walks were in twos with no exceptions. He had lost his companion on purpose along the top of the Downs, ducking down behind some bushes and running down the steep hill, slipping on the chalky winter mud, tears running down his face.

They had killed a cat. It was caught in a rabbit snare they had set. It was a careful snare placed exactly in a rabbit run, camouflaged with great skill and then left until the next day. Or had they placed it the Sunday before? The cat's eyes were wild and stared up at him. It was slavering; saliva bubbling around its mouth. He hit it over the head once and then again. He wanted to extinguish the sight of it. He hit again and again and crushed its skull. Its eyes stared up at him gyrating with pain. In other circumstances he would have loved and stroked it.

He had lost his penknife down the bole of an old tree. He had been carving at a fungus growing on the inside. His fingers numbed with cold and guilt had dropped it into the dark and hidden depths. There was no way to retrieve it. The tree would remorselessly grow around it. The knife would rust and become useless. Eventually when he was old the tree would fall and the rust would be only a slight red stain in the rotting wood.

The lane was silent as he walked. The only noise was the scrape of his shoes on the gravel and the slight moan of the wind in the dying branches of the trees. The sky was darkening, it was about four in the afternoon, and all around him seemed about to die.

At the end of the road was a large house, an estate with wire fences around it. In the house were Nazis left over from the war. They were not dangerous but spent their time in discussion or out hitting the grass with sticks, distant figures. He didn't believe it. It was an invention, a fiction only developed to start a pleasurable excitement, a *frisson* of danger.

He climbed through the wire fence, ignoring a large notice threatening prosecution. The turf was bouncy under his feet, the tufts of frozen grass rustled as he walked over them. The frostbitten landscape extended in front of him, a strange land with no known landmarks. The air made his eyes water. He rubbed them and blew into his cupped hands, his breath streaming out into the air. He kicked a molehill and forgot the eyes of the dying cat looking up at him. He felt warm in forbidden territory.

In front of him was an apple tree. All its leaves had long since fallen. But miraculously all the apples had remained, wrinkled and some shrunken, but still golden. He picked one and bit into it. The cold had concentrated the juices, frozen some of the liquid. His bite released an explosion of taste on his tongue. It ran into his mouth and into his throat, sweet and light, cold turned into secret pleasure. He would not be able to tell anyone. It was not a subject for his kind of fiction, his kind of lies and invention. It needed no explanation. It was complete and absolute. It included the past, present and future. It was the only thing happening to him at that moment, in that fragment of time.

In the distance was the sound of music. The fictitious Nazis were playing Duke Ellington.

The tree in the playground shot out green buds in the spring, but only in its topmost branches. The lower regions of the tree were gnarled and torn, hacked at with expressions of invented love and hate, satirical epigrams and formless ideograms of pure aggression. He hacked at the tree himself, bruising the bark with a stone, failing to impress upon it characters of any significance. He wounded it, a wound with a touch of green. The stone had cut his finger and a little blood had seeped into the edge of a fingernail. He sucked it.

The other side of the playground other, older boys were filling an upturned dustbin with coal gas from a red rubber tube dropped out of the window of the chemistry lab. He watched them, sucking his finger, not understanding what they were doing. They were looking over their shoulders not wanting to be seen. He didn't count.

He hated all bells, the school bell, the church bell. Sirens of any sort made him shiver because of the bomb that landed on the house next door, but bells would end his own time, his rights over himself.

9

Now five dustbins were successfully filled, if that was the right word. He could not work out what was happening. One of the boys was desperately striking matches over one dustbin, cupping his hands round the flame, then he ran off. His name was Hall, the son of a Chilean dictator. An exciting fiction.

The bell rang, he sucked his finger several times more to delay the moment, and wandered past the arbitrary row of upturned dustbins, noticing a small blue flame flickering at a hole in the base of each one. He wandered on unwillingly down dark corridors to his class.

Twenty minutes later he was standing up in his desk attempting to divide a large number, which he had already forgotten, by seven. The Maths teacher was snapping at him, hurrying him on, insisting on the importance of mental arithmetic. He was distracted by the green starting to appear in the top of the playground tree, and immediately afterwards by the sight of the Headmaster standing alone in the playground looking up at him through the window of the classroom. He began to panic. As his long and very public pause was at the point of becoming a subject of future detention, a scandal, an excuse for the teacher to improvise on the subject of the criminal distraction of his pupils, one of the playground dustbins launched itself into the air with an impressive explosion, flew past the window, crashed against the wall and fell with a tremendous noise back on to the tarmac surface of the playground.

He could see the Headmaster, red-faced, glaring with unreasonable aggression at the delinquent object rather than at him. A muffled cheer came from a classroom beneath followed by a murmur of suppressed excitement.

Then, on cue, destroying all mental arithmetic, further dustbins rose into the air with their associated explosions, watched with increasing horror by the distant Headmaster, confronted as he was by crimes without a visible criminal, the contradiction of all reasonable behaviour by mundane objects, and not least a public humiliation.

The Headmaster swept away, temporarily defeated, his

10

black academic gown flicking irritably behind the hedge along the playground. The last dustbin threw itself into the air as he left. The Headmaster's face could be seen peering through the hedge where Michael was still standing looking down at him from his desk by the window. In his face was a look of fear.

Adults loved you and left you. They had stopped being children. But when the rules changed, as rules always did and without consultation, they were afraid. Then they were children again, but dressed as adults. They were absurd.

He had seen the Headmaster once through the window of his study staring down at the contents of his emptied drawer now spread out on the table. It was a collection of more or less sophisticated water-pistols, small black rubber bulbs, bright plastic guns with the reservoir in the grip, multi-shot machine-guns, bags of sweets, worn copies of *Health & Efficiency* and a few American comics, peashooters and catapults. In a rack was a collection of canes, some split at the ends, some thin and whiplash. Behind him was a picture of himself, an oil painting. He was wearing the black academic gown with a red hood, a picture of the future Headmaster.

Just before Michael had to move away for fear of being seen, he caught a glance of pure hate between the portrait of the future Headmaster and the present one. They hated each other. Michael passed on wondering what was expected of him, picking at the black armband sewn on to his grey flannel jacket.

DEAR MUM AND DAD, Something happened in church last Sunday. It was one of those things that changes everything. As we were coming into church the organist was playing one of those pieces with mixed-up hymns he plays before the service starts. Suddenly he died. There was this choking noise and he threw up his arms over the keyboard and came down bang with a loud chord. He was lying right over the keyboard, both arms, the top of his body and his head, all playing notes and chords which went on and on booming round the church. I had a good view. For a long time no one did anything they were so shocked. The chord went on and on . . . Then they pulled him off and, as they did, his hands ran down each level of the keyboard and his fingers played notes at each level. His last finger played one note and then slipped off. We have had to wear black armbands all week and we can't run in the corridors otherwise we get punished. Everyone is very excited.

Michael sat down very carefully on to his chair. The Maths Master slammed a book down loudly on his desk and proceeded to write in chalk on the blackboard.

Michael was beginning to understand that life itself, and death too, was forbidden.

The unfamiliar landscape that lay in front of him, the frostbitten trees that he had not seen before, the distant sound of moorhens, the darkening sky full of the threat of night, was the reason he had to walk that way, stumbling over the molehills, aiming for no place. His flannel trousers were torn, his shoes thick with mud. He was making up the rules.

He fell into the darkness and was found the next morning curled round the bole of a tree, cold but alive. The Nazis took him back to school in a Jeep.

During the night, which was full of birds and numbing cold, his mouth was full of the taste, the acid sweetness of the apple he had eaten.

School was teaching him a strange alchemy: the transformation of conventional knowledge into the techniques of resistance. The fact that coal gas in certain proportions mixed with air made an explosive mixture: that there were substances that were so volatile that they had only transitory existence. These vital facts were written into the footnotes of old and discarded chemistry textbooks, now left out of the conventional syllabus.

DEAR MUM AND DAD, Please stop my piano lessons. Every time I make a mistake the music teacher hits my fingers with a ruler. Soon I won't be able to play at all because my fingers will swell up. I said something wrong in French to our new French teacher and he thought my parents were dead. I can't remember what I said but he suddenly became very kind and didn't give me any more tests. I've still got the Camembert cheese you gave me. It really smells so nobody sits next to me at tea. I like the smell. The latest craze is flicking beans on the ceiling and collecting cheese labels. The point is that you take bets on how many days the beans will take to fall down. I'm glad Dad has a statue to do. Does the Head of State really ride a horse? We don't have turkey to eat here – it's mostly fried bread, beans and porridge.

He decided to write the history of Africa, to make it up, to ignore all other geographies and histories, to write the history of a continent into which all disappeared and were perhaps never found again. His parents were somewhere in the middle of a million square miles of desert that was grey and white and yellow and that shifted and billowed from its own volition ignoring all else. The sense of loss shifted its place and became a source of energy and identity.

Nitrogen passed over pure crystals of iodine will in time and if heated sufficiently produce a compound called nitrogen tri-iodide – a violet and violent crystal that if dropped on the ground explodes, producing an exquisite puff of iodine vapour. It is a transitory compound, existing only in the laboratory and only useful for its clear demonstration that the elements are not all as impervious as granite. So it was with his fictions. They were strategies and tactics to hold at bay the mysterious aspirations that were his inheritance. His mother's name was Violet.

Africa could not be owned. All were lost in it.

After lights out in the dormitory there is a period of alert silence anticipating the House Master listening outside the door. He slips away lighting a pipe. After a time, deep in beds, private activities begin. Small radios are switched on, torches illuminate the spaces between sheets and the voices of Connie Francis and Ruby Murray percolate the hospital corners of the red-blanketed beds: there is the soft crackling of comics.

Then, out of the lumpy inhabited beds, starts an intermittent stream of chatter and the flashing of torches around the dark beams of the dormitory. In the darkness a space of freedom emerges, a collective mode of fantastical speech where the rules of the day no longer hold: tricks, boasts, games and gossip. It continues on and off. The illicit sounds rise and fall until the participants, one by one, drop off to sleep. One pair of eyes stays open blinking in the dark.

'My father has a map of the world. Not a real map but one in his head. It doesn't hang on the wall. It's not geography. The Chinese are damned clever, the Syrians are black-hearted, the Greeks are dirty, the Egyptians are filthy, the Germans are bloody awful and so are the Cypriots, the Sudanese have a marvellous sense of humour . . . the French, the French don't exist, neither do the Swedish. The Russians are bloody secretive, the Americans are bloody awful and overconfident, the Lebanese are not to be trusted. I can't remember if the Greeks are dirty or filthy . . .'

He went to sleep immersed in an imaginary Africa in which all white men were lost. That was where he was at home.

14

2
Brezhnev and Nixon

His imaginary Africa was real to him, like a memory; it
stretched out to each horizon, a flat desert full of incidental
winds and flurries, whipped sand and immemorial rocks,
black granite boulders and tebeldi trees with soft pink
flowers.

The African horizon formed a circle, the curve of the earth's
crust sliced through, the top off a gigantic egg. All the way
round the horizon was a circular mirage, a shifting, merging,
encircling but distant image of water and trees that existed
nowhere but in the imagination of simpletons.

The white-hot surface of Africa was a giant flat saucer, not
quite stable, moving with the scanning of the eyes, tipping
perhaps a little this way or that, giving, despite its vivid reality, a sense of insecurity. This was only to be expected. An
imaginary Africa, properly constructed, is less solid than
what is called the real world, the world of men and jobs, the
world of achieved and realized aspirations, the closeness and
clearness of familiar objects, the calm assumptions of habit
and adulthood.

Above this burning, barren Africa was the sun: a white-hot
hole in the sky that burnt the flesh exposed to it. Even the
blue of the arch of sky around it was bleached to an almost
pure white. The pupils of imaginary eyes contracted to tiny
points trying to take it all in, memorizing it.

Across the diameter of this huge, circular, flat Africa was
an exactly straight railway line. It began in a mirage and
ended in a mirage. It bisected the circle exactly, pleasing any
mathematician watching. A train rumbled along it at about
thirty miles per hour.

Inside the carriage was a white woman peeling an orange. She could have been his mother. She was throwing the peel at the tinted windows as though they were open to the air. The fragments of peel hit the window, dropped to the floor and accumulated. The air was stifling, a hypnotized air that glazed the eyes, slowed each thought and extinguished every regret. The smell of orange was sharp and bitter.

In the dining car Nile trout was being served. The taste of it was firm and full. A fan blew cool air across the eating faces. There was no conversation, an awareness that all was in transition, that the journey might not last for ever. There were white linen tablecloths and the distant mutter of servants. Sounds had a soft indistinctness as though they were being heard behind several layers of glass. All, from time to time, looked out the window at the mirage, a familiar glance, the mirage was a friend, only to be expected, explanations at the ready, a firm laugh, a turn of phrase, a secret touching of one-self to forget that this was not, in any good sense of the word, real. Everything, all appearances, just for the moment, were deceptive. It was something to do with the heat. Everyone remembered to keep up their intake of salt, and remember their relations in England.

There was the African sea. The hard blue Red Sea. It was an edge, a temporary end.

Nitrogen was all around them in the air, invisible. It combines under certain conditions with iodine, used as a disinfectant, to form a temporary compound. Then it disconnects leaving a puff of intense blue smoke that kills memory.

Suddenly it was night. The sky was arched, pierced with stars. From above, as if from a plane arriving, wishing to land, Khartoum was laid out in the form of an illuminated Union Jack, the main angles street-lit, traffic passing along them. Outside it was the desert, inhabited by kangaroo rats with wide nocturnal eyes, the mirage gone.

There was the crackle of an electrical storm, the sudden thump where a bolt had earthed, plunging into the sand turning it into glass. An extraordinary structure could be formed by the intense heat of the lightning, forcing itself into the molten sand up to eight feet deep. The molten sand, now glass, could be drawn out of the sand like an Arthurian sword. It could stand as a trophy on the veranda.

Across the town in a locked and bolted studio was an ancient brass tap elevated on a length of bent pipe dripping on to the top of an enormous and mysterious structure wrapped in damp sacking. It was about eighteen feet high, made of wood, metal and clay. It was the unfinished statue of a man on a horse, not yet ready to be cast in bronze. The damp sacking was wrapped round and round its legs and body, and again around the head of its rider who was sat upright, staring ahead blindfolded. Underneath the sacking the face was unformed, lacking eyes or a mouth. The tap dripped.

There was the scrape and crash of a door being forced, muttering voices and the resounding note of a sledgehammer against metal. The statue tottered as its supports were removed. Then it fell with all the unsupported weight of damp clay. The dark figures around it melted into the night. The tap dripped quietly on the chaos of clay and sacking far below.

Over the town came the soundtrack from the film *Spartacus* showing in the open-air cinema. Sitting on the veranda the white couple can hear the Christians being thrown to the lions, the roaring of the lions, the uprising of the slaves.

Someone is snoring down the other end of the dormitory, not engulfed by an imaginary Africa. Ignoring the sound, Michael sits up and talks in a persistent voice unwilling to be deflected.

'When you fly over Khartoum at night the street lights form the shape of the Union Jack. It was built like that. Avenues crossing one another, like that.' He crosses his two fingers. 'Like that! Khartoum is at the confluence of the White and Blue Nile. It was built by the English in the shape of the flag.'

'Shut up,' says a voice rising out of the gloom of the dormitory.

'A lot of the white women in Khartoum commit suicide. They throw themselves off the Omdurman bridge. The Sudanese have a boat that picks them up before they get eaten

17

by the crocodiles. The Nile crocodiles. You get trout in the Nile too.'

There is a pause. Most are pretending not to be listening. There are some exaggerated snores.

'I don't think they can stand all the cocktail parties. When they pick them out of the water the Sudanese laugh a lot.'

Sleep is advancing upon him too but he continues to talk in a wavering tone almost to himself, in a monotone, his voice being his own company.

'Every time a very important person comes to Khartoum all the white people go up to the airport and watch. They get dressed up for it and wear hats and have drinks as though it was the Queen coming. I don't think much else happens there. They get bored in Khartoum. Brezhnev, the Russian, came and they still came up to the airport to see him even though he was Russian and not the Queen.'

He took a deep breath and breathed out into the cold air. The dormitory was dark and his breath steamed out in front of him.

'The Sudanese had a fly-past with the Spitfires they had just bought. They had the pilots trained in Egypt so they had a new air force and were going to show it off. When they flew past, the two middle ones touched wings and they hit the outer ones and they all crashed. It was like a war film. Then they didn't have an air force any more.'

He got his foot out of the bedclothes and played with his toes.

'A Sudanese with a big smile opened the car door very widely for Brezhnev and he got in very slowly. Then he slammed the door and slammed it on Brezhnev's hand because he hadn't been quick enough. My father said the Russians jammed the Voice of America and the BBC for six weeks afterwards. It must have hurt a lot.'

He lay back in his bed and stared up at the beams above him. If you hung by your arms from one of them you were .supposed to break your arm within the week.

'Vice-President Nixon visited Khartoum. As he drove from the airport he threw out from his car hundreds of ballpoint pens. They had printed on them "Greetings from Vice-President Nixon" in gold. The Sudanese thought it was funny and threw them back. Somebody rolled under his car and was killed. Then a fight started.'

His eyes closed and sleep swept over him. The next day there would be clean clothes from the laundry. They came wrapped tightly in a towel.

Africa reappeared, a lost continent.

His mother stands in the desert next to his father. A huge white sun burns down on them. A kite screams overhead. There are other people around and cars parked at angles near and in the distance. A galvanometer is propped up in the sand connected to huge buried coils of wire.

His mother is talking.

'If I don't get back in the car I'll be ill.'

'It's hotter in the car, it will kill you.'

'Why have we been invited here?'

'They are measuring the magnetism of the sun.'

The galvanometer needle twitches.

By evening when they return home they find there has been a massacre and the Chief of Police has been cut open. Perhaps his head has been cut off.

Memories merged into prophecies.

3
The Champagne Cocktail Party
Part I

Violet's anger evaporated like a puff of smoke. The cream brocade had arrived from London. Brocade was not sold in the Greek haberdasheries in Khartoum. There you could only buy satin in violent shades of emerald green or amethyst. She had a fair skin and needed to wear something subtle. The dress had to be cut just at the knee and it had to be tight. She might have been out of England for eight months but she was not going to be unfashionable.

She sat on the veranda with the brocade on her lap, a cup of tea by her side. She flopped the brocade between her fingers, feeling the weight of it, judging its potentialities. She watched a white egret stalking through the garden poking with its sharp black beak under the lime tree. She could hear the servant polishing the floor in the house with a large cloth on the end of a broom. The floor was black polished tile and showed every speck of dirt.

It was early in the morning but still the heat caught her breath and made her lose concentration. She could hear the Pinochet woman next door shouting at her servant, followed by a metallic crash. Then there was screaming. Above the tree could be seen a column of black smoke. She had obviously overturned the huge and dangerous paraffin cooking stove yet again and was chasing the servant round the kitchen. The egret flew off, disturbed by the noise. Then it was silent again apart from a mysterious tapping noise that she could not place . . .

She could not understand the marriage next door. He was so small and academic, with a wisp of hair and a habit of exaggerated but ironic politeness. She was huge and flamboyant, dressed in violent colours and did not know her own strength. She was not English but came from some South American country.

At some point in the past it was rumoured that she had been his student. One of those academic seductions with the lecturers waiting at the beginning of each year for the new intake of flesh, she supposed. The Pinochet marriage next door was an awesome warning to them and perhaps to everyone. They were probably in exile. No one could possibly put up with them in England. She got a fit of the giggles and had to put her tea down quickly to stop it spilling on the brocade.

The servant put his head round the french door. 'Finished,' he said with a huge grin. 'Pinochet revolution next door, burn the house down next time.' He vanished without further comment but she could hear his deep laughter going out to his quarters at the back. She allowed him to have his wife there, most did not. They probably did not like the idea of sex happening on their premises, especially if sex was not happening in the main house. She was curious about his wife, his woman. She had seen her only briefly washing dishes by the tap outside. When the woman realized she had been seen she vanished as though she should not have been there. A glance passed between them. It was not clear what was the nature of this eye contact.

At the bottom of the garden was a hedge which ran along the edge of the irrigation ditch which in its turn ran along the road that led eventually into the middle of town. The hedge was thin and spindly and it was possible to see the white djelaberes of passing Sudanese through it. They were probably servants as it was a white district of large houses and gardens.

She was thinking of the champagne cocktail party they were going to that night. She would tell the story of the Pinochets and their servant next door. She would tell the story about the discarded brassière from her neighbour's more than ample bosom that her servant picked out of the dustcan, cut in half and used as a new and fashionable skull-cap with frills and boning. He appeared in this new attire, with swank

21

and bravado, at a large and pretentious party last week. It was a public humiliation of the first order and no more than she deserved. Of course, they were academics and their emotional life was bound to be in a mess.

There was more bitch in academic life than anywhere else in Khartoum. They were all the oddballs who could not make it socially in England because of their personal habits or their idiosyncratic theories or even because they were quite obviously completely crazy. She remembered the story of the Professor of Public Health who prowled about Khartoum on Hogmanay, drunk as a newt, visiting his friends he called it. One Hogmanay he crunched up the gravel of a 'friend's' house at half-past three in the morning. His friend, who was half-asleep, identified the huge noise he made as evidence of the approach of a noisy and unsubtle burglar. He got out a gun and shot him in the leg. Then he went back to bed and didn't think any more of it. The Professor of Public Health lay in the gravel drive until morning when his friend, denying all knowledge of the night before, took him off to hospital. From that time on these two and their wives were in a state of constant feud. They took every opportunity to demean the other's academic reputation, to invent or elaborate affairs the wives were supposed to have had, and to imply that the husbands were guilty of financial misdemeanours. The shooting incident was never mentioned. But things were like that here.

One could never rely on anyone, especially one's friends. In particular, and this is what she was worrying about, Ministers in the Government were especially difficult to deal with. There probably would be some of them at the cocktail party that night. They were important and, in some ill-defined way, held the key to the future. The future, to define that more precisely, was a house back in England and a little capital. After the Sudan became independent. Not until then.

The Minister of the Interior was the one to watch. He was the one who pressed white women close to his huge body at parties and who ignored the frightened glares of their husbands. He was the one, at the same notorious party, who fell back in a hopeless state of drunkenness off the veranda into

22

an empty plant pot. The host, it was rumoured, went back on the next plane to London. But nobody seemed to have any specific details. It was an awful warning that hung in the air, full of threat, but not providing any information that was of any use or advice on how to cope with embarrassing advances of this nature.

She felt a pang of guilt, identified it, and thought briefly of her son in England, and quickly of her husband, Thomas, teaching a group of anti-Government students. She dreaded him coming home full of the accumulated problems of the day and the appalling fact of his destroyed equestrian statue. He was an artist and should not be confronted with these kinds of problems. They were only trying to earn a little more money.

The problem was that the dress she was going to wear that night was not made. It was not even designed. She would not even consider going if it was not ready. She was happy to sew it up but the pattern cutting was beyond her. Why had they not sent a pattern from London? She had searched through the parcel for it but it was definitely not there. This was more than irritating, it was catastrophic. Her husband was a sculptor, he would cut out the pattern. He would have to move quickly, there would be no arguments about it. Either he cut out her dress or she would not go. She had another and sudden attack of perspective and giggled again. Then she noticed that the tapping she had been hearing all this time was the servant from next door banging on the shutters trying to attract her attention.

'What do you want?'

'She,' he motioned over his shoulder, 'sack me.'

'Oh!' She did not quite know how to answer this implied plea for help. Was he asking for a job?

'I already have a servant.'

'You need more servant?'

'Not just at this moment.'

'Your servant steal.'

This was worrying. They all knew each other and swapped notes.

'No he doesn't. He is very honest. It said so on his reference.'

'No. All reference written by expert in the market.' He then produced an identical reference to the one she had seen from her servant. She read it quickly.

'Very good. But we don't need another servant.'

'All servants on way to Mecca.' This fact did not seem to be a great contribution to the conversation. He followed it up. 'Need money.'

'We do not have enough money for two servants.'

'Very sad business.'

She was not sure if he was sorry for her or for himself.

'I'm very busy.'

'Busy but very poor white.' With this humiliating phrase he left and wandered up the path. She saw him go next door.

She had a panic. She had admitted that they did not have enough money for a second servant. It was fairly clear that he had not been sacked. Perhaps the Pinochet woman had sent him round to find out if they were as well off as they pretended. She went into a flat spin. Then there was an eerie screaming noise from next door and she heard the servant being ejected. He had been sacked. There had been no plot. She sank back into her chair and closed her eyes with relief. Then another thought struck.

She went out the back of the house, walked round the outside tap, round the grapefruit tree by the kitchen, and into the servant's quarters. There was no one to be seen. The bare room which she had never seen before was clean and empty. There was no sign of her servant or his woman. She was close to tears. Her servant had been stolen by the woman next door.

She walked slowly back into the house, anxiety raging. In the middle of the room was the servant from next door, wearing his unique skull-cap, polishing the floor with the broom. She was going to ask him what he was doing in her house but she decided not to. She walked straight through on to the veranda and sat down heavily where she had been sitting before. How was she to explain to her husband that they now had a different servant? Maybe he wouldn't notice. She could hear a grumbling voice from inside the house.

'White woman with one servant.'

Then there was a deep laugh. She blushed and could not think of anything brisk to say. She still had the problem of her dress. She thought about it and looked out into the garden. The egret was back. There was a man far down at the end of the garden with a spade digging away at the irrigation ditch. The water flooded into the garden and lapped comfortably at the edge of the veranda. 'Hey,' said the man with the spade and disappeared behind the hedge. She waved at him in a familiar way for reasons that were unclear even to herself. The egret hopped and skipped over the water picking at the surface with its long black beak.

4

Statue

Thomas rolled a ball of clay between his hands, squeezed it between his fingers, rolled it hard once more between his palm and the lower joint of his thumb. He pushed it on to the body of the clay horse just above the front leg. It made a satisfying bump, the implication of a muscle, the strength of the front leg.

The studio was dark apart from the brightly burning work lamps. It was quiet. The doors had been locked, a new and huge padlock on the outside. Away at the far end was a guard slumped drowsily against the wall. Thomas had employed him to look after the place when he had left. It was going to be much later that night.

The guard hummed to himself, his head to one side, looking aimlessly at the ceiling. He developed a rocking motion to go with his hum. His turban was shifted to one side and his eyes were half-closed and unfocused. To one side of him was a two-pint glass, empty apart from a thick crust of sugar and a number of insects stuck in it attracted by the sweetness. It had contained the juice of squeezed limes.

The clay slapped on to the horse. He used his aggression to force it into place.

The horse had been levered back into place, hoisted on a chain. The fallen slabs of clay had been scraped off the floor. He had started the process of reconstruction. He was not going to be put off, not going to be diverted.

He was sweating. The constant drip of the tap had made the air humid. Also he was angry. A vein stood out in his forehead. The tap dripped. The clay slapped.

In England, despite all its faults, there was a routine, a set of expectations, a deep conservatism that swallowed the unexpected, edged out the unpredictable, made each day appear a reasonable progression from the last one. In Africa, in Khartoum, it was different. Here every moment of progress had to be fought for with energy and determination. Eventually with desperation. There was the constant risk that whatever had been done would be destroyed in one's absence by factors that it was impossible and even dangerous to predict. The Sudanese sense of humour did not help. Confronted by this shifting sand of what was possible and what was not, they merely laughed. Perhaps their motivations were elsewhere, hidden and not to be shifted by the mere and incidental needs of practical life. Their lives were based on sarcastic theatre and, to him, impenetrable political talk.

Thomas had a sudden image of a Sudanese he had once seen through the window of his car. This tall thin man lay under the shade of a tree, one knee elegantly flexed, his transistor radio blaring, hooked by its plastic strap to a black finger. His tongue was sticking out open to the dry air. In the centre of it was a large, slowly dissolving pink sleeping pill, the sort that were fashionable amongst the insomniac European wives. His tongue was curled insultingly around it.

There was something about this sight that irritated him beyond measure. It was satirical, it *was* insulting, it threw into relief his intense work, his struggle to be conscientious. Also, even worse, it made the lives of all the white expatriates seem absurd: the expenditure of that universal and characteristic anxiety, homesickness, happening in the midst of the desert. He worked the clay between his fingers, forcing it into place, forcing it home.

The work on the statue generated images like dreams. The harder he worked, the more his body was totally engaged, the more intense the images. It was a sharpened memory of a trip he had made to the Northern Sudan.

The heavy, dusty green shutters of the train were slammed shut for much of the trip to prevent the white travellers seeing the poverty along the way. There was a famine in the North and most of the scattered occupants of the region had clustered along the railway line hoping for something, hoping for anything. In the dark and embarrassed recesses of the train, rocking slowly through the desert, their hands could be heard scraping and banging on the outside of the shutters. They were running along the line after the slowly moving train. He had wished, as had all the others, that it would move faster, that it would leave them behind. For hours the scraping and banging continued. Inside the train was a deeper and deeper nightmare, the pale white faces staring at each other not thinking, only enduring. He remembered it, but could not think what was the purpose of the trip. He stopped work and glanced at the sleeping guard.

The only thing to see in the Northern Sudan was the house of a long dead District Commissioner. He had built it close to the Nile and, in the way of the time, had an individual irrigation canal dug to supply his dwelling with water. Now the building was deserted, left like the *Marie Celeste*, unchanged. The water supply continued to water the lawn but it had grown wild and uncut, a neglected English garden in the middle of the desert. They had stood on the lawn bewildered. He had looked down and seen a single daffodil growing in a clump of grass. He had looked at it for some time.

The house was open, the doors banged in the wind. Nothing had been moved from the house. It was untouched and rotted quietly on its own as though it was the site of a past but virulent disease, avoided by all sane people.

The shutters were left open on the way back. Skeletal children ran along the lines for short distances shouting. The train left them behind and they disappeared, crouched black dots on the yellow and grey sand.

The guard made him another *limoune* and put in too much sugar. He stirred it with a long spoon, his eyes still only half-open, and handed it over with a gesture of condolence, as if the sculptor was subject to a great and terminal illness.

The horse and its unformed, its ill-defined rider loomed over them. Work was finished for the moment, for that night. He would return home leaving the security to the guard, who would stay there all night and protect the horse and rider from his students. Thomas could not grasp why for them his work was an insult.

He got into his Volkswagen and drove into the night avoiding the wobbling bicycles without lights that wandered into his path. To cool himself he hung one hand out of the car window and trailed it fingers open in the passing air like the Sudanese did. His hands were tired and ached from working the clay. The air was full of Arabic music blaring from radios in dimly-lit shacks and sheds.

He parked the car in his drive and sat silently for a moment. England seemed very distant. The lights were on in the veranda. His wife was waiting for him. The champagne cocktail party approached.

The guard swung a hammer knocking out the supports for the statue. It fell with a crash, then was held lopsided, caught in the chain from one of the hoists.

Quietly he went out of the studio and locked the door carefully behind him, weighing the padlock in his hand.

5

The Kiss

The glaring face of the Headmaster appeared from behind his lectern. He put on his glasses and looked out, nailing Michael with what seemed like a ferocious glance.

The last hymn was finished in evening assembly. At one side, a few feet away from the Headmaster and in full view of all the boys, was an ancient priest in white and black vestments with straggled white hair that stuck out either side of his face. He was sound asleep and snoring.

A ripple of giggles passed over the Assembly Hall. The Headmaster was hidden behind his lectern. He blew his nose loudly hoping to wake the priest. In return there was an even louder snore. At this point in the service there was meant to be a sermon, a regular event on Sunday evenings. The evident unconsciousness of the preacher seemed to make this impossible. There was an awkward pause while the Headmaster attempted to make up his mind what to do. Obviously, Michael thought, if he walks over and wakes the preacher there will be some time before the old man recognizes what is expected of him. There would be an opportunity for indiscipline. Someone, not him, would laugh.

The whole room appeared to be absorbed with the same problem, struggling with the possibilities, trying to think what they would do in the circumstances, attempting to think up the most entertaining next move. As if at a signal everyone began to cough. This had no effect whatever, only drowning the embarrassing noise of the snoring priest. Michael looked down at his feet, at the chalk that was still on his shoes from the Sunday afternoon walk. He tried to rub the chalk off with his finger.

There was a sudden change of mood in the Assembly Hall. The situation had forged a solidarity in the assembled company of teachers and boys. It had become a mutual embarrassment, with little or no opportunity for any kind of subversive move, confronted as they all were by the eyes of the Headmaster.

The Headmaster shuffled his papers, about to make a decision, stood up, and smoothed a sheet on the lectern in front of him. He had a better view from there. He eyed the assembled company, daring them to laugh. The priest shifted in his chair and suddenly let out a shout. 'Sanctimonious fool!' he shouted and disappeared back into unconsciousness. This intervention was so unexpected that it produced a deep silence, a heavy atmosphere of foreboding, a premonition that at any point the conspiracy that made the school function would collapse. Whatever dreams the priest was having might produce further outrages, however accidental. The Headmaster's face was bright red and, as if in sympathy, the more sensitive members of the assembly blushed too. The temperature in the room appeared to rise, collars began to be tight. Michael found he had a deeply-felt need to leave the room, to hide in the privacy of the lavatories.

The Headmaster glanced at the priest hoping to quell him with the ferocity of his look, to kill his dreams, to silence him. The Headmaster was acting on behalf of all of them. Michael could see the neck of the Biology Master in front of him growing redder and redder with each moment. The Headmaster began to speak.

'A number of disturbing items have come to my attention. They are matters of some weight . . .' He glanced across to the now silently sleeping priest. 'This will not be the usual passing on of information for you to ignore. I want you to listen, for I will not repeat what I have to say. For some of you this constitutes a last warning. Mind what I say. I will not tolerate certain kinds of behaviour.

'This school has a long history. As you know it was founded in the fourteenth century, an august establishment then run by the Church. The inventor of the division sign was taught here . . . the school has a tradition, a history . . . it has standards which I insist have to be kept up . . . standards which it appears are under threat . . .

'I am establishing a committee of prefects who will, in future, supervise all behaviour in the showers. There will be no repetition of certain disgraceful scenes reported to me. You will bear in mind that showers are a convenient means of cleansing yourself. Not an opportunity for depravity.

'On an unconnected matter, you may have become aware that the school has become a subject of attack. Louts, apparently from Brighton, have taken to attacking the school with, I believe, apples. Several windows have been broken. I discover, thanks to some research taken on by Mr Laker, to whom I am most grateful, that these attentions are due to the totally illegitimate presence of certain sixth formers in Brighton several weeks ago. Some rivalry has broken out.

'You will notice that some well-known members of the Sixth Form are not present tonight. They have been expelled forthwith. Take it as a warning. Some of you who are still here are walking on very thin ice. I refer you to the quite explicit school rule regarding conversations with young women. It is forbidden. The rules for the School Dance will have to be reiterated. If you wish, and this applies to the Sixth Form only, if you wish to invite a young woman to the Dance, then her parents should contact my wife and discussions will take place on the matter. That is all I have to say on this matter for the moment.

'Any future attacks on the school will be immediately reported to me and then totally ignored. Retaliation is forbidden.'

The priest let out a loud snore as if to emphasize the point. Michael, confronted with this set of moral paradoxes, contented himself with feeling mildly guilty, not personally but on behalf of anyone involved in these extraordinary events.

'We will be changing our hymn books next week from *Songs of Praise* to the *Public School Hymn Book*. This will mean that Hymn 123 will now become Hymn 437, Hymn 84 will become 189, Hymn 47 becomes 544 and so on. I'm sure you will soon get used to the change. You will leave the old hymn books at the back of the hall when you file out.

'I have had some complaints from parents that boys are not writing home on Sundays. Letters home will now be inspected before tea on Sunday and will then be posted. Please remember that duffel-coats will not be worn to church on Sunday morning.'

During these comments Matron had slipped down the side aisle and was now sitting close to the still sleeping priest. Another problem was about to arise. The visiting preacher was always escorted out by the Headmaster at the end of the service. The Headmaster could not walk out leaving the preacher behind. If he woke him up there would be problems as the time for the sermon had now passed. It was not a good time for misunderstandings. Matron with a fine exercise of native wit had found the solution. The sleeping preacher was, of course, ill and was therefore escorted with all due ceremony out the door by the woman who was concerned entirely with sickness and the more intimate needs of the school. The priest, who staggered a little, looked back at the Assembly Room and, as if he were still dreaming, shouted at them, 'Vicious little prigs!' As the priest passed, Michael caught a whiff of spirits on his breath. He was drunk. That explained everything.

Michael had kissed one of the village girls that afternoon. He still had the taste of her metal braces in his mouth. He had been rather disappointed with the whole experience. He was homesick for Africa.

6

The Champagne Cocktail Party
Part II

The invitations had gone out. They had been printed in the town in the style of a wedding card, flowery script and a large RSVP. The name(s) had been written in what looked like a schoolgirl's best handwriting.

The hostess was a tall willowy woman who had once been an anthropologist. Now, she dressed with the utmost formality in long evening gowns draped to the floor. Her interest in the many hundreds of dialects still existing in the Nuba Mountains had been long forgotten and she now concentrated on the development of her husband's career.

He was a physicist whose abiding passion was the measurement of the magnetism of the sun, its variation during sunspot cycles and other solar events. He was not at all interested in the development of his career and was an unwilling participant in the extended cycle of social events that his wife generated, seemingly on his behalf.

He was very happy doing what he was doing, laying giant coils in the desert and measuring the induced electricity thus created. Hs wife, even during these purely scientific operations, somehow managed to turn them into social events. Isolated parts of the desert outside Khartoum sometimes became the venue for picnics and drinks parties. The guests, who had no knowledge of or interest in the magnetism of the sun, drank and drank in the heat of the day and sometimes suffered heatstroke with its associated hallucinations after returning home.

Somehow she had the gift of making each of these social events essential, almost mandatory. There was a strong but hard to explain anxiety in the back of everyone's mind that if for whatever reason they were not to be seen at these events their careers would be mysteriously blemished, their expected salary increment would not be paid or, worst of all, their place in the academic hierarchy would be taken by a newly-trained Sudanese and they would be on the next plane back to England. This was based on no firm evidence: the hostess, nevertheless, continued to operate her mysterious power to a background of resentment and intense competition from those who wanted to take her place.

She managed, and perhaps this was the basis of it all, to imply that she had an unimpeachable source of information about what was really going on. Though nothing specific would ever pass her lips, the mere mention of a name in a particular tone would imply a series of sexual irregularities, an inclination of the head would imply a career prospect not to be fulfilled, a minute lowering of her eyebrows would imply the darkest of secrets that had been passed to her, probably by a member of the Government. This was the reason that her face was the subject of deep and intense but surreptitious scrutiny by all except her husband. If she had all this information then the only way of finding out was to decode her multiplicity of facial expressions. Over time this concentration on her every facial movement had made her, in anticipation of instant interpretation, unable to respond spontaneously to anything. She would, when not in a frenzy of organizational activity, stand on her veranda facing the garden, frantically exercise her face, open her mouth wide and issue a silent scream. Her husband, having once observed her in this condition, shook his head and wondered if he should return to England sooner than he had planned. He put off the thought to the end of his next experiment.

All over Khartoum, there was a frenzy of preparation. There was the Champagne Cocktail Party and there were all the other parties that had been swiftly organized by her rivals and those who had not been invited. The Greek drinks shops suddenly had their shelves stripped. There was not a single bottle of champagne to be found in the town, except perhaps in the American Embassy stacked away with their mountain of frozen steaks. There was a run on glacé cherries.

In other parts of Khartoum much more serious activities were taking place.

Violet could see from her position lying prone on the cold surface of the table that the servant was watching, lurking in the dark outside the door to the veranda. He was craning his neck attempting to work out what was happening. She had insisted that her husband cut out her brocade dress for the party that evening. It had resulted in a flaming row, he had thrown an ashtray in the opposite direction to her that had made a dent in the wall, she had screamed at him loudly, but not so loud as to be heard next door. Now they were both silent. He was cutting out the cream brocade to the shape of her body, treating her as the pattern for a three-dimensional piece of sculpture. A great deal of time had been lost. It was already getting dark and the party started at nine. She still had to sew the garment and make sure that it fitted.

The light that he was using to work by was on the floor. It shed a magnified image of them both on the wall. He with a huge pair of scissors, she reclining. It appeared in the shadow play that he was cutting her body into pieces.

'Keep still,' he said as she giggled. She did as she was told, having won the argument and demonstrated, without fear of contradiction, that none of the other dresses she had in her wardrobe would be possible or sensible for her to wear.

'Bloody Greek importers are making a fortune.' He was alluding to the cream brocade and to the cost of its importation. 'You realize it's all one family, don't you? They have it tied up.'

'I'm not interested in the Greeks. I want to get this dress finished. I've still got to have a bath.'

The hot water for the bath came from a water tank fixed high up on the roof. The water heated during the day and could then be used pleasantly warm in the early evening. Later on it had to be supplemented by an electric water heater. As the electrical connections for this heater were now in a dangerous state it could not be used, so if she were too late the bath would be cold. It was more the idea of a cold bath that disagreed with her, its actuality was quite pleasant. Baths should be hot, that's how they were meant to be.

She could still see the servant watching, perhaps waiting for a repetition of the previous loud scenes. The servants depended, she knew, on the strange theatre of the family rows of the whites. They surely swapped notes on the drama and the action they observed from their privileged position. One was forced to trust them. There was no alternative.

She waved a hand awkwardly at the servant. The hand movement was trying to tell him to go away, to brush him out of her sight. It had the opposite effect. He came in the room eager to have the opportunity to have a closer look.

'Guns,' he said as an item of factual information. 'Guns firing in the town.'

'I can't hear anything,' said her husband.

'Massacre,' said the servant.

'Go away.'

'Upturn the apple cart,' said the servant with some pride.

'Get away,' she said through gritted teeth. She did not like being in front of the servant in this peculiar and humiliating position. She was also worried that her husband might notice that he was not the same servant they had had the day before. She had not tried to explain the situation that had arisen next door.

The servant wandered away offended. He kept in view, slowly polishing the tiles on the veranda with the broom with a rag stuck on to it. She could hear him muttering to himself, 'Massacre.'

For some reason while she was lying there she found herself idly thinking of her brother who was nearly killed on the last day of the Second World War. He was shot by his own side as he was driving out of the gates of the Company stores with a car full of contraband Forces watches. He had omitted to acknowledge the shouts of the guards at the gate and they had immediately opened fire. What had she forgotten to do?

As she lay there on the table she was thinking of the black market, the illegitimate way of making money. She remembered the spivs in the war, making profits while the others were fighting. Was her life exciting? Or was it a struggle without any virtue, without vision? Was it a sly mean struggle with tiny triumphs and great failures, the compensatory attempts to be important? For money only? Perhaps a little status? She could not make up her mind just then. The table was comfortably cool . . .

She had married an artist because that was interesting and worthy. Now, were they spivs? No, they were unsuitable people for this role, they would be unhappy in it. They were not stripped of all they felt to be valuable. They, whatever the difficulties, made the best of it. She would walk out on to the veranda in the morning and say ritually to herself, 'It's another lovely day.' Her husband would remind her before going off to work that it had not rained for two years. It was a joke between them.

Later that evening she was sewing the dress. Her husband was attempting to mend the connections on the water heater so she could have a hot bath. The sewing machine that she had brought from England rattled and clattered. It was now dark and they had little time before the party started. They were not talking to each other.

The servant stood in the door looking at her. She felt there was something sinister, something resistant, in his gaze that made her feel uncomfortable. He drifted away leaving an emptiness, something unsaid. But she did not have time for enigmatic arrivals and departures.

The dress fitted. It was a little tight but it fitted. She smoothed the seam she had just sewn.

She went to have a bath, taking a last look at the dress on its hanger. Her husband had given up the attempt to mend the bathroom heater and was doing something angrily to the car outside in the drive. He was worried about the sand getting into the engine. Perhaps it was the *haboob* coming.

A *haboob*, a great wind that raised the dust of the desert and carried it in great clouds into the town, was due. The first signs of it were apparent: a fresh wind and an unaccustomed drop in temperature. The tops of the trees in the garden were moving. She could hear him swearing over the car outside. He would not have much time to get ready.

Not long after she squeezed into the Volkswagen with some difficulty because of the tightness of her dress. They drove in preoccupied silence through the town. It seemed to be quiet. No sign of guns. No massacres. The new material against her body made her feel better and more content. She must not be too talkative, especially after a few drinks. That was dangerous. Too much hidden resentment might be exposed. She giggled. Then they would not be asked again and would sit rejected alone in their house. She told herself how childish it all was. When they got back to England they would be adults again.

The reason why they had been asked to the party this time and not before must be because of the equestrian statue. A direct link to the Head of State. It was, of course, and a thumping anxiety started to give her a headache, not a commission that had any written contract. It had come through an intermediary. At least he was supposed to be coming tonight. Then a real contract could be organized which included a proper but not exaggerated fee. That would be a step in the right direction.

There was nothing wrong with the party. She found several friends there. There was the girl (was she still a girl?) who always dressed in the uniform of the Polish Resistance. There was the man who dressed in Nazi uniform. They either hated each other or, equally likely, loved each other. Everyone knew them. They were a theatrical reminder of Europe.

The champagne glasses were carried round on trays. Each had a stick with a glacé cherry impaled on it. She drank several of them, relieved that the party was really quite pleasurable, her dress had been admired and envied, and even the hostess's face had indicated, if she had got it right, that her performance was entirely appropriate and apposite and perhaps they might even be friends. There seemed to be some talk about a coffee morning and sharing a few secrets and a complimentary reference to her husband and his exciting work and the great difficulties for creative people working in

39

Africa. The colours of the dresses around her merged a little and became an exciting blur. She stood her ground, only a little drunk, her legs crossed. Her husband was only just across the room having a serious conversation about, she thought, public schools in England. It seemed, after all the anxiety, to be a success. Then she found that she could not uncross her legs.

The brocade dress was tight when she was cool. It had now become a little damp and perhaps it had shrunk. In any case the hem of the dress had become a tight band round her knees. She could not move at all. She was, at the point of this discovery, having an animated conversation with a Sudanese civil servant who she fondly believed held the key to her husband's future in the Sudan. He also appeared to be rather handsome.

She was astonished to find that, having discovered her predicament, her own feelings towards the Sudanese she was talking to rapidly changed. She was trapped into a conversation she did not want. He had a strangely cold eye which she found repellent. She wanted to get away. She smiled at him and stopped listening to what he was saying. She was holding a champagne glass out in front of her with one hand and attempting to motion, to signal to her husband with the other. He would not come. The Sudanese seemed to be getting progressively uneasy. She was not sure if this was because of her or because there was something about the absence of the Minister, the guest of honour, which was causing anxiety.

Her husband and the expert on English public schools carried her by her elbows through the nearest door into a bedroom. Then she was alone with her husband, who seemed to be very angry and anxious. She still could not move her legs. Even more irritating was the fact that there was no other door out of the bedroom. They would have to go out the window.

He pushed open the window and looked down with horror. The newly-irrigated lawn was fresh with black Nile mud.

He stood in the centre of the lawn lost in the darkness holding his giggling wife in his arms. His white evening dress was splattered with mud as was the brocade of her dress.

There was a gunshot and the path to the house was full of soldiers carrying guns. There was screaming from inside the house and a body was carried out. It was the Sudanese she had been talking to. They crept out through the hedge and he fed her stiff body into the narrow door of the Volkswagen. As they drove away she giggled once more. Thomas, her husband, was not talking to her.

7

Revolution

Thomas had spent the whole night awake, walking about the house, turning over the events of the past evening in his head. First he was in a fury, an uncontrollable rage. He broke glasses, pots and ashtrays. He overturned the heavy terrazzo table with the iron frame. The rage was succeeded by a silent cold fear: each noise in the house becoming a premonition of a further catastrophe.

His frail cycle of normality was broken, there was, now, no knowing what could happen. His fear about the state of his career was quickly overwhelmed by a fear about his physical survival, a fear of death. He had become unravelled. The delicate web of politenesses, diplomacies and repressions necessary for survival was laid waste.

It had been cumulative, not just one event but many humiliations over the last twenty-four hours . . . He had crunched his hands together in the darkest part of the night, the trees blowing outside, attempting to reform, to reconstruct, a personality that would be able to cope with future catastrophes.

Now he was sitting in an unstable wooden chair in the early morning in his studio staring at the devastation caused by the fallen statue.

It seemed peaceful outside. There was the screaming of a black kite high in the air, wheeling over the desert looking for small animals or carrion.

He could still feel the effort of lifting his wife through the door of the bedroom. He and the education adviser had taken her by her elbows and, while pretending to carry on a conversation, had carried her a little at a time towards the door. It seemed, at the time, that they had not made too much of a diversion. They were trying to be inconspicuous. His wife continued, even while she was temporarily airborne, to smile and converse as though nothing had happened. She had had far too many cocktails.

The educationalist was using an expression of professional concern when he caught sight of a soldier standing outside the window holding a gun. Throwing caution to the winds, they had lifted up the cream brocade dress and its occupant and hurried her into the bedroom. The educationalist had then slipped back through the door and closed it quietly. Husband and wife had been left together.

Thomas had not seen the soldier in the window. He was reacting to an investigative glance from the hostess who had, at that moment, noticed that his wife had her feet mysteriously off the ground. It was that glance that he had caught. He had only afterwards seen the armed soldier through one of the bedroom windows when he was peering through the shutters to see if the coast was clear.

He blocked out the rest of the evening. The present was painful enough.

He had talked earlier that morning to his servant. After they had discussed the *fait accompli* of exchanged servants with next door and he had come to terms with his new servant he had been told, or rather it had been explained to him as though he was a simpleton, that the Sudan now had a new Government, a new prospective Head of State. His mind was blurred from the night before so he had to spell it out to himself. His attempt to make a little extra on the side by the construction of the equestrian statue had failed just at the point when it was within sight of completion.

He had walked up the path to his car with a feeling of elation, he had been let off the hook. He was free of his own soured project. He would not have to barricade himself in his studio night after night. He could plan his students' trip to the Nuba Mountains, apply for jobs back in England, order a new series of art books from Zwemmer's.

Looking at the devastation of his work in the studio

reduced him to mental silence. Sand blew through the door. The *haboob* had begun.

As he was driving through the town the sand was blowing in waves across his path. Figures scurried in front of him with cloths and scarves over their heads running for shelter. Soon the whole town was enveloped in the dust storm and vanished from sight.

DEAR MICHAEL, I'm afraid that your father's statue of the future Head of State hasn't worked out. First his students broke into the studio every night and broke up the armatures and clay figure he had built. Then he put locks on the doors and went there every night to check. The students still got in. They are all anti-Government you see. But yesterday he managed to nearly finish it by staying there all the time, all night. Today we have just heard that there has been a *coup d'état* and we have a new Head of State. I don't know what we are going to do. Your father has gone to bed. Sometimes we can hear the noise of guns in the distance. We don't really know what is happening because there is a dust storm and no one can see anything . . .

8

The New Elizabethan Age

The mirror had exploded in Violet's face, the tiny fragments embedding themselves under her skin and tearing the tissue underneath. She had been making up one face, getting it ready to go out, and then it was gone. It was only a ragged bleeding area with no reflection. It had to be reconstructed patiently with new techniques, piece by piece, using fragments from the skin of her thigh. Then a new face was born, a post-war face, still scarred, perfectly recognizable, but blurred, somehow indistinct. The face emerged and existed in the present, looking out on England.

It had not been possible to extract all the fragments of glass so they swam in an internal sea, were worn down like pebbles and arrived at the surface of the skin years later, were taken out with a simple operation and placed like souvenirs of a seaside holiday in a small glass jar which was kept on a shelf in the kitchen. She spent some time each day looking at her face, familiarizing herself, documenting its faults and possibilities. The new face came with a small war disability pension, a re-entry grant into a new universe.

But all this was hearsay. Michael had not been allowed to see her. She had been taken off in an ambulance and had become invisible.

In retrospect he imagined himself as being immensely calm. He had looked up from his safe position in the Anderson shelter, with his eiderdown, the Libby's milk tin full of chocolate fingers and an orange, and seen soot falling down from the sky. The staircase that once went upstairs now extended crazily into a grey sky out of which fell a continuing stream of black soot that soon covered everything. He had no memory whatever of the explosion, the caving-in of brick walls. It was only afterwards that he was told of the flying bomb that had landed on the house next door. When he was taken out of the house there were huge pieces of polished wood lying in the road. He imagined that they were the fins and wings of the bomb.

Still immersed in this immense calm of memory he could see two women in the street crying. They were being comforted. He could not imagine why they were crying. They went to a street shelter made of brick with a concrete roof. They sat there for a long time. Then he could remember nothing else. He looked up intently from his bed, up into the darkness of the dormitory roof with its criss-crossed black beams. There was no further evidence.

In the morning it appeared that the school had suddenly become the object of a series of 'patriotic' donations. It was not at all clear what had precipitated this burst of generosity. The walnut cabinet containing a television was clearly to do with the Coronation as that was to be everyone's first glimpse of the new medium. For some reason Matron had been put in charge of it as though it was a potential epidemic and was, therefore, contagious. She had no idea whatever about electrical appliances but accepted her new role with her usual stoicism. No one had really worked out the etiquette of who was to open the walnut doors, turn the switches, and decide who was to watch it. The Headmaster had clearly thought that it was beneath his dignity to take such a theatrical role.

A less explicable donation was a set of *The Collected Works of Aldous Huxley*. These remained in the library untouched for several weeks until it was discovered that certain volumes, in particular one called *Ape and Essence*, contained material of such an explicit sexual nature that within a short space of time all the volumes had been rapidly scanned for further material of the same type. Soon afterwards the complete set disappeared from the library for good. At the same time the *New Statesman*, which had been ordered by the History Master, was cancelled.

Quite suddenly there was talk of a New Britain, the Headmaster lectured on the Stock Market to the Sixth Form, and there was to be a new emphasis on Geography following on from a further donation, a huge and sweetly smelling *Atlas of the Universe*, which contained maps of a post-war world and detailed drawings of the surface of the moon.

Another quite illegitimate donation was a worn, fingered and scrappily typed but totally unexpurgated version of *Lady Chatterley's Lover*. This circulated amongst the dormitories and was read avidly with torches under the bedclothes. No one knew where this arcane document had originated and it vanished as mysteriously as it had appeared.

The New Elizabethan Age was upon us, said the Headmaster, as a brief and awkward introduction to the new walnut cabinet that stood in the Sixth Form meeting-room. Matron stood to one side of the cabinet waiting to open the doors. The Headmaster sat in the central chair, the House Masters either side of him. Then Matron opened the doors to reveal a small and bulbous screen with a flickering and dense black and white picture that was almost negative.

Behind the Headmaster stood a group of Sixth Formers and behind them a selected group of juniors, very few of whom could see anything at all. Matron stood behind the set watching them all benignly in case they should suddenly fall ill. Michael was at the back looking out the window at the mulberry tree and so caught only a glimpse of the ceremony. When it was over Matron moved in from her position and closed the walnut doors. There was an atmosphere of slight disillusion, even embarrassment, and the room rapidly cleared. Matron polished the top of the cabinet and left the room. Michael was left to stack the chairs.

The New Elizabethan Age produced a flood of enterprise amongst the pupils. One boy, Green, was expelled for running an insurance scheme to which most of the Lower School had contributed. If any of the insured persons were beaten during that term they collected what was equivalent to a month's pocket money. Profits were heavy and were never traced. The scheme continued in the absence of its originator but with heavy security.

Michael pored over the new atlas and stared again and again at the two full pages that were devoted to Northern Africa. The huge area of the Sudan was almost blank, a few names, El Obeid, Kassala, Juba, Suakin, Port Sudan, Khartoum, Omdurman, scattered thinly over huge areas of nothing but a featureless relief map of a flat country. He stared further at it, investigated the graphs and figures of cotton exports, the ins and outs of the Gezira Scheme. Nothing he found was what he wanted to know. That did not stop him going back at every available opportunity to look again. He was looking for the face of his mother. It had begun to fade. All he could remember was a photograph of her before the war with a hat and a black veil. He tried to conjure up her face but it slipped away leaving him with a feeling of guilt, a blind featureless relief map with mysterious towns and rivers and the looming mass of Ethiopia down in one corner ravaged by rivers.

He could remember everyone else, his aunts and uncles, his cousin who was always falling out of windows and shouting for chocolate, even the surface of the moon was familiar, he had looked at it through telescopes and on the map in the atlas. The Sudan was blank and he was sure he would not recognize his mother even if he met her in the street.

This burst of remembrance and outbreak of forgetfulness were motivated by his imminent flight to the Sudan. He was to fly from Blackbushe Airport on a charter Viking plane, or perhaps a Dakota. After his visit he would have to return to the school, that was made very clear. He concentrated above all else on Geography.

The fog brought them down in Lyons instead of Nice. They stayed overnight in Malta in the gigantic Hotel Phoenicia. Then after a short stop at Benghazi they flew over desert for most of the day. The desert was white and brown, sometimes black and was almost as featureless as the map.

They had a break at Wadi Halfa which was, according to the atlas, on the border of Egypt and the Sudan, a dot in the desert. They walked across the burning hot concrete pad to a tin shack. Crates of Fanta bottles were stacked outside. They all sat in metal chairs with hot plastic seats: they arranged their legs as though they were on holiday, put their hands behind their heads, half-closed their eyes to block out the burning concrete.

If you touched the metal of the chairs it burnt the skin. The drinks were hot. Most of the liquid fizzed out of his bottle of orange Fanta when it was opened by a somnolent Sudanese and evaporated instantly on the concrete. The Sudanese blinked in slow motion and wandered away.

Michael looked out over the landing strip and watched the heat shimmer. In the distance was a gleam like a distant fish, a plane, a silver glint caught by the sun. It landed and stood on the hard pad. The stairs were pushed up to it, the door opened and a priest in black emerged. Behind him was another. Soon they formed a continuous black line, a black crocodile of missionaries, advancing to the tin shack where mortals were drinking, hypnotized in the heat, trapped between one civilization and another, emigrés from the New Elizabethan Age.

Soon afterwards another plane landed and parked symmetrically to the first. From this plane emerged a line of nuns dressed impeccably in tropical white. The two lines of white and black figures were like a mirage, distorted by the heat. They did not join the other passengers but stood in separate groups, apparitions not in need of refreshment. Soon they returned to their planes and took off into the sky.

It was dark when they reached Khartoum. Through the window of the plane the lines of lights made a facsimile of the Union Jack reproduced in the desert. The door of the plane opened and the African night rolled in, tasting of cinnamon and singed flesh, the taste of sin itself, pleasurable and frightening simultaneously.

The airport road flashed past the car window, and led on to trees and hedges.

There he was lying in bed on the roof, a thick mud roof to keep out the heat from the living quarters below. Above was a dense black sky pierced with unnaturally brilliant stars. Over the city came the sound of roaring lions, reverberant screams. *Spartacus* was playing at the open-air cinema. There were cheers from the audience. The branches of the lemon trees swayed above him. The air was heavy with scent.

He dreamt of the atlas, its smell seemed to be in his nostrils, the soft crackle of its pages filled his ears.

His mother's face was familiar after all, it was as he had remembered it, the post-war face that contained its own fragments of mirror swimming within it.

This African chasm carved out of the sky was now, for want of a better word, home. In all the houses along the road expatriate New Elizabethans considered the problems of their servants, their salaries and the date of their return to England.

9

The Nuba Mountains

In the distant past (he had been told) there were volcanoes in the Nuba Mountains where they were to go in just a few days; a different, wilder and more active landscape than he would see. The desert had advanced over millions of years, swallowed the volcanoes, leaving only the dead peaks pointing above the surface of the flat sand, the valleys filled, the level of the land raised, a geologist's paradise.

The windblown sand had eroded the peaks, grinding away the surface of the hard black granite, leaving the tops of the dead volcanoes stricken, piles of gigantic black boulders, monuments, dramatic sculpture waiting to be recorded for posterity.

The scattered Nubian tribes (whose languages and dialects had, without their consent, become of great academic interest) had built their villages into the gaps between the boulders, outcrops of conical huts with straw roofs that appeared to grow out of the rock.

Nearby (he had heard with some interest but with a glazed expression) grew miniature trees with conical silver trunks and pink flowers on the ends of thin branches, the roots deep in the crevices. They were poison or tebeldi trees of great interest to botanists, or at least the one who was talking to him. The land around the boulders was flat scrubland inhabited by baboons whose social structures and hierarchical organization were interpreted by zoologists.

The roads were pot-holed and strewn with stones, not much more than tracks, making access to the area for European academics a matter of great difficulty. They regretted the absence of railways in the area and went on to have private conversations about the dearth of academic funding.

The white community in Khartoum was full of educational content, brimming over with it, spilling it at every opportunity. If they were academics they took pleasure in the expounding of information in their specialities, their civilized obsessions (their means of livelihood). Michael was of the right age for them to feel that they had *carte blanche* to fill his mind with worthy and uplifting botanical, geological and even anthropological detail. He was, like all the other emigrés from boarding schools, on an excusable educational trip, a fully justified absence from the righteous and necessary routine of the Ordinary or Advanced Level courses at school. Physicists would get him into a corner and subject him to impromptu tests on the structure of the atom, teachers of French would carry on one-sided conversations with him in that language, even lecturers in English would question him lightly on the sexual uncertainties of *Hamlet*.

His answers, or lack of them, would then become part of incisive critiques of the dropping standards in English schools, an indication, in itself, of the decadence of the Home Country (which had only occurred in the absence of them personally and the lack of the high standards of work that their personalities, learning and dedication had generated in the past).

He detected a competitive edge between the parents of recently-arrived children. Their answers to these questions were compared and used in an obscure game whose main move seemed to be an excess of sympathy for his lack of academic brilliance. It was always blamed on the vicissitudes of the educational system but with a condescending air as though this system must be severely impaired having to cope with such dullards as himself.

Violet and Thomas looked strained. He retreated constantly from them, his parents, into the garden under the leaves of the lemon tree. From time to time he could not be found at all and there was a succession of short-lived panics until he was found, on the roof or in the servant's quarters.

He watched the white egrets poking around in the garden

52

with a temporary and excessive interest to take his mind off it all. It was not what he had expected. Even the woman next door had asked him if he realized that he was now at the confluence of the White and Blue Nile in a particularly patronizing tone. He said he had not, didn't care, and ran away. When they talked to him they were obsessed with Geography, the great opportunity he had to see Africa, to see what the maps meant. They, hardened travellers, already knew all there was to know about Africa. Their atlas lay untouched in the pile of books stored back in England, no longer needed.

There were things that he liked. The smell of hot sand, the hot nights, the bleached sky in the day, the brightness and proximity of the stars at night away from all the talk. It was the sensuality of Africa that drew him, all the talk was, under the surface, provocative, hiding secret passions, the dangerous smell of potential sexual partners, the brief touchings of hands and legs, the coolness of skin in evening air. He sensed it but was not part of it. But, if he was on his own, he could embrace it all, experience it fully, cut out the interference.

The railway from Khartoum going south curled a little and then stopped at El Obeid, facing across the Sahara, six thousand miles to the Atlantic. Below it was a flurry of dots with unpronounceable names that was the Nuba. The rest of the journey took place in huge Ford lorries, tied together with thick wire, the site of innumerable reconstructions and improvisations to keep them going in the absence of spares. When they finally died they were quickly transformed into other useful articles. The axles were beaten into spears and decorative knives, the seats appeared in huts transformed into thrones, the door handles opened other doors. The remains collapsed into the desert as though they were being drawn under the surface by colonies of termites.

The students were crammed into the back of the lorries and the front seats were retained for the whites. Battered by the mysterious games of the academics back in Khartoum his parents had agreed to take along Ted and Beryl from Construction, a non-academic institution, who were not engaged in competitive exercises of any sort. In fact they were extremely grateful to be allowed to come at all as Construction people were, in general, not to be seen in the social life of the University. It was rumoured that some of them did not yet have servants.

The lorries bounced and groaned over the increasingly rough tracks, hitting boulders, swerving, grinding to sudden halts. The driver talked constantly in Arabic, grinning to himself, a running commentary on the condition of the lorries and this one in particular. At the end of a steep descent the steering wheel came off in his hands. He rammed it back on to the steering column and continued to drive down the precipitous bank of the *wadi*, a dried-up river bed. The lorry could not make it up the other side and got stuck half-way. The driver got out and lit a cigarette, wandered around and inspected the lorry from all angles and then disappeared behind a bush to evacuate his bowels.

They sat in silence in the front seats, waiting for the other lorries to arrive to give assistance. A kite wheeled overhead. Ted and Beryl were in a state of shock and stared without hope in front of them, bruised and battered by the journey from El Obeid. This was not what they had expected.

She was a plum-shaped Cockney who pronounced continually on the physical and mental well-being of her husband, gave detailed run-downs on his happiness, the state of his ingrown toenail, the details of their friends and financial prospects. This commentary happened in his presence but apparently without his attention. He seemed to be in a constant state of semi-consciousness, his eyes half-closed. He would sometimes burst into activity and get engaged in a technical problem of some description. Beryl would then lapse into a disapproving silence and watch him with disdain. They appeared never to converse, their dialogue was always carried on via other unwilling and embarrassed partners. He talked about 'she', she talked about 'Ted'.

Beryl had packed very carefully, considering this trip to be a social event of the first order. She had packed as though she were to put on her best appearance, a little like a party that was to be important to her husband's career. She had even packed a party dress, a little black number with spangles that she relied upon to give the right impression. She had secretly packed a dinner jacket for Ted as well as his best khakis. She had no idea that the trip was to be less than an excursion, more an expedition. No one had told her. No one explained anything to anybody. You were expected to know.

She looked out at the baked wall of sand in front of the lorry and toyed with the impossibilities of her cocktail dress in this hostile environment. Ted was incommunicado, his eyes half-closed, lost in a secret world of joints and clasps and fasteners. Violet and Thomas's son was looking at her in a peculiar way. She could not think of anything appropriate to say to him. He was explaining to her what a *wadi* was. She drew herself up together and began to take his explanation as a condescending if not a hostile act, but decided that this was too much and gave him a comforting smile right for his age. He gave up in disgust, got out of the lorry and wandered off, looking up with interest at the kite wheeling overhead. The heat round the lorry shimmered. She had to shake Ted to make sure he was still conscious. He was snoring.

Later, when they had been rescued, she felt a bit brighter. The road was flatter and they were bowling along, hitting the occasional rut which sent her bouncing up into the air hitting her head on the roof of the cabin. She giggled at the memory of a distant fairground and tried to make the others join in the joke. In the absence of any response she enjoyed the bouncing by herself and whooped each time she was thrown up into the air. She was a small woman with little gravity to hold her down.

In the back of the lorry the students sang and banged on the top of the cab.

They stopped in a village near the *jebel*, the pile of black granite boulders. The lorries were surrounded by girls, naked apart from beads about their waists. Their hair was plaited into spikes and in between they had screwed in Pepsi-Cola tops as decoration. Their heads were shining, other-worldly. They were laughing with large white teeth, their bodies were grey with dust. Michael ate them with his eyes, lovingly gazing on their perfect small breasts, taking in breaths of their gaiety and curiosity. It was the first time he had seen naked women outside the covers of *Tit-Bits*.

The sight stayed in his eyes all the evening, blocking out all else. He stayed away from the company just to remember, to savour the sight, the bright eyes, the smooth dust-covered limbs, the oval faces gleaming up at him with a total absence of guile.

Beryl strung a line between two tebeldi trees and hung her cocktail dress on it, so the creases would drop out. The dress was black, shimmered a little and was almost square to fit the small but ample shape of its owner. It moved quietly in the evening breeze with a background of the *jebel* and the setting sun. It was Christmas Eve.

In the village lived an anthropologist. They visited him in the only proper house in the village. They knocked, the door opened and there was a man in white evening dress. In the background was a woman, his wife, in a long willowy green evening dress. She was standing by the side of a Christmas tree.

10

The Canals of Mars

The image moved, spots on its surface travelled and went in and out of focus. His eyes strained at the oval shape of light as it turned on itself, defying identification, a revolving unresolved patch with no definite boundaries, no real existence. He moved his position at the eyepiece and immediately the phantom image leapt away leaving blackness and a bright sharp sphere in the midst of the circular field of view.

Michael had been looking at the reflection of his own eye. Now he was looking at Mars through a telescope. It was on the roof of a house in Fulham. Everything had dropped into place. Mars even had something of a red glow as, according to the books, it should have.

He should have been at school but he had developed a conspiracy to extend his period of absence. He was, as far as the school understood, still in Africa. In fact he was in London staying with indulgent friends of his parents. They were artists, a little of the bohemian, so had the correct attitude to his stories of beatings at his boarding school. As they had a telescope on the roof, a collection of opera records, a loom in the kitchen and a number of Japanese swords it was felt that this was sufficiently educational an environment to delay his return. They had discussed it and it seemed very sensible and to the point. He was filled with unreasonable joy, but wondered how long it could last.

He spent a lot of time on his own, either on the roof or pretending to listen to Verdi. He was reinventing the Africa that he had just left. It made little sense without further thought and reflection. A bundle of experiences with no coherence. He needed time to sort it out.

To extend his options he developed a cold (of the right degree of severity or mildness) which he could draw upon if necessary as a further delaying tactic. He practised a slight cough in private before displaying it as a symptom in public.

Downstairs there was a small set with a number of clay figures standing in it. It was unfinished. It was for a museum, a representation of life in Neolithic times. The unexpected thing about it was that it was made to be seen only from one angle. In order to establish the right perspective from the necessarily foreshortened viewing angle from the front, the figures had to be made so they were distorted from any other angle. He spent some time moving slowly round the figures so they changed from 'normality' to a monstrous elongation as though they had been blown by a cosmic wind. This was something of a privileged view for, as soon as the cyclorama at the back had been put in place and it had been boxed and put into the museum, no one would know the strange other forms the Neolithic men and women were hiding as they crouched around their fires.

The cyclorama was lying about in separate pieces, not quite finished. It represented the background to the fireside scene. He looked at it very carefully. It was almost identical to the scene he had witnessed in the Nuba Mountains. There were the black granite boulders piled high, rising out of a flat plain. There was even a glimpse, as yet not fully painted, of a tree with pink flowers on it. The only thing missing was a clothes line with a black cocktail dress hanging in the sun.

He had been in Fulham a week. Perhaps they had picked up the idea from his description.

He looked through the telescope and saw, as before, an oscillation between the image of his own eye and the sphere of the planet Mars. He imagined the *jebels* of Mars, the worn tops of dead volcanoes, the rising swirl of sand, the expectant faces of Martian baboons yet to be investigated by Martian zoologists.

The strange thing about the canals of Mars was that they did not exist. Despite a historic series of exquisite paintings which he had examined and which clearly demonstrated their existence, structure and changing form, they were not really there at all. They were 'an effect of the process of observation'. If you looked at something and had no idea what to expect then you were subject to 'mistakes' as the object wandered about without clear identity. It was only when you were told what to expect that you then, dutifully, began to see it, as though it had always been there. Your first impressions were wiped out and lost all significance. They were only mistakes.

This, of course, gave unreasonable power to whoever it was in the end who decided what was 'really' there. Everyone else lost sight of their first impressions and went along with the new revealed 'truth' or identity. On the other hand whoever looked at anything was, in the end, subject to 'effects' of observation. The 'truth' was therefore just a matter of power and influence.

Michael began to use the eyepiece of the telescope to look at the structure of his own eye.

In an excess of introspection he took to inventing his 'experiences' in the Sudan. He invented a story of how he was attacked by a snake, then almost poisoned by a scorpion, chased by baboons. These stories were invented for the audience at school. The trouble was, he had no idea what they wanted, or expected, or would be likely to believe.

Michael's state of mind began to cause concern and it was decided that it was about time that he went back to school. This produced a bout of hay fever, coughing and a series of mysterious symptoms all with the common characteristic that they could be turned on and off at will. Eventually he agreed to return to school, the symptoms vanished, and with the strange request for one more look at the Brompton Road Air Terminal fulfilled, he was on his way.

He went straight into sick-bay on arrival at school. He was in isolation, of course, as he had developed a tropical infection of uncertain identity due to his brief visit over Christmas to an African country. He explained his illness to Matron by startling her with his description of the local African bread that had, according to his description, baked-in cockroaches.

It seemed to fulfil all her expectations of African disorder and lack of hygiene.

Then, ironically, he had a real fever. His temperature shot up, his skin burnt, and he was having hallucinations. There was little distinction between the images he was hallucinating and his dreams. He seemed to be awake and asleep simultaneously. The dream and the hallucination went something like this:

There was a war between the North and the South. He had, unwillingly, become involved in it as a witness, not as a participant. The railways sank into the desert and were replaced by huge lorries that jarred and ground their entrails and came to a halt. There was a war but the warring groups could not reach each other as the transport had failed. Dust storms blew between them so they could not see each other, they struggled blindly to find the enemy who could not be found. So the war happened in the heads of the participants, their brains boiled with antagonism for the invisible enemy, they struck out into the air to damage or to kill the opponent. But their blows fell through the air and had no effect. Their faces were distorted with hate, their guts curdled with fury, but they could do nothing as the enemy was too far away, too distant to be affected. Soon they were immobilized with frustration, still trying to burst at the seams, but now unable to move. Sand storms blew between them and they were like statues, arms raised in attack, faces lit up with the anger of their cause.

During these series of events Michael was locked physically in one position, like a statue himself. Matron and Nurse spent some time trying to disentangle his stiff limbs.

Just a few hours before the school was having to decide whether to inform his parents of his strange condition, he suddenly and completely recovered. He was released from sick-bay and was immediately absorbed into the routine of the school. For a few days he was given a wide berth by some on the premise that he probably still had an infectious tropical disease. Soon they forgot all about it.

A few weeks later he met the Headmaster coming down the stone stairs that led up to the Assembly Room. The Headmaster fixed him with his customary steely glance over the top of his spectacles and made some comment about his habit of wearing a duffel-coat to church on Sundays. To Michael's own astonishment this produced in him an unstoppable flow of speech directed at the person of the Headmaster and in a very public situation. It was a calculated flow of invective, during which Michael discovered all kinds of ideas that he had been perfectly unconscious of before but which arose spontaneously, perfectly articulated, a flow which for a period of some minutes froze the Headmaster into silence. At the end of it Michael just walked away in a daze. He had said everything so there was no more to say on either side. Strangely, immediately afterwards, Michael could not recollect a single word or idea that he had uttered during those moments of calculated delirium.

The Headmaster, taken aback by this outburst, beat a hasty retreat, and conscious of his public position settled his face into an expression of calm and sympathetic understanding. He, needing to make sense of it, put it down to a stray effect of Michael's tropical fever. Nevertheless, he made no mention of it to his wife or to anyone else. From then on he treated Michael with some circumspection befitting someone who was undoubtedly mad and whose behaviour could not reasonably be predicted.

Michael developed an intense interest in astronomy, perhaps because no one else in the school knew anything about it.

11

The Red Sea

His ear pressed to the pillow was a seismograph, it picked up noise that reverberated through the earth, through the structure of the building, not through the air. From time to time he raised his head and listened, checking what he had heard through the pillow. There was the light breathing of the others in the dormitory, the patter of rain on the high windows, nothing else. Buried back into the pillow he was picking up other sounds entirely, the distant slam of doors, footsteps advancing up staircases in some distant part of the school, the growl of a passing lorry. Beyond that there were mysterious sounds, deep scratchings, slow evolving reverberations with the odd, high-pitched grate. He heard them as the movement of worms under the mulberry tree outside, eating through the earth, swallowing it, eyeless and responding only to vibration. He hovered on the brink of sleep, attempting to piece together what, exactly, he had said to the Headmaster. (His anxiety ticked away, censoring it, making it almost polite.) Then he gave up and succumbed to sleep accompanied by the rumble of the excavations of distant and obscurely sexual worms.

Don't say that to me, said Michael to the Headmaster, I don't accept anything you say. You are a comic figure I have imagined. I invented you (when I was sleeping in a bed in your school). You stand in a punt wielding a gun, blasting the water-fowl off the surface of the lake, playing a country gentleman, ordering your students to uproot the weeds blocking the lake to increase the fishing potential, poisoning the moles on your lawn, confiscating water-pistols, advising us on the Stock Exchange, stopping us talking to girls in the village, covering up your fear of having a heart attack, inspecting the cleanliness of our hands, instilling in us the virtues of your hypocritical Christianity, lying about our progress to our parents, failing to stop the rest of the staff becoming alcoholics, ignoring the sexual habits of the Classics Master, importing Irish girls as maids and paying them minimum wages, pretending to be a hero when the school is flooded by wearing thigh-length boots and wading into the playground, pretending not to be intimidated by the Chairman of the Governors, pretending the school is a public school with a long history, glaring at all of us during the School Dance, covering up your distaste for your own wife and children, spending too much money on the Honours Board, trying to hide your own sense of failure and not succeeding, failing to control your uncontrollable anger while facing your pupils who, underneath it all, taking everything into account, you hate.

Then, lapping around the edge of sleep was the Red Sea. It was crystal blue, sparkling, transparent, alive with fish, full of flickering sardines, bursting with manta rays throwing themselves into the air (hiding stingrays and sharks): the air was full of dark-pink flamingoes and fluttering bats, the white pointed wings of terns were etched against a darkening sky, the distant cries of kites could be heard as they wheeled overhead, completing a dream ornithology.

By the deserted harbour black cats fished, flipping their catch out of the water and over their thin elongated bodies, racing to snatch their prey from the waiting kites. From the Turkish buildings round the silted-up harbour the bats streamed, like memories.

The palace by the harbour crumbled, its three hundred and sixty-five rooms containing the bat-winged memory of that many wives, that many erotic encounters in baked dry rooms. The sun sank, first turning the deserted town of Suakin golden yellow and then extinguishing it in night (in the blink of an eye).

Then the sea opened up and swallowed him (until the bell rang at seven-thirty).

12

Home

In the middle of the bare, black-tiled floor of their Khartoum house was a pile of photographs and typed sheets from an English estate agent, the only things left after the thieves had left. To stop them blowing away someone (the burglar?) had placed a heavy and old-fashioned iron on the top, holding them down. It must have been brought in from the kitchen; a conscious act. Why did they want to stop the papers blowing away? Was it an incoherent political message, put in a prominent position, asking them to go home, back to their choice of country house?

Violet and Thomas had returned from the Red Sea, from Suakin, and had arrived at the house to find it stripped of all furniture and all their possessions, but for this insolent pile of paper describing houses that they could not afford. They wandered round the house, at a loss, but could find nothing else left behind.

The intruders seemed, though this may have been an illusion, to have cleaned the floor afterwards; it was gleaming. If they had, it was by far the most sinister element of the burglary. If a mess had been left they could have been usefully outraged; the opportunity would have arisen to talk comfortably about the political and economic anarchy in the Sudan and the consequent need for stability. It would have helped. But this cruel neatness, the gleam of the polished floor, took the wind out of their sails and left them speechless. It had something of the sense of an official act, by order of a government department. They felt helpless.

She wandered round the house passing from room to impeccably empty room, as if upon re-entry she would find

64

everything as it had been, miraculously replaced. The servant followed her with an exaggerated expression of profound sadness, taking it all as his failure, his lack of vigilance, just as he had been told. They had already assigned to him the responsibility for the theft; there was little more to say on either side. It was no good sacking him, that would have left her without any assistance, another nightmare. Her husband had gone to see the police.

Violet picked up the iron and handed it briskly to the eagerly waiting servant, who dutifully took it away to the empty kitchen. After a great deal of thought he placed it in the middle of the floor.

She leafed through the sheaf of paper, the pencil drawings of desirable but unattainable cottages and mansions. She was still suffering from the dull hypnosis induced by the long train journey to Khartoum. All her perceptions had slowed. She had spent much of the journey peeling oranges and throwing them at the tinted windows as though she were throwing them outside into the desert air. The slow progress of the train had sent her into a dream-like state from which she was not yet fully recovered. She flicked through the pages not seeing them properly, but feeling a dull pain at the sight of an English cottage.

The servant, wanting to be of assistance and conscious of his now uncertain future, had found a rough wooden bed and a mattress. He carried it into the bedroom and awkwardly arranged the suitcases round it, a substitute for the missing and familiar furniture. He stood there wanting her to rest, a picture of concern. It was the afternoon, the hottest and blankest part of the day.

Dutifully she lay on the bed and stared up at the fan whirling gently above her. The moving air flicked the hair across her face. She flicked it back and almost immediately was asleep. The pictures of an estate agent's England blew around the floor having dropped from her hand. The servant picked them up and put them under the iron in the centre of the kitchen floor; a quest for an irreproachable and healing neatness.

For her, sleeping, England was home, but for her son, lost in a English winter, it was more a place of exile. Michael regarded the Sudan as his rightful place, his home. It smelt right, it was hot, it was sufficiently unpredictable to match his emotional condition, his emotional geography.

Each embellished the absent place with sights and tastes that were magnified by distance, salted and peppered with unsatisfied desire. He and his mother suffered a parallel but opposite homesickness, dreaming one of an imaginary Africa and the other of an imaginary England.

She slept an exhausted sleep, ignoring all noise, the arrival and departure of vehicles, the sound of voices, the clatter of packing cases, even the tense tones of her husband, the tone he used when dealing with Sudanese whom he had categorized as incompetent. Then there was silence apart from the swish of Thomas's shoes as he passed from room to room. There was a clink of a glass as he moved out to the balcony to have a drink.

She woke suddenly expecting to look up and see the clustered bats hung in the corner of her room in Suakin. She expected to see the pile of droppings that had accumulated beneath them. Instead it was her bedroom. There was a dressing-table, a mirror and a chair in front of it. But there was something wrong. It was not her chair, her mirror, her dressing-table. She got up and, confused, walked into the living-room.

There was a table, chairs round it and more around a coffee table in the room beyond. But they were not the same chairs or tables. Everything had been replaced and was in the same position but nothing was the same.

She felt an almost physical jolt to her identity. Perhaps it was not the furniture that was wrong, perhaps it was her. Was she the wrong person in the wrong house? Overcome, she began to cry and shout at the same time.

The explanations given by her husband in the faint hope that she would be pleased did not help. He had replaced everything from the market, from the selection of effects culled from other burglaries that were available in certain places, if you knew the right people. In this way, they said, there was a constant, and advantageous, circulation of furniture and effects and a constant profit to the middle-men.

The explanations went on, she stopped crying and took on an ironic and slightly quizzical expression as though nothing in the future would be entirely certain. Her head was slightly on one side as if she doubted her capacity to hear or do full justice to the absurd simplicity of it.

The servant had discovered the empty house when he wandered in after a particularly deep afternoon sleep. Descending rapidly into a panic, and unable to think of anything else to do, he had set to work cleaning the house, polishing the floor several times over to cover his neglect, his blatant lack of responsibility. He had placed the iron and the estate agent's sheets in the centre of the floor as they were the only two objects that had been left behind. Putting them in the centre of the floor had made the house seem less empty and had reduced his rising anxiety about the possibly dramatic effect the burglary might have on his employers when they returned.

He had omitted to mention that it was he who had told his friends in the market when the occupants would be away and when they would be back. He also failed to mention the cut of the profits that he would soon be collecting. It was a dramatic confirmation of the political and economic anarchy of the Sudan. The circulation of furniture that took place in this way financed annually several hundred devotees several steps further to Mecca in the long, slow migration of which Khartoum was only one stopping place. So a few moments of anguish and disorientation for a few brought many others closer to a state of bliss. In any global economy of human happiness it hardly required further justification.

But none of this was part of the explanations Thomas gave to her, his wife. It was only those who had spent many years in the Sudan who knew what was going on behind the scenes. They, in their state of deepest cynicism, regarded it as final confirmation of the frailty of the African conscience and therefore the final justification of British imperialism. This carefully nurtured intuition they would take back with them to England and tapping years of experience would settle into retirement believing that they had a deep insight into the vagaries of the African character and a true understanding of the underlying moral superiority of the white races.

But for her it was a moment of deeper disorientation. The simple explanation of the reorganization of her Khartoum house with its interchangeable objects threw into relief her lack of purchase on her own place in it. Was she interchangeable, too?

The only objects that Thomas had failed to replace from the selection in the market were the beds. Consequently, she was lying on the servant's bed in the bedroom where she had slept that afternoon and her husband was slumped in the next room in one of the chairs. She could hear him snoring.

Her father had told her and her sisters, all six of them, that they were destined for great things. He had omitted to say what great things he had in mind. All of them had inherited from this constant paternal refrain that they were not quite of this world, that they had 'destiny'. The progress of their lives resisted dramatic and conclusive evidence of any such special status. But they were still on the look-out for it and wrote obsessively to each other, not, of course, in any competitive spirit, swapping notes on their husbands and sons, believing that if there was any destiny around it would be embodied in them. Constant disappointment had created amongst them all an ironic and humorous tone as they looked out on the world and were amused at their position in it.

This time she lay in bed, still wafted by the slowly moving fan, unable to generate any amusement or irony, even to herself. She felt swept along by events, powerless on her own account, changing to fit the needs of others her ideas, clothes and attitudes. It swept her clean and she felt emptied out as though she would at any moment be blown gently away by the air moving around her. She was weightless.

She was woken from the reverie by the dark and silent figure of her servant carrying a bed. He had taken pity on them and had recovered one of the stolen ones. He put the bed down and melted away. Her husband came in wondering what was happening.

They, like lovers, spent the rest of the night sitting on the bed talking together about the house in England that they had not yet discovered. She spent the rest of the next day writing to her sisters describing the home they would have in England.

13

The Proper Study of Mankind

It was nearing the end of the summer term and a taste of anarchy was in the air. The relaxing of certain rules after the examinations brought a general sense of disregard for all arbitrary restrictions which were, perhaps, appropriate enough for the winter but anachronistic when a summer wind blew smells and perfumes and pollen into the brain.

Members of the fifth form broke out at night and somehow got to Brighton where they were astounded, impressed and not a little shocked to find a group of French students blowing up condoms into balloons round the Clock Tower and then bursting them. Normally such objects were treated with exaggerated respect, even veneration, a sign of entry into adulthood. They were usually carried, pristine, in secret pockets, the subject of sophisticated chatter and knowing glances.

The School Captain took to winding his girlfriend up to his room at night using the asbestos rope of the fire escape and then dropping her back down to the street much later. Rulebreaking at such an elevated level loosed an erotic charge in the school that became focused on the School Dance.

The rules concerning invitations to girls were Byzantine in their complexity and involved the parents of the girl getting in touch with the Headmaster's wife and, if asked, the prospective invitee and her boyfriend would be entertained to tea at the Headmaster's house to ascertain the suitability of the relationship. A prospect as quelling as this excluded any of the willing village girls from taking part which, of course, was the intention. Instead, as was the tradition, a coachload of girls from a nearby school would be imported to introduce the boys to a suitably constrained and supervised heterosexual environment.

The Headmaster's wife instituted ballroom dancing classes, at which she was the only woman, to get the boys used to mixed company. As the dance instruction consisted of her grappling with recalcitrant fifth and Sixth Formers, trying to pull them as close to her body as she could, using the weight of her authority and the considerable strength of her arms, these events became extremely unpopular and in the end had to be made compulsory. The only answer to this appallingly embarrassing problem, the proximity of the Headmaster's wife's body, was to tread very hard on her toes and then apologize with such sincerity that recriminations were impossible. Those who failed this last stage found themselves hanging, tortured, on the wallbars of the gymnasium where the Dance was to take place. The Sports Master came to see fair play and a proper regard for womankind and the slightest reaction to the Headmaster's wife's body odour would be punished immediately by the wallbar treatment. He would watch carefully to see that feet were kept off any support and in the air. Arms stretched in this way, agonized faces looked down on the dance below as it went through the St Bernard's Waltz, the foxtrot, the waltz itself. Even this series of anaphrodisiac activities failed to quell the rising tide of sexual expectation. In some ways it developed it in masochistic directions.

This loosening of the rules also had its equivalent in the classroom during the day. The Biology Master attempted with some success to convert his Sixth Form to Catholicism, presumably on the basis that the experience of original sin was so prevalent that everyone would know exactly what he was talking about. The Divinity Master had decided to give religion a break. He was, during the main part of the term, subjected to difficult, disturbing and intentionally subversive questions about his own faith; someone had discovered that he was in the process of losing his calling. He and his girlfriend were pursued all over the Downs hoping to catch them in a non-divine position when they thought they were alone. He had discovered a book called *The Proper Study of Mankind* which let him off the hook. He became a late enthusiast for a liberal, humanitarian education as he had noticed that it sent his class into a sullen and resentful silence.

Michael did his bit for the general atmosphere of levity by setting light to the South Downs. He and a friend, Day, who had a similar anarchic streak, were lying staring at a burnt blue sky through the dry yellow grass of the Downs when Michael took it into his head to light the patch of grass next to him instead of lighting the next 'Passing Cloud' cigarette. It burst into flames immediately and a gust of summer wind carried the fire rapidly up the hill towards the beech woods. They took off their jackets and beat uselessly at the flames until the jackets themselves were starting to char at the edges. Then they gave up in desperation and ran down the hill in a panic back into the village and back to the school. They were already late for tea so were already in trouble. Behind them the fire spread rapidly until the top of the hill was aflame and the woods themselves were beginning to smoke.

In a burst of inspiration they developed a story, an improvisation, between them. They had come across the fire and realizing the danger had immediately started to try and put it out. This story worked well until the battered packet of 'Passing Cloud' dropped out of Michael's jacket and gave the game away.

This seemed to be the signal generally for a clamp-down. It was realized at a high level that things were getting out of hand. Even the Classics Master had caught the air of levity and had moved on from a mild and affectionate touching of junior boys to attempt the full act of buggery on a particularly articulate and intelligent boy who was quite capable of a horrifying description of what had happened to him together with quotations from Plato. The classical allusions somehow made it worse, it brought the academic side of the school into disrepute. The Classics Master vanished and was not heard of again, some boys who had been caught on their way to Brighton were suspended, and Michael was not allowed out after class as there was some remaining doubt if it was the cigarettes that had caused the conflagration. The Headmaster called the School together and sent a shock through the assembled company by threatening to cancel the School Dance. This had the desired effect and breaches of School Rules happened then only in darkest secrecy.

Instead, there was a sullen and sexualized silence about the school. Female partners for the Dance were fantasized for the moment and then evaporated, names of willing village girls were mentioned under the breath and condoms were accumulated secretly as it was only right to be prepared. These items were not seen as methods of preventing pregnancy but more as the only way of getting the appropriate heterosexual erection. A great deal of practising went on after which the condoms were carefully rolled up again and replaced in their cardboard packets. Classes in *The Proper Study of Mankind* went on in an atmosphere of deep gloom as the Divinity Master read from the blue-covered book with enthusiasm. A whole lifetime of sexual activity could not possibly fulfil the expectations that were placed on the Dance let alone the Dance itself. Such was the energy generated by the prospect of meeting girls that it was bound to destroy itself.

At last the Headmaster found the excuse for which he had been waiting. One of the Sixth Formers was discovered during the day on a bed in full sexual intercourse with one of the Irish maids. Worse, the event was witnessed by a group of juniors and Matron herself who had burst in through the door engaged in an explanation of the distribution of laundry parcels. For the juniors it was an event of the first order. They would not be able to forget the sight of the girl's legs pointing straight up in the air while a naked bum between her legs was contracted at the point of orgasm.

The Headmaster spoke to them in tones of deep regret but managed to avoid mentioning the event that had triggered his regretful and resentful frame of mind.

'The School is under a cloud that may take some time to pass [a deep frown and a raking glance taking in the first two rows as though they collectively were the guilty parties]. The school depends on its good name, its standards of behaviour, its smartness in public, its integrity in private. The school depends on its academic record, its standards of excellence, its moral standing [the word 'moral' was emphasized so that everyone was compelled to imagine in graphic detail the event that had set off such ringing phrases].

'The future of the school is indeed uncertain, the future of some of you who embody values that are alien to the school will not only be uncertain but will, as far as this school is concerned, be at an end. [He held up his hand as though it was the wall they were running into.] No one can say that they have not been warned.

'The School Dance, in the past a chance for the school to show itself in its best light, will not now take place. [A shiver of physical disappointment ran through the Assembly Room as developed and carefully-grown fantasies died.]

'That is all I have to say at this moment but I shall insist on high standards of behaviour at Speech Day, a great deal higher than I have come to expect.'

At this the Headmaster turned away dramatically and left the room down the central aisle, looking neither to right nor left, his academic gown swinging behind him. He left a deep and impressed silence behind him as the enormity of the unspecified but well-known events were confronted by all and turned over judiciously in the mind. Those who had condoms concealed about their person were thinking how they could suitably dispose of them in case their accidental discovery might constitute guilt by association.

There was one item which caused the most optimistic to retain some belief that the Dance would, in the end, happen. For some reason the Headmaster's wife continued to hold compulsory ballroom dancing lessons. The more cynical thought this was only a punishment and changed their attention to the synthesis of mysterious compounds not in the chemistry syllabus, in particular nitrogen tri-iodide, the volatile violet crystal that several terms of work out of hours had finally succeeded in creating. It was stored secretly in dark-blue bottles for future use, a small quantity in each bottle.

Michael had found a way of getting into a classroom where he had a view of the dance classes taking place in the gymnasium. It was a summer evening, the lights had just been put on and there were glimpses of the tortured fifth and Sixth Formers dancing either with each other or with the Headmaster's wife. Under the playground tree he could see shadows of unfamiliar shapes, leaping and gesturing, running over to look through the glass door of the gym and then whirling away in a mad dance. They were the Teddy Boys from Brighton who had been arriving from time to time to bombard the school with rotten apples or sometimes to break a window. This time they had got into the school itself.

Michael watched the satirical dance with great concentration as they laughed amongst themselves, flapping their long jackets and bouncing up into the air off the thick soles of their shoes. Finally they threw a stone at the window, smashed it, and vanished into the summer darkness, laughing and jeering to each other. The door of the gym opened tentatively and the face of the Sports Master looked out. Then all the ballroom dancers and their tutor filed out into the playground and talked quietly to each other as though they had been in the presence of the Devil.

For Michael this event immediately had a strange effect, perhaps an identification with the Devil he had secretly glimpsed. The flickering figures he had seen, with whom it was impossible to talk or have any relationship, were free of his rule-bound world. He was not sympathetic to them, did not consider them potential friends. It was their existence, outside his closed world, that had the greatest effect. He realized that he only took pleasure in the illegitimate, the world outside the school. He was underneath, not publicly, a traitor, he was a conformist by fear and not conviction.

He pinched his arm to remind himself of his physical existence and stared out into the now empty playground. But he still felt different. He carried this feeling back to his dormitory and almost immediately fell asleep, a dreaming imposter who had only accidentally set the Downs alight.

Speech Day was an appropriate conclusion to the errancy of the end of term. The platform which was to bear the weight of the Governors, the Staff and the Headmaster, had been liberally dusted with crystals of nitrogen tri-iodide. Any movement on the platform caused an immediate miniature explosion and a puff of delicately purple smoke. The Headmaster, defiant, at least until the end of the term, insisted on continuing and getting his closing homily on the record.

The prize-giving went on, punctuated by decorative explosions and suppressed laughter from the assembled parents and pupils. The faces of the Headmaster and Governors grew red and enraged though it was noticed that the Biology Master was in a state of contorted physical anguish trying not to laugh. This sequence of events had the advantage, for those who had set it up, that it was impossible for any of the victims to make any allusion to the strange phenomena that had unexpectedly beset them. If they had done so it would have released the rising tide of laughter that was rapidly building up and Speech Day would have come to an end in a frivolous and undignified manner. The comic tension of an event of such dignity being subverted for such an extended period caused some of the more susceptible to creep out the back of the hall in paroxysms of suppressed laughter and then, released, to leap around the playground like dervishes. As the event wore on the playground filled with those who were physiologically incapable of holding back their laughter any longer. This crowd, who were talking their heads off about the nature of the exquisite interruptions, became a further source of distraction for those who were still inside. Nevertheless, the Headmaster relentlessly continued, being unaffected constitutionally by a sense of humour and taking the events, quite rightly, as a personal attack on himself.

The ritual wore on until the hall was only occupied by those of hardened physiology, those who were deaf and short-sighted and those who accepted it all as the normal course of events. These were the people who finally experienced the full weight of the Headmaster's considered words.

'The proper study of mankind is man,' said the Headmaster, throttling his anger at the half-empty hall. He repeated it at higher volume for the benefit of those outside. A puff of violet smoke passed ironically and engagingly in front of his face.

'But my study is of post-war man and of the future of man and the future of England. We have, as teachers, the future in our hands: your children, who have been born into a New Elizabethan age. We share a responsibility to them, to point them on to the right path, to describe the dangers and the evils that lie ahead. I am about to describe those evils and I will not be interrupted. [This was an allusion to a sharp crack under his left foot, the first time anyone had admitted that anything was wrong.]

'I will speak of two evils. Two evils that come from the war. Parents will have fought in it, pupils will have been born in it. We have a generation of war-babies anxious to forge, to construct, a new England. But two evils, two temptations, stand in their path. Both arise from the constraint, the terror, of the Second War.'

A wave of gay chatter rose from those in the playground who were discussing in an animated manner the nature of nitrogen tri-iodide.

'Evil comes in two forms, first the evil of Communism, second the evil of the Black Market. They are opposite but equal, do you hear what I am saying? [This was directed to the distracted audience in the playground.] The first, the evil of Communism, came from the experience of the Blitz and the perverted example of the Russians. The communality of people in the street, good in itself, people attempting to look after each other, a good thing you might think, now comes in the form of sentiment and bureaucracy, the conditions for Communism.

'Next, the need to make a living in desperate circumstances creates a Black Market, the illegitimate distribution of goods, the criminal appropriation of what is not due to you. These are the combined inheritances of the war, bureaucracy on the one hand, criminality on the other. If you do not listen to me you will find that these sins will haunt us until the end of the century, and the war will never be over. England will become a dissolute power in the world. It has already lost India. It will lose its moral status, its reputation for fair dealing, its sense of fair play . . .

By this time no one was listening as the platform of Staff, Governors and local dignitaries had had enough of the farce in front of them and had made their way to the back entrance to the accompaniment of assorted explosions and puffs of smoke. The Headmaster slumped over his rostrum and decided, for a fraction of a second, that this would be an appropriate time to have a heart attack. Unfortunately this was not to be and by force of internal and external circumstance he had to continue his prophetic utterances to an ever-decreasing audience numbed by either bewilderment or repressed laughter or both.

'Bureaucracy will sap the initiative of the people, greed will distort its sense of measure, its rationality. Institutionalized charity will stem the post-war hope for a better life, for opportunity. Criminality will make England a place that is no longer worth living in.'

But it was all too late. The Headmaster's last stand was to no avail. The hall had emptied as even the most accepting of the parents had realized that something was wrong with their investment in school fees. The Headmaster was left with an audience of first formers who had stayed in their seats from sheer lack of confidence. Desperate, and now having no way out, the Headmaster addressed them directly.

'For those who were born after the war I can only say this – '

He never managed to give the last piece of advice as the longed-for heart attack arrived, Matron came into her element, and, by force of circumstance, the Headmaster, a prophet in his own time, was retired. At least this made a reasonable conclusion to these extraordinary events. He had of course, been working too hard.

He was taken into his study before going off to hospital so was confronted by the arrogant stare of his own portrait before being whisked away by sympathetic ambulance-men.

The Divinity Master was seen cycling off on holiday with twenty-six volumes of *The Proper Study of Mankind* strapped to the basket on the back of his bicycle. Perhaps he was going to take them on a bicycling holiday with his fiancée.

14

The Minister of the Interior

In the summer most of the wives went back to England. Those that were left either had no children or had been so absorbed in Khartoum life for so many years that they were apprehensive about returning, a bit touchy about it, perhaps preferring to let England remain a desirable mental construct of the home country rather than having to face its reality. But even they stayed at home and the social life ground to a halt apart from the odd visit to the Blue Nile Club to use the swimming pool.

The men who were left behind without the social support of their wives were at the mercy of their servants, who were unsupervised during the day. The consumption of alcohol rose and some men spent the whole day in a state of semi-consciousness before collapsing into an alcoholic daze in the evening and total unconsciousness at night.

Men visited each other and had desultory conversations on each other's verandas before saying that they really had to get home. While saying it they were aware that they were not at all sure why they had to leave. It was as though there was a phantom wife back at home who would want to know where they were at this late hour of the night. However, such was the low state of awareness brought upon by the heat and the lack of social stress in the white community that the existence of mildly demanding phantom wives was not questioned.

Of course, there were those who broke ranks, frequented the Italian Club and other dubious haunts and made it quite obvious that their wives, phantom or not, were not at home waiting for them to return. But everyone knew who they were. They were treated with some disdain on the few occasions that they surfaced from their less than secret assignations with loose women and alcohol. When in this more constrained company, their faces were stretched and tensed. Perhaps it was merely due to an excess of alcohol. In any case they soon would beat a hasty retreat and let their expressions drop in more entertaining company.

The phantom wives, collectively, operated considerable power. Their wardrobes, full of tropical clothes, stared out at the bedrooms making sure they were not used for illicit purposes. Lists of instructions were sometimes put up in the kitchen for the servants and further instructions and warnings could even be found on the dashboards of cars, in the bathrooms, and in the lavatories at the ends of the gardens. They were all to do with the keeping up of standards, an attempt to hold at bay the anarchy that was likely to break out in their absence.

Thomas had picked up his post from the post-box and was on the way down his drive holding the letters, already anticipating the descriptions of the boarding houses in Brighton and the fruitless pursuit of the house in England. He was brought to a sudden halt by the sight of the huge bulk of the Minister of the Interior sitting on his veranda, attended by his servant, drinking a large glass of *limoune*. He was dressed in a djelabere and was slumped back into his seat with every sign of having been there for some time.

'There you are,' said the Minister and added unnecessarily, 'I've been waiting for you.'

A creeping feeling of anguish came over Thomas. He was, after all, only a tenant of the house and on sufferance, a temporary resident of the Sudan. Had he somehow crossed the Government? What could possibly have induced the Minister of the Interior (not even the Minister of Education) to invite himself to his house without warning or appointment or official letter? It was a dangerous enigma.

'Sit down and have a drink,' said the Minister and waved at the servant who was lurking apprehensively behind him. The tenant sat down dutifully and apologized for not being home sooner and therefore keeping the Minister waiting. Then Thomas stood up again, very suddenly, not liking his own boot-licking tone that was brought upon by shock, if not actual fear. The Minister waved his polite remarks away as though men of their sort, men of their culture, should hardly find it necessary to indulge in meaningless diplomatic banter.

'Immortality,' said the Minister, 'is a prize that is given to few men,' getting the conversation at the level that he wanted it.

He was waiting for a response but none came. The Minister looked across at his host or guest or tenant and noticed an expression of utter bewilderment pass across the face. He ignored it and continued his remarks while inspecting the sky closely, as though it was about to produce a cosmic ratification. He leant forward to see if the roof might have obscured such a sign. The sky was still unmarked blue. He sighed deeply.

'You work with materials, with substance, with matter itself. You are an artist.' He sighed again, weighed down, it seemed, by the ineffable nature of creativity.

His host was wondering about the order he had just made to England for new materials. Perhaps it had got caught up in some government bureaucracy and had been questioned at a higher level. He began to compose a concise explanation of his order with precise figures and a closing remark about the essential experience for his students of working with many and various and unfamiliar materials.

He began, 'The order was, of course, authorized.' Then he was interrupted by the Minister who was fixing him with an intense and searching stare.

'You believe in order, then. Beginnings and middles and endings. Who do you think authorizes them? Don't tell me you believe in God? The English are a conventional race.'

Thomas, the conventional host, had become fixated by his suede shoes, not a displacement activity after such a bewildering response, but because his shoes indeed did have a relation to his conventional or unconventional behaviour.

In fact, they were the means by which he had left home from his army family and become an artist. His father, a strict disciplinarian, had insisted that the shoes of his sons should be left outside their bedrooms each night for his inspection. One night, among the immaculate black polished shoes and boots, there was an alien pair of brown suede shoes. The row that developed from this rebellion caused him, in the end, to leave and go to art college. But this was not the end of it. The Second World War upturned his decision for he was promoted in the field to a higher rank than the rest of his more conventional brothers. This made his initial break with army ambitions less certain, less absolute, less final. He retained his army moustache after the war, a certain military bearing, and a deep confusion about the condition of artist. Technically he carried it off by investing his creative work with a certain military discipline and eschewing completely any idea that his work might have any value in itself.

His fixation with his shoes caught the attention of the Minister, who put it down to tiredness. 'You should sleep, my dear man, we will talk again.'

At this the shoes and their owner immediately got up and took themselves off to bed leaving the Minister still unsatisfied, looking up at the sky and drinking deeply yet another lime juice.

(Thomas's response, to do immediately what he was told, might seem peculiar or too subservient. But the unexpected visitation had thrown both the artist and the military man into a hypnotic state emphasized by the peculiar nature of Khartoum life at that time of the year. Everyone had too much time to think so were prey to elaborate and usually paranoid fantasies about their careers, their servants and their phantom or actual wives.)

Having left the veranda the artist peeked uncomfortably from inside the house at the slumped figure of the Minister; he was showing no sign of leaving. He watched for a long time, well into the darkness, as the Minister sighed and stared into the sky on a stranger's veranda.

Finally, through fatigue, he retired and slept uncertainly,

conjuring up the huge face of the Minister staring into his own. He felt an ill-defined guilt as though there was something he had forgotten to do. With these last moments of conscious thought before sleep he had been struggling with a list of possible reasons for the Minister's presence. As he slipped into dream he thought he had the answer, but when he woke up in the morning it was gone and there was nothing he could do to retrieve it.

In the morning he crept out on to the veranda half-expecting to find the Minister still in his place staring at the morning sky. He was not. The events of the previous evening retreated quite reasonably into the category of dream, leaving only a little uneasiness. As the day wore on, the events of the previous night rose up again with their unanswered question. What did the Minister want? His colleagues were equally mystified. Their comments and speculations, he noticed, had a tinge of jealousy. Why had he been picked out for this visitation, they were thinking. Even if the reasons for it were sinister and they were glad it had not happened to them, the event was still invested with a peculiar prestige. They began to wait for a resolution; it must have an outcome and could not for ever remain an enigma.

Suspicions began to be aroused and developed about his conduct and a possible blow-back from the authorities. Certain people began to be insufferably knowing about the whole event, pretending that they had the inside story, that they had realized for a long time that it would have to come to this in the end. They had known from the moment that he had arrived in the Sudan that there was trouble ahead, that it could not possibly last.

By the end of the day most people were expecting him to pack his bags and make his way to the airport to pre-empt his certain dismissal. There was a flurry of excitement too about who might take his place, and the possible chances for advancement that his dismissal would open up. There was knowing talk of increments and future plans for the department. All this took place out of earshot of the holder of the potential vacancy and all he experienced was a strange cooling off and a feeling of absence. He stopped conversations when he walked into the room as though he were a ghost.

A few of the more charitable members of staff made a particular effort to talk to him but their conversation was stilted and the expression in their eyes evasive. They would not look him in the eye, as if they had news for him of such a disturbing nature that they would have to choose the time to tell him very carefully indeed. The fact that they based this disturbing behaviour on almost no evidence at all did not worry them in the slightest. Some were, towards the end of the day, even planning what they would say to him about the excellent nature of his work when he was packed and ready to take off for an uncertain future in England. They started to feel a burst of sentiment and loss at the leaving of a valuable partner in their pioneering educational enterprise.

When they left for home their heads were full of their own career advancement and a certain feeling that their conscientiousness and talent were about to be rewarded. It was a comfortable certainty, they thought, toying with a drink on the veranda, indulging in new and brisk authoritarian tones with the servant.

When Thomas arrived home he found the Minister in the same position as before, the servant fawning over him with a tray and a bowl of ice-cubes.

'You are a difficult man,' said the Minister and, fixing him with an interrogative eye, lurched round in a seat that was far too small for him. 'You are, what shall I say, enigmatic. I shall assume that it is the condition of artist that brings this condition.' This last phrase definitely had threatening overtones. It was the word 'assume' that implied his superior position in the conversation and almost, to exaggerate a little, the power of life and death.

'I am being as straightforward as I can,' said the sculptor, with as much dignity as he could muster. 'I cannot respond if I do not know what you have in mind.' That was it, he had asked the question. What did the Minister want?

'Ahh . . . ' said the Minister, 'you want a definite request through the regular channels. I'm not sure that is possible. I was thinking of a more personal arrangement. Something outside the regular channels.' There was a hint of anger in his voice. 'I wanted to talk to you about the fine form of the horse, its musculature, the form of the human leg.' He pulled up the hem of his djelabere exposing a huge and scarred calf. 'This leg . . . now do you understand!'

Thomas did not understand at all and had formed the conclusion that he was in the presence of a dangerous lunatic. He weighed the huge physical bulk of the Minister against his own strength which was rapidly ebbing away. He pulled up his trouser leg and slapped his own calf, a momentary inspiration. The Minister stared at him.

'Of course . . . of course . . . that's better.' The tone taken on by the Minister was now sympathetic, as if he too were tolerating a madman. 'I would prefer,' said the Minister, 'to take a dignified position with perhaps, symbolically speaking you understand, an arm outstretched indicating an interest in the future. We are talking about the future, are we not.'

He said this very slowly and stood up to demonstrate. He turned to look back at the apprehensive figure below him who was sipping his drink to give himself time to think of his next move. The Minister threw himself into his chosen pose once more and seemed to be waiting for approval of some kind.

The internal artist and the military man struggled silently with each other over rival courses of action, none of which seemed entirely appropriate. He stood up and almost shouted his next comment out of sheer nervousness and now with a hint of aggression.

'I would have thought a finger pointing would be more appropriate.' Thomas stretched out his arm and pointed into the distance to describe what he had in mind.

'Good,' said the Minister, 'that's more like it.' He slumped back into his seat then raised himself once more and started to make his way up the drive.

'Good session!' said the Minister. 'We will meet again to discuss further details and our private arrangement.' A car drew up that had been waiting round the corner and took him away.

He had emphasized the word 'private'. Did this mean that he should not discuss these strange meetings with anyone else? Was he becoming involved in Sudanese politics?

Apart from a brief flirtation with communism in the Thirties he was not political at all. He had views, a mixture of egalitarianism combined incompatibly with a strong belief in British power and a total cynicism about British political parties. His main attitude was that people should be allowed to get on with it, whatever it was, with the least possible interference. He was trying to make sense of the two meetings with the Minister. He could not take any further intrusions of that type. He was not being told what was expected of him. He knew very little about Sudanese politics although there were certain circles that talked of nothing else. As far as he was concerned it was dangerous and none of his business.

The next day he came down the drive expecting to see the, now familiar, figure of the Minister. This time he was not there. He did not come the next day or the next.

Thomas arrived home on the third day and, as he was walking down the drive, realized, with a sudden inspiration, what it was that the Minister wanted. He looked over at the veranda and was upset and disappointed to see that he was not there.

The fragments of conversation with the Minister had been connecting and disconnecting in his head without him being aware of the process. The crunch of the gravel under his foot soon after he stepped out of the car had triggered something in combination with the anticipation of the giant body on the veranda. Now he had the answer.

The Minister wanted an equestrian statue of himself, to be placed God knows where, but clearly part of his political ambition, his attempt at immortality. The arm pointing to the future was something he liked, something he wanted to be incorporated. Everything fell into place, his anxiety fell away, and he hoped that the Minister, who was after all a cultured man, would appear and they could do a deal, come to an arrangement, whatever he liked. Even his experience with the last Head of State did not put him off, such was his need to get on with something substantial, something that would use his skills to the utmost, something that would take him out of his loneliness and make him part of some world, however strange, however unpredictable and African.

But the Minister did not arrive. Thomas ate, drank a few drinks and went to bed. Soon after, he got up again, looked out on the veranda and went to bed again. He did not sleep but lay there in a state of indecision wondering how he should get back into contact.

Soon after he had second thoughts. He realized that he had embraced this new project too soon, that it was fraught with dangers and frustrations like the last one. The only public sculpture in Khartoum had been the statue of Lord Kitchener. All his work teaching sculpture had been in opposition to that statue, in opposition to his first-year students who wanted to start their course with a full-size bronze of a man on a horse. He had emphasized basic design, the sphere, the cone, the cube. Such was the strength, the power of that perched absurd statue, that imperial bronze, that his work had been frustrated and he still felt that he had not made the impression on his students that he should. He had expected that the Muslim attitude to three-dimensional images would have created a difficulty but he had not imagined that he would be pursued by bronze equestrian statues, a kind of imperial vengeance.

He decided not to do it.

The next day, still full of conviction about his decision of the night before, he was treated by his colleagues with a respect verging on fear. He trod around in this atmosphere for some time before asking explicitly what was the matter. He was taken to one side and asked if he knew that the Minister of the Interior had been assassinated in a particularly nasty way; his gut had been slit open with a knife. Thomas was so shocked by this that he had to return home immediately.

He walked down his drive with the absurd feeling that today, of all times, the Minister would be there to have further conversation about his statue, his immortality. He was not there. The servant was standing there with his drink. Things were all as normal and he was not to be pursued by the dead, demanding statues of themselves.

He sat for the whole evening smoking cigarette after cigarette in a concentrated reverie. He ground each butt into the floor as he finished it and immediately started another. Deep into the night he was still sitting there, the wind blowing through the trees summoning a dust storm to wipe it all away, to start again.

He felt battered by history.

As Thomas sat, he attempted to understand what had brought him here, what had happened to his original impulses as a child, as a young and successful artist in the Thirties. He put it down to the war. How could he start again, how could he continue his proper trajectory with a shrapnel wound in his back, the rank of Captain and the hollow sound of bronze hooves beating in his ears? He realized that the sound was his heart beating. The Minister of the Interior was in hot pursuit.

15

The Sanity of Anthony Eden

Michael woke up in the wrong place, surrounded by ticking clocks, with no idea of the time. He could hear the sound of sand trickling, an intermittent and anxious sound, as though the desert was about to empty into his bedroom and engulf him.

Through the leaded windows of his room were moonlit, frost-etched trees, leaning silently, chilled to the roots by the November air. There were a few cottages, their roofs white, their windows dark. He drew on his window, a circle with a dot in the middle, like a target.

He opened the window and met a wave of icy silence and the shiver of his own apprehension. There was an eddy in the frozen landscape. It was a distant sound like two blocks of hardwood struck firmly together to make a resonant note. It was hard to place in the landscape as, at the point of hearing it, it seemed to come from all directions at once.

He closed the window but it could still be heard, muffled but distinct. It was not going to let him sleep. It would not let him indulge his desire, his passion, to wake up elsewhere. It demanded immediate explanation and identification.

He dressed quickly and crept down the stairs, holding his shoes in his hand, still unconscious of where he was, what country, what circumstance. It was a kind of delirium in which he had become expert; it made him a tactician of unknown landscapes, of bubbling ambiguities.

He stopped outside a bedroom, one foot on a creaking board, and listened to the sounds within. There were two adults sleeping, an aunt and uncle. As they slept they cleared their throats as if at the point of making a pronouncement.

Nothing came, as though they had thought better of it. Then the throats cleared again, as if after further thought they had indeed now decided to speak. But nothing came. It gave the impression of deep but hesitant thought, a sentence, perhaps, that should and must be said although there was an insuperable difficulty contained in how to say it. It left an impossible tension in the air. What could they be wanting to say that was so embarrassing, so difficult, that they spent their sleeping hours with it on the tips of their tongues? Both of them had the same habit; an embryonic conversation between them for which the day did not give proper time or space and the night, no solution.

He felt like bursting into the room and demanding that they came out with it and told the truth to each other finally and completely. But they would not. They remained teetering on the brink of spelling out their sleeping secrets, the door closed.

The uncle was a film producer, recently returned from South Africa, where he had been involved in the production of a film about diamond smuggling that had mysteriously evaporated amongst complex financial problems of a very inexplicit nature. They had, however, been out there long enough to have developed an obsession with the dampness of the English countryside. When they arrived they had hung out the carefully aired sheets on their bed, hung them across the room on lines they had brought with them and subjected these already crisp sheets to a further process of drying out. There seemed to be some strange element of competition in this process. They had been in South Africa only a few months but they were acting as though they had little experience of the cold humidity of the English climate. Perhaps the clearing of their throats was only confirmation of the deleterious effects of a cold English November, a conscious and guilt-provoking noise indicating that they were not, if the truth were known, even unconsciously, used to such conditions.

The board under his foot creaked again. Then he was outside, bathed in moonlight, his hands clenched against the cold. The resonant noise hung in the silence of the village. He scraped the soles of his shoes on the cold tarmac of the road to make a noise that he could clearly identify, then set off down the hill towards the river. He pursued the noise, or, more disturbingly, the noise pursued him.

He plunged into dark thickets off the road in an attempt to place the origin of the sound, to identify its source, to nail it. He was scratched and bleeding from flailing brambles and was no nearer the solution.

He was looking down into the river sluicing past his feet, bubbling over the rocks, where he knew crayfish hid their transparent grey forms. He hung his hands into the water until they were numb, cold and white, then shoved them back into the pockets of his duffel-coat.

Over the river was the house of the village doctor, Dr Hope. There was a light on at the top of the house and his stout, striding figure could be seen passing backwards and forwards. Michael stepped over the rocks in the stream and walked over the lawn closer to the house trying to see what he was doing.

When he was in his most exposed position in the middle of the lawn, the window of the upstairs room was suddenly thrown open and the head of the doctor emerged as though he was about to greet him.

'Gamel Abdul Nasser,' shouted the doctor, as if in greeting, and slammed the window feeling the cold outside. He seemed, in immediate fearful retrospect, to be in a mood of jovial fury, a theatrical jousting mood, playing with the absurdity of the Arabic name. He continued to talk behind the secrecy of the window to a guest who could not be seen.

Michael was pressed close to the surface of the lawn, terrified of being seen and bewildered by the nature of the outburst. He moved slowly to his feet and made his way back across the river, stepping-stone by stepping-stone. 'Gamel Abdul Nasser' rang in his ears, the water swirling past his feet. He said the name to himself.

He crunched up the hill full of thought, still pursued by the mysterious clapping of distant wood blocks, a sound that he thought he had once identified at some time in the past but whose real nature he would not now discover. Perhaps it was the snapping of icicles overloaded, overcome with their own weight.

In his bed, still warm in parts, he felt the sand of the desert envelop him, the blankets the heavy weight of a grey dune above him. He fell asleep dreaming, with a mild sense of revenge, of the broken tooth of his History Master, a public and very obvious flaw that had plunged him, an adult, into silence and humiliation and, soon afterwards, into oblivion.

The school had a new Headmaster. He was of the new managerial class and was immediately immersed, with scrubbed red face and crisp shirt, in an investigation of examination results. He called them 'our measure of success'. Having discovered that the passes in History were not of sufficient standard he interviewed the History Master and demanded changes in teaching practice and a consequent improvement in results. The History Master went into a sullen mood, obvious to all, and reacted by refusing to talk to his pupils. Instead he handed out duplicated sheets of questions which the pupils were to tick or cross in absolute silence during the course of the period. During one of these lessons a large piece of his front tooth fell out, leaving him gap-toothed. He held the fragment of tooth in his hand for a long time looking at it and feeling the hole that it had left. Then he crunched it under his foot and walked out of the room.

He could be seen through the window of the public house over the road from the school mournfully drinking and staring out, gap-toothed, into the unwelcoming street. Soon, in the way these things happen, he was not seen at all and he was assumed to have left. He was missed. It was believed that he may have, at some time, voted Labour. But no one would have suspected him of being a supporter of Nasser. Before he left he was seen reading the *Daily Mail*. It was too late.

In his sleep Michael struggled with the necessity, the barely conscious demand, to find himself awakening in an African dawn, the midnight-blue sky edged with soft pink, the soft dry warmth stirring the leaves of the lemon trees, the distant sound of Arabic music spreading from the markets of Omdurman over the river. But it was not possible; he opened his eyes each time to the darkness of an English dawn.

He imagined the crayfish stirring under their stones, the water swirling past them, their antennae waving, searching for cold food amongst the grit.

So he thought it through, half-awake, the Somerset village around him, a retreat from Africa.

His mother had discovered the house and it had become for a short time the apple of her eye. It was the return from Africa, the return to England. It was country living, an implication of privilege, the intimacy of village life and friends to be made. It was, for a time, a perspective on the confusions and shifting sands of Khartoum life; that cocktail party in the midst of a million square miles of desert.

But the village itself was, unfortunately, crippled by an errant and untimely feudalism. It rejected newcomers with waves of indifference. They, the vicar, the doctor, the Lady of the Manor, thought nothing of Africa and less of those who had returned from it. His mother found she had no one to talk to (except their bank manager in the nearby town) now that her husband had returned to his work. She cleaned the place often and read the *Radio Times*.

He, of course, was meant to be ill. That is why he was away from school. He pretended, while walking through the village, to be gripped inconsolably into an expression of terminal sickness or, at other times, to limp. If he passed anyone in the street he would apparently be overcome by a fit of tubercular coughing. For a time he toyed with the idea of mental illness and took to rolling his eyes and publicly exposing his tongue if inspected with curiosity by any of the locals. They merely averted their eyes. Sometimes he would forget and would be consumed by a coughing fit when his potential audience had already passed. Once, after a few weeks of this kind of exercise, his fit of imaginative coughing changed into a fit of laughter when he had, all in a moment, recognized how absurd his whole tactic had become. While he was laughing uncontrollably to himself he realized that he was being watched with curiosity by the girl who worked in the local shop. This was a serious matter. She had become the focus and crystallization of a number of his jumbled sexual fantasies, strange combinations of Grace Kelly and Brigitte Bardot. He had slunk away. From then on he forgot his pretence of illness and experimented with an ancient bike left at the house by the previous occupants.

He stared at his reflection in the closed window. He was smoking a crushed and bent 'Passing Cloud' cigarette, blowing the smoke against the cold glass behind which was the dense black of the dawn. The moon had disappeared; the smoke billowed back at him.

His father had gone back to Africa in disgust several months ago after a series of embarrassing events to do with a right of way. Michael could not go to Africa because the British Air Force was at that moment bombing Port Said and Alexandria; Nasser was sinking ships in the Suez Canal; the charter flights from Airwork could not fly over the war zone. He and his mother were trapped in England; his father was trapped in Africa listening to the World Service of the BBC.

In the meantime fourteen- and fifteen-year-olds were bombing Russian tanks in Budapest with Molotov cocktails.

He could not even ride a bike.

More disturbing was the question of his cousin. He hardly remembered him. There was his capacity to fall out of windows and eat vast amounts of chocolate. What else? The two sisters had lived together in Brighton just after the war. There were other sisters, five more of them. One was staying at the moment, putting up with damp sheets . . . she was the eldest and knew how things should be done. She did not have any children and was a film editor in Soho.

His cousin was now in America, an American teenager. The family compared them, their various achievements and disasters; real and imaginary . . . He did not want to be compared; he did not want to be under scrutiny; he did not want to be the subject of airmail letters to anywhere in the world. If anyone was going to make up things about his success or failure it should, in natural justice, be himself. And it was he who should blur over embarrassing events, disasters and the like . . .

For the first time he felt spied upon, under surveillance, an object for some kind of international family game of consequences. Up the road was a man called Hollis who was rumoured to be the brother of the Head of MI5. No doubt he was implicated. Michael saw him wandering down the hill trying to look in through the front windows of the house, waving his stick in front of him, trying to appear as though he were not curious about the events and the people within.

On the outskirts of the village was a small line of council houses. Most of them were inhabited by farm workers. One was the house of a communist, an engineering worker from the nearby town. His windows had been smashed with a brick. It had something to do with the Russian tanks in Hungary. Michael was the only person in the village who would talk to him. He was persecuted too. Perhaps someone would throw a brick through their window soon and they would have to leave. All the signs pointed to it. They were part of Africa which was now being bombed by the Air Force. They were the allies of Gamel Abdul Nasser. It was the same part of the world and all who worked there were automatically part of it.

He stubbed his cigarette out on the window sill and then spent some time scraping off the burnt paint with a penknife. He opened the window and smelt the air. There was no sound coming out of the darkness except, perhaps, the hum of sleeping conspirators. He closed the window and crept into bed, his thinking done. There was no doubt that he was in a panic.

He dreamt of Molotov cocktails and barbed wire. The Molotov cocktails originated in Hungary and the barbed wire was the barbed wire that his father had unrolled over the right of way in front of the house. It was this barbed wire that had trapped the Lady of the Manor in the middle of the night when she was trying to demonstrate her public rights and quell her curiosity. She had screamed very loudly and there had been an ugly scene. Tanks rolled in from up the hill only to explode in sheets of flame in front of his window. The enemy was everywhere. The problem was to discover who the enemy might be. He ran through the streets, the petrol slipping over his hand making it greasy, slippery, difficult to hold the bottle. In a doorway his mother was reading the *Radio Times* ignoring it all. There was the beep of the time signal for the news. It was Saturday and the Russians had come back. He was going to die.

He woke with a start just at the point when the streets of the village were crowded with young women tightly holding the hands of black children. The village was in flames and a tank had run into the front of their house. It was still burning.

He had seen these children before. They were the sons and daughters of black USAF staff stationed close to the village. In the village they had a kind of half-life led by the hands of disgraced village girls dressed in poor skirts, who had the twisted mouths of those who have had too much to put up with. They always took the side roads, the pathways through woods and were never to be seen in the main street. They were like ghosts, never acknowledged but always there, a living reproof, a warning that the foreigner was never to be trusted. Now their children had become, illogically, the children of Gamel Abdul Nasser.

It was Sunday. He was late down to breakfast.

A pale cold light illuminated the kitchen where his aunt and uncle were laying a full-scale breakfast. There was the aroma of frying bacon and toast.

'Your mother has a little headache,' said his aunt by way of explanation for her unaccustomed activity. 'She's in the other room.'

His uncle released a 'hrrrumph' of agreement as he polished a knife and placed it on a white serviette. They were demonstrating how things should be done. He had shaved only one side of his face as though he had been interrupted half-way through.

They did not seem to want to talk, busy as they were preparing breakfast. His uncle inclined his head towards the room where his mother was having her headache. The movement seemed to indicate that he should go in to see her. There was a rather mysterious atmosphere. He wandered out the front door. It was closed violently behind him. He had been causing a draught. England was a draughty country, the wind got everywhere, nothing was airtight, nothing sealed.

Leaning against the wall was the old black bicycle just where he had left it the day before. The grass was frosted on the front lawn.

He looked back through the window and caught a distorted reflection of his mother's pale face, immobile, looking out at him. He approached the window and looked through at her. She seemed to be absolutely still, sitting in a chair looking straight in front of her, her arms neatly on the arms of the chair as though she had been arranged in that position. She did not seem to be blinking.

He went quickly back into the house, ignored the wafting smells of breakfast and went into the other room.

'Breakfast's ready,' said the voice of his aunt in a gay tone. 'You sit here, then we can start.' There was some whispering between them and a mutual clearing of throats. Michael was looking at his mother. She seemed to be paralysed. Her face was dead white and her breathing was sharp and shallow. She did not respond to him. He felt her hand. It was cold.

He went back into the kitchen.

'We thought we would call the doctor after breakfast,' said his aunt. 'She will be better then. Much better to get some breakfast inside us first.' She started to pour the tea.

He was out of the house on the way to the doctor. Without thinking he grabbed the bicycle, mounted it and wobbled off down the hill. He heard the door slam behind him. He was causing a draught again.

The hill down to the river and the doctor's house was steeper than he had remembered it from the night before. The bike wobbled and rapidly increased speed. He did not brake but allowed the bike to freewheel. The trees rushed past him, his fingers twitched on the brake but did not squeeze. He would not brake until the very last moment. Molotov cocktails were bursting in his head, he was in the streets of Warsaw dodging the fire of Russian tanks.

At the last moment he wrenched on the brakes at the point where the road swerved to cross the river. The brakes did not work. The bicycle continued in a straight line, hit a stump at the edge of the road and threw him into the air, head over heels, to land in a muddy patch at the edge of a field.

He was dazed, in Budapest and Somerset simultaneously. He fell back, his hands over his face, the bruises and abrasions of his fall turning into pain. He heard the resonance of distant wood blocks, the rush of the river, the rub of branches swaying in the trees. Fear trickled like sand.

The doctor had to be woken from his Sunday-morning lie-in. There was a confusion as to who it was who was in need of treatment. Michael was covered in mud, with scratches and cuts, and would have kept the doctor occupied on his own, a more congenial Sunday-morning occupation than an emergency up the hill.

'We'll walk,' said the doctor. He had recovered his rude attacking attitude to emergencies once having deciphered the real nature of the problem.

'Exercise,' said the doctor by way of conversation as he strode energetically up the hill. Michael followed him painfully looking back at the wreckage of the black bicycle. The doctor stood at the top of the hill and looked down at Michael. He seemed to have reverted to the thought patterns of the night before.

'Nasser,' he announced, 'is a bounder.' He seemed to be pleased to be engaging in this kind of conversation on a cold Sunday morning in November.

As the ambulance was about to leave, his aunt and uncle announced that it was essential for them to get back to London so they would not be there when he returned. He shook hands with his uncle and uncomfortably kissed the powdered cheek of his aunt.

'Keep up the school work,' said his uncle.

It was an aneurism, an expanded, flooded blood vessel in his mother's brain that was causing her paralysis. Nasser had sunk ships into it, blocking the passage of blood, stifling movement, disallowing thought.

Michael refused to allow the hospital to put his mother into a private room. He was sure that they could not afford it. There were school fees to pay and his father's flight back from Africa. The hospital staff swallowed this strange militancy, sure in their own minds that anyone returning from Africa would have, for all practical purposes, unlimited wealth and would demand a private room. In the end they came to a compromise. She had the room but would not have to pay for it.

They extracted samples of spinal fluid and chatted to the paralysed woman about her experiences in Africa.

Michael returned to the house and was enveloped in plans to make love passionately to the girl in the village shop, the girl with the cold, passionless face and long limbs who had earlier in the year promised to marry Prince Rainier of Monaco.

16
Shrapnel

Now they are all talking to Thomas as though he is the only person in the room. What is he to them; a piece of driftwood to which they all cling? What possible confirmation could he give them? He knows no more than they do.

They are out of their depth, thinks Thomas, they are sinking, their grabbing expatriate arms and flailing legs are searching for a resting place. It is not going to be him. Their lungs gasp for air, they want to be saved and sent back to England; refugees from the war zone. They use up his patience. Damn them all!

Thomas is breathing more quickly. He's angry. He's drunk enough to confuse anything, jumble the present, past and future.

There is that peculiar metallic smell in the dry air, it gets behind the teeth, coats the tongue: the smell of bullets from a thousand miles away in Port Said; puffs of smoke on a desert horizon far away in Egypt. The crunch of bombs.

He is catching their fear. There is no doubt about it. The wound in his back is starting to ache.

He was falling, a long time ago, into a ditch in Normandy, covered in wet khaki and blood, a piece of shrapnel passing through his body, smashing the face of the man next to him. It would send him back to England where he wanted to be. He rolled over and over, then, in the distant past, without feeling the slightest pain.

He has drunk too much. Everyone is talking too much. They are bilious with talk, brimming with alcohol, chock-a-block with anxiety, cock-a-hoop with patriotism. Why? He wants to get home. Home? With the Suez Canal jammed in the way, flights cancelled, and a wife paralysed in an English hospital ward? It's not possible.

Basic design, pyramids, cones, cubes and spheres; bloody squelching clay, battered iron, hardening cement, splintering stone, flowing blood, dripping sand; bloody pyramids, frozen hands, hot breath; electric arcs, melting metal, broken bones, broken bloody hearts. Bloody English villages. Shrapnel. Too much talk.

Thomas trips over the veranda and almost falls flat on his face. Yes, yes, he says to himself, I'm pushed out, falling out, back to England. I'm off to England. Driftwood with spivs hanging on to it, that's England, floating around in the North Sea. Nobody, but nobody, is thinking clearly. Thought and elucidation, that's what's needed in Khartoum. Elucidation and basic design; a flight to England as though nothing has happened.

Why is this man Mapplebeck sitting on the veranda? Everyone else is eating inside.

This representative of the Schermuly Pistol Rocket Apparatus Limited, suppliers of pyrotechnic apparatus to the Army and Air Force (and the Police Force), is pretending to be legitimate. Here he is. A firework rep in a war zone! Why isn't he inside gathering information? Everyone is hysterical and will tell him anything he wants to know. Why isn't he investigating the extent of the support for Anthony Eden, the hatred of the Americans, or the conditions over the border in the Belgian Congo where the Belgians are murdering the natives? He is a spy, why doesn't he do it!

All information is loose in the city of Khartoum, Thomas can feel it, all kinds of games being played, all kinds of secrets up for grabs. Everyone is pretending to be the source of knowledge, knowing the real intentions of the British Government, Nasser himself, and above all the Americans. Everyone is an insider now. The events themselves are happening only a thousand miles away to the north!

Why is Mapplebeck sitting out here with every appearance of calm, stroking his moustache, juggling a drink in his hand as though he were relaxing at home, inspecting the night air, calmly turning over his prospects, sniffing the wind, gently engaged with his own future? That is what Thomas is thinking. Mapplebeck, a statesman, always calm in a crisis. Who is paying him? Has he got a way out of here? Or would they have to depend on the RAF? Is he working for the Czechs, supplying arms, or is he an Israeli agent keeping an eye on the Sudan? Whoever it is, is paying him well. He has a new shirt with gold cufflinks. Perhaps there has been a run on firework displays?

Mapplebeck winks conspiratorially; that is a habit of his. He clears his throat; another habit. Thomas is trying to remember where they last met.

'War wound playing up,' Mapplebeck says. It is more of a statement than a question. 'It seems to me,' he continues, leaning forwards in a conspiratorial fashion to go with his habitual wink, 'that war wounds all over the world are throbbing like billy-oh. They expect a few colleagues to join them before twelve months is out. More wounds, you see. War on the horizon.'

He settles back, screwing up his face into an expression of great knowingness. What does he know?

'The Russians start with Hungary. Then, sweeping all before them, they invade Europe. The yoke of communism. Then, back in England, my dear fellow, we will be ruled by home-grown communists who will come out of the woodwork when the Ruskies take over. That's the way it's going to be. Better, on the whole, if we stay out here. Move down to Rhodesia or on to South Africa. Take it from me, Europe's had it. Wiped off the map. Eisenhower will wipe his hands of it all.'

Mapplebeck is leaning back again. What is he after? Thomas winces in expectation of further nuggets of wisdom.

'I have work for you.'

Here it comes, he's recruiting, thinks Thomas. Would you believe it?

'I need a bit of welding work on one of my lorries. On the underside. Need someone I can trust. Little bit of welding, here and there. You have the equipment, skills and all that.

102

Do something for the cause. Slipping some bon-bons out of the country hidden away in the chassis. Over the border. Maybe I'll go off to the Congo.'

Mapplebeck lights a cigarette, shading the flame as though he is under fire in a wartime trench, his eyes flicking from side to side in case they might be overheard. God in heaven, he is off his head! Why else would he be asking a sculptor to assist his smuggling operations?

'Communism has had its last day. Tanks in the streets firing at civilians . . . it's not good enough. It's not good enough. Even I thought there might be something in it in the Thirties. Muddy waters, eh? Joe Stalin misses out in the Mapplebeck brain.'

He is tapping his head with his finger too long to make it seem a normal gesture.

'Strain of it all, gets to you in the end. War wounds, war wounds. Can't think what we are all doing here. Can't unravel it at all.'

He is looking out into the garden as though talking only to himself. Then he looks back. He looks weary.

'England, my dear man, is a wonderful country. It has green fields and hills. It has the Queen. It has a fine democracy. It has a Conservative Government. What else do we want?'

Is there a steely glint in his eye?

'See this.' He is putting a revolver on the table. 'It's a souvenir of the war. Heavy. Feel it!'

He is mad, thinks Thomas. He is going to kill himself, wander down to the bottom of the garden and blow his brains out. He's tinkering with the gun, thinking about it, turning it around in his head. Is he married?

On the other hand Mapplebeck could turn the gun on others and put them out of their misery. He could run riot, become yet another incident demonstrating the collapse of nerve that affected them all, starting when the Sudan became independent, reaching its apogee now, when the British were in action at Suez. They were lost in a no-man's-land, not happy in England, homesick in the Sudan, always waiting for news from home. It was an aneurism, blood escaping into the brain. Was she going to die?

'It's not the circumstances that are getting me down, old son. You must understand that. It's inside. In here. It's the feeling that something's gone, never to come back. Can you feel it? It's like a lump, here.' He presses his heart.

'It's not the money problems. Not at all, although those are bad enough. It's just that I can't seem to see the point, if you know what I mean. Money's only money, after all. Somewhere or other I seem to have lost the point of it all. I think [he is leaning forward talking in a whisper] that it's spiritual, you understand. None of it makes sense [he is waving at the stars]. There is no way I can get the bitter taste out of my mouth, however much I drink. It's a spiritual crisis.

'Do you believe in God, old son? Bent the knee a bit when I was young. I know enough to know a spiritual crisis when I see one. I see it every morning in the mirror under the shaving brush. You would have thought we would be immune out here, Godless wilderness that it is!

'Don't take to the Sudanese myself. Never know what they're thinking. Very polite. Oh my God, are they polite! But mark my words are they watching you . . . are they watching you! Little black eyes on the look-out! Checking on the tie-pins. Few little phone calls and the game's up. The game's up!

'Like a few hymns myself. Grant to sailors tossing on the deep blue sea. Wanking on the waves. Britannia rules the waves.'

Thomas goes into a sudden reverie while listening to this nonsense. Tiny veranda trapped in the middle of the universe. Why am I listening to this man? African stars burning down above us, the chatter of drunks from inside the house, the glimmer of light flattering the profile of this fraudulent commercial traveller as he plays with his moustache and tries to involve me in his jokes, his games, his unpleasant pursuits; his pathetic recourse to his knees when he is found out. He is a phantom, transparent in all his workings, a joke but not a joke. A grim jester.

What is it that matters to me, thinks Thomas? We all, all

the drunks, all the commercial travellers, all the spies, want to get out of this place. I want to get out of this place. Away from this remorseless jester, this fool without wisdom.

'Let's face it, old pal. We don't belong here. Who knows where we belong. We are has-beens. They have caught up with us, seen through us. What do they say? Not much to say about him. Don't see how he holds his job. Empty vessel, hollow man, straw man, con man. He'll have to go.

'At the same time, who is it who's in the driving seat? The real con men, the real tricksters, the ones who have got the situation tied up, who have tied us up, who pack it all away in Switzerland in a numbered account, air tickets in the pocket, just in case something goes wrong.

'Suez. Take that as an example. All about the contract for the Aswan Dam. Who will get the pickings? The Americans, the Russians, the Egyptians, the British, the French, the Israelis? Do you get it? The tricksters have got it tied up.'

Thomas looks at Mapplebeck's wet, drooping lower lip and tries to out-guess him. There are tears in Mapplebeck's eyes. He is fingering the place where his tie-pin should be. Has he taken it off to hide the evidence?

Now he is fingering the cufflinks affectionately as if they are of sentimental value. He is taking them off and putting them on the table. More evidence of his diversion of funds for all to see. He lays them next to the pistol and takes another drink. He brushes away a tear with the side of his hand.

'The tricksters have got it sewn up.'

Out of the house comes a burst of baszooki music. Mapplebeck is launching himself out of the chair into a parody of a Greek dance, making even more of a fool of himself. He's drunk beyond redemption, all dignity gone. The music finishes and he is back at the table holding the pistol, lolling back into his seat. His eyes are a little wild. He has got a gun . . . should someone have taken it away from him?

'This way,' he says pointing the gun at the garden. 'You follow me. It's time to blast my brains out. Can't get out of the country. Can't take a Sudanese prison, that would be bad for my health, don't you agree?'

In the darkness of the garden Mapplebeck points the gun at his own chin, releases the trigger and falls back into the night, his face smashed, his arms limp.

Mapplebeck is not Thomas. Thomas is alive, thank God, feeling no pain, there he is falling back into a trench in Normandy, the shrapnel passing through his body, missing the kidneys by a hair's breadth, passing through and smashing the face of the man next to him. He is rolling over and over without feeling the slightest pain, hearing nothing, keeping his charmed life. They would send him back to England this time if he wasn't too drunk.

Thomas knocks the cufflinks off the table. He picks them up, puts them back and stares at the crowd in the garden that has clustered round the body.

17

Lumbar Punch

Violet was in a war-zone, receiving contradictory instructions, confusing explanations and commands from doctors and nurses, staring out at the hospital ward.

Cerebro-spinal fluid is a clear liquid (full of thought and retrospect) that surrounds the brain and passes down into the spinal cord from where the nerves pass into the body (which is racked and anxious). It is there to feed and lubricate the nervous system, to protect it, like a buffer, from shock (to protect it from fantasies and thoughts that turn in unexpected ways). It circulates, moves by minute ciliary hairs within the nervous membranes (carrying thought to thought). It is separate from the blood system. Consequently, if blood corpuscles are found within it then there has been a leakage somewhere in the system (the secrets are getting out somewhere). To test if this has happened a sample has to be withdrawn from the lower spinal cord in the lumbar region. A hypodermic is inserted in this region and the cerebro-spinal fluid is withdrawn and taken off to be inspected (who would know what to make of it, it belongs to someone else). This is called a lumbar punch and is unfortunately a little painful for the patient (she treats it all with some distance, as if it were someone else's war). It is a routine hospital task if, for instance, the patient has an aneurism in the brain and it is necessary to check on its progress, to see if blood is still leaking from the site of the original lesion (the damage happened much earlier, this is just the effect, not the cause).

It's nice to be fully informed, keeping a check on the stability of one's fluids, the state of one's blood pressure, the exact contents of one's urine, the rhythmic activity of one's brain, the possibility of evacuating one's large intestine, the possibility of one living or dying, or if one is to be operated upon, or not, according to the best medical advice and always in one's own interest. However, one's head is full of other things that do not appear on the charts at the bottom of the bed in written or graphical form. (How do I pin them down? They emerge in my thoughts and dissolve like clouds, like the weather. If you watch a cloud for long enough it melts away and you have the impression that it was your will that made it go.)

Cerebro-spinal fluid under the microscope. They are looking for those microscopic fruit gums, red blood corpuscles, that shouldn't be there, that have got out. They are evidence that something is wrong, confirmation that something has to be done about it, that the skull has to be lifted off and strangers have to work inside it, inspecting, parting, maybe mending. Sharp stainless-steel implements parting nerve from nerve, thought from thought, memory from memory, desire from desire. I don't know what I think about the lack of privacy. I may even panic at the thought that they may find secrets that I know nothing about, that I have kept out of mind, behind membrane walls, behind sensible and normal thoughts. But there's not much point worrying about it. As long as they don't tell your friends or family, I suppose it doesn't matter. The main point seems to be to keep a grip on things, tell stories to myself, find warm comfortable things to tell myself and try not to cry. Would I be able to feel the tears running down my face?

I'm worried about my eyes. Are the pupils dilating too much? The light seems very strong, the windows are whited out and blurred. Perhaps I have lost control over the iris, so all I can see is overexposed, badly framed, a moving album of faded snapshots that stir some remembrances, while other glimpses of passing people like the faded photographs of forgotten aunts produce only an obscure feeling of guilt. I don't recognize what is happening in front of me. I am moved by things that don't appear to have any meaning, that I don't recognize, that nevertheless stir feelings and emotions that I cannot identify. When I blink the world suddenly vanishes in a cloud of pale darkness and there is nothing but the whirls and spots of my brain working on its own outside my control struggling with memories and origins, distances and proximities, revulsions and faint desires.

Someone has brought me copies of the *Brighton Evening Argus* because my relations live there by the sea. I can hardly read them. The new Astronomer Royal says we will never get to the moon. Will the Government resign? There is a seagull in Shoreham that they call Hat-Grabber Nasser after the Egyptian. He flies down and steals the hats off fishermen's heads.

All I can think of Brighton is the sound of the shingle being drawn back by the waves, the music of rounded stone upon rounded stone, drawing and retreating; the grey white spray of the winter sea hitting one's face walking along past the bandstands, the groynes; the black metal skeletons of the West and Palace Piers with their battered silver domes looking as though they were at the point of being overwhelmed by the rough water underneath them. The Shiverers Club at the swimming pool. The smell of seaweed from Black Rock is called ozone, although Michael says it is not possible and said something about three molecules of oxygen joined together in the outer atmosphere. I don't always understand what he is talking about. Has he been to see me?

Brighton is my sisters and my father. I remember the boarding houses and the upraised wooden hands used for making gloves in my father's factory. Why did he say we were not Jewish? I can hardly remember him; I can't remember his voice. Why am I guilty about my aunts, what did I do to them? Were they poor or were they rich? Where did they come from?

The *Evening Argus* was brought to me because I used to live in Brighton and they thought it might jog my memory and keep me alive. But I can't spend the time looking at it; I don't have the time, there is so much to do inside without being bothered with headlines and the state of the world.

Did they find any blood in the sample, am I still leaking secrets to doctors and medical technicians? I could giggle about it if I had time to get round to it. I've still got the splitting headache but then I suppose that's what it's all about, the reason I am here. Given a bit of time it will go away and there will be silence and the sound of the shingle at Brighton moved back and forth by the waves.

I must look a sight. I wish I could put on some make-up, brush the eyebrows a little, otherwise I look sightless and confused. It's this pale skin and blue eyes. They vanish into the face without a little help. If only I could brush my hair, give it a good brush, even give it a set if I had the time. I must have brought something with me to brush my hair. I don't like the idea of using someone else's, it's so unhygienic. Before the war I had a hat with a veil, a black one. Before the war I didn't need a veil because I was pretty. The war ruined all that. I suppose the new face is all right but I still haven't got used to it. I wonder if the bits of mirror got into my brain and I'm really a war casualty more than ten years after it finished. No one will treat it like that now, there isn't the sense of urgency. Even Winston Churchill wears more make-up than I do. He drove through Brighton waving at us last year. He passed close by and waved his cigar at me sitting in the back of an open-topped car. He looked old and confused and he was gripping the side of the car tightly, as though he felt he was going to fall out at any moment.

The lumbar punch is so painful that I don't know how to cope with it. It is so painful that it wipes out memories completely. They come back slowly floating into an agonizing fog. I wish I could pin them down, so there was something firm I could think, something I could follow to the end, something firm, solid, real.

I can hear the clink of trollies and the talking of the nurses. There is a blue cabinet next to my bed. Someone opens the drawers in the night and takes things out of it. Are they stealing my things? What things have I got? Have I my own hairbrush? Are they taking that? I must have brought some things with me; a dressing-gown, nightdress, things like that. They can't steal those, it's not possible!

They steal cerebro-spinal fluid from me, the pain is like

giving birth to my son. He was taken out of me, or did I push him out? He didn't struggle out himself! I made him and pushed him out there. He is going to do what I can't do.

Before the war it was different. I had a different face. Everything was working out. There was the war, I had a son, all at the same time. It's hard to explain how quickly things can happen, how quickly bombs can fall, how little warning everyone has before their lives are uprooted and they have responsibilities, all of a sudden, that they had hardly thought about before. Of course, it's unfair. Just when you have got used to something nice, it vanishes. You have had no time to take pleasure in it, put it neatly in your memory, nicely framed, part of your life, part of who you are. Things have not been like that.

Now I have another war to cope with, in between me and my husband. Wars spoil people's lives.

The nurse is talking to me about Africa. She knows nothing about it. Nothing about the effort it takes to go from one day to the other. It's not about looking at the Pyramids, doesn't she know that? She doesn't even know where Khartoum is! She should go away, I don't have time to talk to her, there is something I have to think about, such a lot of work I have to do. I have to lie here and think things through without interruption from those who know nothing about it.

Why is it that things will not work out? Why is it that I spend my life hoping that at last something pleasant, something invigorating, something hopeful, will happen? Why is it that I, myself, can do nothing about it? Can't make it happen, can't stop things going wrong! Men do things but they are hopeless at it. They don't make things work in the way that I want them to. Never, never, in the way I want. Never, never in the way that they want. What is the matter with them all, have they all lost control? Are they all mad or ill like Anthony Eden? I can't stand sickness or ugliness. I want people to have perfect teeth and not talk with accents. I want people to understand what I am talking about. I want people to listen, and listen properly, and then go and do something about it. I can't stand indecision and men who can't even make a phone call to get things moving. There is always something in the way. Some reason for not getting on with it, some reason for going off and talking to so-and-so about it first. Before you know where you are the situation has changed and it's too late. It's always too late. Before you know where you are it's all out of your hands and all you can do is put up with it. That's what women are all about. Putting up with this and that, with births and deaths, and hospitals. Women are always ill; they are ill because they are always disappointed and fall ill from the weight of it, their wombs collapse from disappointment, their skin wrinkles, they get short-sighted and faint-hearted. Women feel all the pain, all the frustration that the men cannot feel because they are off thinking of something else, waiting for the right moment. Then when they do finally decide to do something, it's always wrong, they've chosen the wrong time, they've worked it out wrongly, they've tried to influence the wrong person at the wrong time. Men are wrong. Always wrong. Women don't have a chance to be right because men don't listen to them.

What's the good of me talking, no one is listening!

So you flirt with them. That's the only way to get their attention. That's the only thing they respond to, the only thing they want, to be flattered. But it's not to get the things that we want, because once we've got them they don't mean much. It's not that. It's to get them to listen, to get them cracking on the right track so they are in a position to be in control of things, right out of this acceptance of everything that hits them out of the blue. Nothing comes out of the blue, not really. You must be able to predict something, to have a plan to cope with it, have an idea where you want to end up.

So women, all my sisters and I, flirt and flirt and flirt hoping that there will be some change, that things will settle down and become predictable, that there will be some happiness and control over what happens. That's what we want. Why are things so different?

Through a peculiar haze I am trying to flirt with the doctor who is telling me something. Perhaps he is just being polite. I must look terrible. I can't move enough yet to sort myself out.

He seems a great distance away. It's difficult to smile or make a joke. What is he saying? Why doesn't he speak up? The nurse is talking to him about Africa. She doesn't know anything about it even though she is black. It's only people who have been to Africa who know what the problem is.

The problem of Africa is that it is a desert.

Cerebro-spinal fluid is a clear fluid (suffused with doubt and anxiety). It surrounds the brain and the spinal cord from where the nerves pass into the body (allowing an arm to be raised to brush the hair). It is there to feed and lubricate the nervous system, to protect it like a buffer, from shock (to protect it from the unexpected damage that comes out of the blue). It circulates, moves by minute ciliary hairs within the nervous membranes (carrying secrets). It is separate from the blood system. Consequently if blood corpuscles are found within it then there has been a leakage somewhere in the system. (The secrets have got out and have drained away somewhere. Were they ever really secrets? Perhaps everyone knew them all before.) To test if this has happened a sample has to be taken from the lower spinal cord in the lumbar region. A hypodermic is inserted and the fluid is withdrawn and taken off to be inspected. This is called a lumbar punch and is, unfortunately, a little painful for the patient. (She treats it all with some distance as if it were someone else's war. But, in truth, it is really her war she is fighting.) It is only a routine hospital task.

18
Plankton

It was a moonlit night, glittering on the black metal of the end of Michael's bed. He had got out of the school, secretly, quietly, swearing under his breath, and was walking to Brighton. He wanted the sea and, in any case, could not allow himself to sleep. If he slept he dreamt and he was afraid of dreaming, for in his dream his mother was dead. He would do anything to avoid it. He tricked himself into believing that he was in control of himself at every moment, that he owned his thoughts, and was subjected to nothing.

He was trapped in Sussex, and had lost all sense of what was expected of him. He had tossed and turned trying to find a relaxed position. He got out of the school instead. It was not possible to relax anywhere.

The trees loomed at him, threateningly, along the way. Foxes yelped. Occasionally, the road was shaded from the moon by hedges. Then he had to aim blindly, crunching noisily towards a dim patch of moonlight at the other end of what seemed like a dark tunnel. When in the almost total darkness he could feel the incline under his feet, the dips and hills. When going up hill, he listened to the increase in his rate of breathing and heard it relax on the way down. Then, when into the light, he glimpsed bobbing moonlit horizons over fences and walls, the shapes of houses. Others had drawn their curtains, locked their doors, located their pillows, and disappeared into unconsciousness, their windows blanked out, their eyes closed, dreaming of kings and queens, the corpses of great men.

He had developed and worked up this habit of going out at night into an obsession. He loaded himself with experiences

114

before the day cracked open his head and lost him in routine (bells and duties and work periods and more bells). He wanted to stare at the world when no one else was looking at it. He wanted to carve his initials on it before it turned into something else and slipped away. His stability (this is how he explained it to himself) was based on his experience of the night, his explorations into an amnesiac world that nightly forgot everything that was real and replaced it with dreams. It carried him through the day without flinching (but with an oblivious and sleep-starved stare that drew adverse comment from some members of staff who wondered about his sanity and wondered also if he was really suitable to be a prefect).

The outskirts of Brighton were deserted. It was half-past three in the morning and a wind had got up, skirling paper through the streets. He put his collar up and skirted through the whirlpool of the bus station behind the cinema and came out on to the front. There was no one in either direction. He crossed the road, looking to right and left before he crossed, the wind blowing in his face. Then he was down the steps, on to the lower Promenade and was crunching over the salty pebbles on the beach. The deep smell of pitch rose from the shadows of the wooden boats around him, the cobweb tracery of fishing nets lay drying on the pebbles or heaped in ragged piles.

Then he was over the rise of shingle and faced the cold and moonlit sea between the piers. It was another universe; its wind and smell, noise, rumble and undertow, its wind-spun surface, taste, its depth and dimension; that was why he had come. A car passing along the front soon droned away into the distance.

Further out, beyond the piers, was the black ocean. He faced it as though he were confronting his own fate (the purpose of his night walk). He expected a revelation, a crystallization of his purpose. There was nothing in the cold sea to inform him. He shivered.

He forced something to happen. He imagined the sea bolt upright, a vertical wall in front of him, its surface stirring ominously, its surface disappearing sheer into the sky, dividing the universe in half. He closed his eyes while looking deep into the vertical sea, the delicate shells of dead crustacea falling away from him into the depths, the pulsating bells of medusae weakly moving in the cold salt water. Larval forms suspended themselves in front of him, microscopically luminous creatures, struggling to prevent themselves falling away into the depths. The vertical currents of an imaginary sea swept them away. He opened his eyes and the sea had returned to its proper position. He had felt drawn into it, as if he were his own pelagic larval form fighting the constant threat of a slow drop into the deep.

He squatted on the cold pebbles, suffering from lack of sleep. The sea was striking into the groynes and breakwaters making an eerie hollow sound. The wind was whipping, blowing the tops off the waves. Driftwood was being thrown up on to the beach. He had tar on his finger. A small pebble was stuck to it.

Despite himself he felt that he was falling into the black ocean in front of him. He was at the bottom looking upwards, a rain of the tiny calcareous shells of foraminifera getting in his eyes, settling round his legs, their accumulated weight holding down his arms. Around him were black fish with luminous eyes, huge jaws and whiplash tails angling for their prey. They loomed out of the dark, disconnecting their jaws, ready to swallow anything. Looking upwards there was the dim light of the moon shining on the underside of the surface. There was silence. He had his hands over his ears. It had started to rain. The moon was blotted out with whirling clouds and he was making a break for shelter over the beach, past the boats, up the steps and into a shelter where he could watch the rain beating on the deserted road and wonder distantly what he was going to do next. There was tar in his wet hair.

He walked and walked, dodging for shelter wherever he could find it. He stood in a doorway up a few steps and through a gate. He leant his back against the door. It moved. He turned away from the swirling rain and tried the handle. It turned, the door opened in front of him. It felt warm inside.

There were no lights on in the house. He crept in and closed the door silently. He stood absolutely still for some time soaking in the warmth and listening hard for any signs of life. There was a grandfather clock ticking, the stairs led upwards from there. Further down the hall, alongside the stairs, a door was open. His clothes dripped.

He was compelled, without thinking, to creep up the stairs as though he were going to bed. On the second landing he stopped. Another door was half-open. From inside came the sound of deep passionate breathing. He listened to it and then moved towards the door, drawn towards something, wanting to see it.

The door was sufficiently open for him to put his head round without pushing it open even further. He did not want to make a noise. It was darker inside and he was aware only of the wetness of his clothes, a run of water down his leg. The darkness cleared, the soft shadowed shapes inside came into focus.

There was a bed in the centre of the room overshadowed by a huge wardrobe with a mirror that dimly reflected his image holding the edge of the door, his head silhouetted by the brighter light in the hall. Also reflected in the mirror were the shapes of two bodies, moving slowly as if they were moved by a gentle current in an aquarium. They floated together.

She was crouched over him, her knees close to his chest. Her head lay to one side, her eyes closed. Her white back glimmered, he could see the regular pattern of the vertebrae under the skin as she moved, pressing deeply on to the body of the man beneath. They were oblivious to their nakedness, the bedclothes thrown back.

He crept down the stairs in a state of shock, astonished by their difference, the fact of other bodies in a deserted world, the fact of a sexual calm where he had always imagined a drastic cataclysm, a moment of desperate risk entering adulthood.

He sneezed at the bottom of the stairs and held his breath, frightened that there might be more to come and he would be confronted by the man and woman he had seen in the bed looking down at him from the top of the stairs wrapped in sheets and asking why he was there.

He moved along the side of the stairs and went into the room at the end of the hall. The house held him in a conspiracy.

The room was a study. There was a desk with papers and a chair. There was a sofa with papers thrown carelessly on to it. The wallpaper was printed with huge chrysanthemums in gold and red. The desk was mahogany. There was a light on the desk which he switched on. He tried to read the papers but he was tired and his eyes would no longer focus. He put them down. He slumped on the sofa and was almost immediately asleep, his clothes still soaking wet from the rain.

It was still dark when he woke, out of habit, out of fear of dreaming, before the fragments of dream thoughts coalesced. He got up in a panic and switched off the light. He waited and calmed a little though he was in a strange house and the rain battered on the window, the wind blew the doors upstairs. He had no idea what to do. He sat at the desk and began to read the scattered papers switching the lamp back on as the light from outside was too dim.

But these were private papers! This was not his house, he was a burglar, a potential thief, a subject for complex misunderstandings. He was a Peeping Tom, a voyeur, an exploiter of the privacy of others. Enough warnings had been given about his peculiar excesses, not indeed of the usual sort, but excesses of a strange kind that were hard to name and find due reason for in the conventional phrases of supervised boyhood. The very strangeness of his behaviour, the purposeful refusal to sleep, the hallucinations that followed, the irregular nature of his work, all gave credence to the implication that he was homosexual or was certainly over-doing the masturbation. Homosexuality was a word for general deviance of an ill-defined type so did not add much to the understanding of his peculiar behaviour. They did not know what to do with him.

It would, in some senses, have been better if he had gone to Brighton to steal something that he wanted. That would be understandable, if deplorable. Had they made him a prefect out of desperation, hoping that responsibility would put him on a straight course? If so, it had not made the slightest difference. Now he was investigating a complete stranger's papers in the middle of the night.

The papers in front of him were notes on the role of Ernest Bevin in the formation of the post-war condition of England. Some were written in red ink and there were pencil notes in the margins. The rest were typed with further annotations in red ink. There was one piece of ruled paper completely covered with drawings of Bevin. They were unflattering, emphasizing his corpulence and his beady short-sighted eyes. A pin was impaled into one of the drawings fixing the paper firmly to the table underneath. There was a pencil sharpener, a bottle of red ink and a fountain pen without its top. The waste-paper basket under the table was full of screwed-up pieces of paper, discarded comments on the role of the North Atlantic Treaty Organization and further drawings of Bevin with the annotation 'a turn-up in a million' or 'the working class represented on the international stage'.

In front of him was a page full of notes in pencil. One, it said, diversion of the correct role of trade unions into a social contract with the State. Two, NATO and the submission of Britain to the needs of the USA. Three, legitimization of the post-war imperial role in the Middle East. Four, sheer lust for power. The last one was crossed out and under it was another drawing, in pencil, of the beady spectacles of Bevin with the pupils of his eyes dotted in red.

One type-written sheet began: 'The end of the war gave the opportunity for Britain to look towards Europe and the USSR rather than continue in a close relationship with the USA; a relationship which will, in time, become humiliating and inequitable. The war destroyed Britain's imperial role and in the post-war period opportunities have been wasted by pretending that it still exists. Britain is, and will be, frozen within the relationships, internally and externally, of the war. It will not get over the war.'

The papers on the sofa had absorbed the dampness from his

wet clothes. Some of the red ink had run and soaked into the cover. He rubbed at it but had no effect on the spreading stains. He gave up and looked out the window at the rising dawn. He would have to leave.

He walked out the door and on impulse, slammed it. He slammed it as if it were his own door that would not close properly if not shut firmly. Then he ran down towards the bus station to catch a bus back.

19

Blizzard

The sand had got into Thomas's mouth. No matter how many times he rinsed it out, again and again, it came back, crunching between his teeth, drying his tongue. It had a taste he could not place, not exactly.

He spat in the basin and ran the tap. He ran his finger round his gums feeling the grit that was still there. It was a little salty but there was something else that made him instinctively spit again, and again, as though the sand was intrinsically repulsive, something that repelled him physiologically, something that was wholly antagonistic to his body. It was like tasting his own death.

The sand had no smell, except that of dust. It needed to be dissolved in his mouth to evoke in him such feeling. It dissolved its surface in his saliva easily. He spat it out clean as though it had been washed by the sea. He was left with the taste of the dissolved and liquid veneer. He felt it was being absorbed by the inside wall of his cheeks. He was not swallowing; he did not dare. He spat instead and washed his mouth out again.

It was bones and skin, sweat and shit, flies and scorpion tails, all desiccated, burnt to a frazzle, ground and pulverized until it was absorbed on to the resistant silicon surface of the sand. It was the bark of dead trees, arsenic and iridium, stains and mysterious putrescence. It had a touch of sump oil, a metallic flavour of worn engines, beaten crankshafts, burnt straw and scorched mud, the ashes of the desert driven from all points of the compass into his mouth. The sand was lying in between each page of his passport.

As he gently revolved his finger around his ear there was

the familiar amplified crunching of the sand that was deposited there. The grains were stuck to his finger.

It was dark. The black polished floor was covered in patterns of blown sand with his, occasional, footprint that was soon obscured, wiped away by the wind that blew under the closed shutters. The sand storm roared outside in its own rage. He felt the desert would absorb him, swallow him up, carry him across Africa, desiccate him, pulverize him until he was only the integument of a single grain of sand to be spat out when dissolved, an intolerable taste.

The storm had vanished the outside world. It had delayed his flight to England. It held him in no-man's-land; neither at war nor at peace, suspended between different futures and different pasts, with only scraps of memories. There was a carved wooden centrepiece to an ornate bedback hung over buttoned satin. It was gilt and represented a large bunch of fruit, apples and bananas. Then there was the outflow from a power station, the warm water flowing by carrying a cargo of dead fish. His passport stared at him giving him no rights whatever, no protection, no passage from here to there, no protection from his inconsequential memories. Her Majesty's Government was not involved in his predicament. They had other things to do.

He had packed. The suitcases were around him, dusted with sand. The sand would erode all of it, make it anonymous, wipe out his grip on things. He had released the servant. He had given in his resignation. He had cut his ties. He had drunk toasts, shared in jokes about the return to England, smiled at people who had not been friends until they knew he was leaving. He had sold his car and most of the furniture. He had given up the house. But he was still in residence, a bird of passage fluttering in the lobby, the awkward guest who could not, somehow, get through the door and away, all goodbyes said, the compliments exchanged, the smiles left too long on the face, the next item of conversation frozen on the lips depending on the absence of this person who would not, could not, go.

He remembered only the decision, his decision, to leave;

his wife's illness, the needs of the house in England, the house in Somerset. The storm outside thundered like the hooves of a gigantic horse driven by the wind, panic-stricken, snorting, out of control. He was overwhelmed by it, its rider full of rage, pulling at the reins, its face invisible and impenetrably obscure, covered by a cloak of darkness, engaged on some mysterious purpose, some quest of which he had no knowledge and now, no interest.

He hid his head in his hands waiting for a telephone call to tell him that the plane would take off soon, at such a time, whereupon he would have to present himself in good time at the airport, with his luggage correctly labelled, his face organized into an expression of regret at leaving, a touch, but not too much, of sadness, some implication of gratitude at the hospitality of this country, a suitably diplomatic joy that his Sudanese students would be taking over from him, a little concern that standards would be kept up in his absence, a promise that he would be there *ex-officio* to help if he was required, a sensation in the stomach that here was a job well done that could be referred to in the future with confidence and knowledge but not arrogance.

He felt none of that. The sand storm had blotted out all hope, all energy. The heat, the noise and the delay had sapped him and he was oblivious to everything but the palpitations of his heart, the taste in his mouth and the amplified crunching of the sand in his ears.

Then, standing in front of him, there was a Sudanese, Ibrahim. He had arrived out of nowhere, perhaps an outrider of the storm. He was standing there in his robes, a scarf wound round his mouth against the sand. He unwound it, and spoke, as he always did, impeccable English. It was unsure, given the nature of that night, if he was there at all such was the unexpected nature of his arrival and his subsequent delivery, his speech, his farewell.

'Perhaps you will remember,' said Ibrahim emitting what seemed to be a perfumed aura of hot skin, 'that we are grateful but unmoved by basic design. You know that our art starts from the traditional, that we use our own resources, that

Arabic art has a history and a future longer than that of the English. Your art is only novelty, your art eats the history of those it has conquered and spills it out again as its own. It is full of disgust, may I say, self-disgust. You attempt [he waved his arms around as though the house itself were full of attempts of some description] to engulf the history of others, while you have no history of your own. You are the last colonized people, having eaten the history of others, you now proceed to eat your own history. Art is history and the future. It is sad to find a nation that has neither. It is the one thing that you do not understand. You have no reason to make art, we have every reason. For us art is life.

'As a human being we have been glad and honoured to have you here. I will, speaking like this, give up art and become an Ambassador.' Then he vanished leaving the footsteps of his sandals in the sand. The telephone rang. He had left a whiff of perfume in the air.

Ibrahim was in the taxi with him on the way to the airport, humming quietly to himself, hanging his hand out the car window, cooling his fingers. The wind had died, the sand had descended to earth; a silent electrical storm was playing in the sky. They said nothing to each other.

The flag on the car aerial fluttered in the passing air, the driver grunting at each passing car as if each were an affront to him personally. The airport road was deserted, swathed with sand, lit from the sky and the failing, flickering headlights of the car. Africa was vanishing into the night. A trickle of sand ran down his sleeve as he moved to open the car door.

'Macmillan,' said Ibrahim as though he had been carrying on a conversation all the time, 'is a different white man from Eden. He has both intelligence and cunning. We shall see if it makes any difference.' Then he shook hands and laughed ironically.

The Viking aircraft chugged across the airstrip and into the air shuddering, vibrating its rivets. It hung there as if deciding for a moment whether to drop back to earth. Then it was gone into the night.

'The extraordinary thing to me,' said the man next to

him through the overwhelming noise of the two thrashing engines, 'are the tricks that time plays on you, do you know what I mean? When you are travelling, you understand.

'I find myself believing when I take this journey that I'm travelling backwards, it's absurd I know. When I get to Benghazi I think that the next stop is Wadi Halfa instead of Malta, back to front, d'you see! So when I am leaving the Sudan I think I am on the way there, do you know what I mean. Perhaps it is due to homesickness, not that I suffer from it, or something of the kind. Or a sense of tragedy. A grand sense of tragedy. When you are flying in the dark you can't tell which way you are going, you can't tell what height you are. We may, as far as I know, be flying upside down!'

There seemed to be a tear of anxiety in the corner of his eye, but it was probably a permanent fixture, a tear gland reacting for ever, perhaps, to a past sadness. He grunted, getting no answer. He was gripping the edge of his seat with one hand, holding a loosely tied brown-paper parcel with the other. He still had his seat-belt strapped. Then, giving up, he closed his eyes, relaxed, and appeared to be sound asleep, forcing himself towards England and the familiarities of the ground. His finger picked unconsciously at the parcel.

The engines thundered and grated around them. The plane flew a few thousand feet above the desert, a gleaming rattling construction renowned for its reliability.

They reached Benghazi not long after dawn. The passengers stayed in the plane in the various contortions of sleep and travel-induced exhaustion, culture-shocked. During the night lightning had played around the wings of the plane and it had dropped, several times, a few hundred feet, as it hit air pockets. These events had been uncomfortably incorporated into a dozen or so nightmares and had dramatized sprawling anxieties about absent wives, burnt houses, drowned children, and salary cheques lost in the post. But Thomas had stayed awake.

He looked down at the last strip of Africa bordering the Mediterranean. The land was green. The sand was yellow. The sea was blue. He could see lines of waves rippling on to the land, miniaturized by distance, etched by the morning sun into radiant and excessive detail, as if painted by a single hair of an obsessive cosmic brush. The morning was too brilliant. The sun shone with a hard light into the cramped fuselage of the plane, sweeping around it as the plane banked. It lit too much, too cruelly, of the tired faces and crumpled clothes of the travellers to England. They looked grey and anguished, with lined foreheads, as if on the way to hospitalization, the human load of a flying ambulance. There were the hard blue distant ripples of the Mediterranean beneath them and, just distinguishable, the toy shape of an American warship locked into the waves. The engines hammered on the way to Malta, vibrating the passengers' eyelids down, making them hard to keep open, insisting that they dissolve again into unconsciousness.

He could not remember if it was lunch or dinner. There were white napkins in front of him and silver cutlery. Two wine glasses on a white tablecloth. They were sitting in the huge dining-room of the Hotel Phoenicia in Malta, chandeliers hanging high above them, their small grey group waiting awkwardly to be served, placed most embarrassingly in the most exposed position in the centre of the room. There were no other diners. All the other tables were empty, glistening with unmarked silver and glass, their chairs parked neatly. A waiter dressed in red stood moving from foot to foot keeping an eye on them as though they might, given the wrong signal, damage something.

Behind him, but some distance away, was an impressive and ornate arch, decorated with intricate plasterwork. Beyond that an imposing staircase swept upstairs with a deep-red carpet patterned in gold covering its marble treads. A gigantic chandelier hung above it, glistening with glass pendants.

Opposite, the man who sat next to him in the plane was, with the accompaniment of knowing glances and murmurs of satisfaction, opening his brown-paper parcel. It contained a grey knitted pullover.

'This,' he said, 'is my protection against the elements.'

Then, he removed his crumpled tropical jacket and proceeded to pull the garment over his head. In the process he knocked over a glass which fell to the floor and rolled under the next table. The other passengers stiffened as if a serious breach of etiquette had occurred. His head emerged, triumphantly, and found the others watching him with disdain. He pulled the arms down and rolled them at the wrist.

'You'd think it was Buckingham Palace, wouldn't you? I suppose they are all dismissed academics with an elevated opinion of themselves. They'll be lucky to get work back in England. That's all I've got to say to them!'

He looked ready to sit in front of an English fireside. Perhaps he was going to bring out a pair of carpet slippers and confirm his lack of proper dignity. A tear from his active tear gland on one side slid down his cheek. He wiped it away, unaware of it, and proceeded to reorganize the cutlery on the table. He had forgotten the glass under the next table.

The group lost in the centre of the dining-room had begun to talk rather louder. It was the particular sound that the English make when the arrival of food is delayed and not explained. The waiter, recognizing its threatening harmonies, vanished behind a screen, and from certain viewpoints could be seen lighting a cigarette. Now the braver voices had emerged from the general background and could be heard loudly protesting at the constant delays and even, at times, they would draw back their chairs, as if about to make a violent sortie into whatever background service-rooms there might be.

'The English are afraid of servants, both their own and anyone else's,' said the man across the table in a moment of reflection over the cutlery he had rearranged. He looked up while polishing a knife with the unfolded napkin. 'I think I'll talk to them. Instil some confidence.'

With that he walked off behind the screen. There was a muttered but, it seemed from across the room, friendly conversation. Then he appeared again, folded his arms, and confident, dowdy and resplendent in his grey pullover, filled everyone in on the current situation.

'It appears,' he announced generally, 'that as our flight was unscheduled and has arrived at an inopportune moment the hotel is in some difficulties, d'you see, about providing us with food. Are we having a late lunch or an early dinner? Have you worked that out? It seems that we may be better off having sandwiches for the moment, dinner at the correct time, at seven, and breakfast in the morning before we take off for Nice. The hotel is used to flights arriving at convenient times for meals and is therefore in some confusion at the moment. Gentlemen, we are inappropriate, d'you see!'

Then he went back, picked up the remains of his parcel and its associated string and strode out into the foyer where he brazenly ordered sandwiches and coffee, his tropical jacket slung over his arm with something of the devil-may-care about him while he was doing it.

One by one, after several moments of intense and collective resentment, most of the other passengers followed, and ignoring the instigator of this blatant act of effrontery, ordered sandwiches themselves in a discreet and off-hand manner as though they had been thinking of doing this all along. The ones who were left in fear and indecision were thrown into momentary confusion and later triumph when the waiter arrived and handed round menus for a late lunch. The hotel had come to its senses and written out a new menu. The lucky ones had both lunch and dinner and therefore slept replete in gigantic and resplendent bedrooms and woke to have a further course in the form of breakfast before the flight to Nice and then on to England. It caused a rift amongst the passengers that was not to be healed by the approach or the prospect of home. More than half of them had missed lunch.

There was fog over Nice. After several passes over the sea attempting to spot the runway the pilot decided to land at Lyons instead. It appeared that there was fog or, worse, even snow over England and they would have to stay in French hotels in Lyons until the weather lifted and they could continue.

In the hotel most behaved with exaggerated politeness. They withheld with great difficulty their deep-set antipathy to anything French. The sound of the language itself froze them in mid-sentence and caused them to glance knowingly at each other. Afterwards they would talk more loudly in English as if in this way they would stamp out the Gallic atmosphere, erase it from their minds and even silence momentarily those who spoke the infernal language.

The fog descended on Lyons. It was yellowish, thick and choking. Nevertheless Thomas walked out into it to get away from everyone. He did not like being part of a travelling circus, the compulsory intimacy irritated and embarrassed him. He could not distinguish their thoughts from his own. He had, for reasons that he did not quite understand, to laugh with them (just for the moment), join their infantile prejudices until the strain was too much and he had to get out. It was not that he objected fundamentally to what they were saying. He did not like being part of a group. He liked to evolve his perceptions slowly, work at them, make them his own in the same way he worked at clay or stone and made it into a unique object irreducible to any other. He wanted friends, did not mind conviviality, but not at this cost. That was why, he explained to himself, he was alone in the night streets of Lyons staring at the yellow lights shining in the fog, the row upon row of indeterminate French houses and flats without a light to be seen in any room. The streets were empty and he wandered from desolate district to district, his eyes blinking with tiredness, unable to focus, his mouth still sour with sand and the ironies of his departure from Khartoum.

He dreamt compulsively that night. The dream continued throughout the flight to a fogbound and snow-covered England, the plane humming through dark cloud, the ice building up on the wings. He was struggling with it, each time he dozed it re-emerged; he opened his eyes and it was gone.

It was a letter he had to write, something he had forgotten that was essential, a letter that had to be articulated with exactly the right phrases otherwise the consequences would be devastating and irrecoverable. He was struggling with the words, writing them down, crossing them out. Each time he finished water would spill over the letter, falling from the ceiling, turning it into a blotted and incomprehensible mess. He would start again and the words would not flow from his pen, they turned into drawings, sketches (of animals, of birds and insects) that he did not want. The lines of ink on the page would writhe on their own, change the meaning of what he had written, turn into scribbled insults and obscenities that stared up at him. He did not know what it was that he wanted to say, why he was anxious about it. But this was a letter that had to be written. Why should he be writing it? He was resentful that this had been imposed on him. He did not know what had to be said, what was the importance of the letter or even to whom it was addressed. He hated the task but he was compelled to continue on this useless quest to finish a letter that continued to self-destruct. His head was full of spidery, writhing lines that blotted and spat at him as though the lines themselves were full of hate and venom. He could even see the lines when his eyes were open looking at the snow-covered airport when the plane was bouncing and shuddering to a halt.

Someone was talking to him from the front of the taxi. There was a snowdrift ahead and the car could not get through. He would have to walk the last few hundred yards dragging his suitcases through the snow.

He made it to the front door and stood there for a moment breathing heavily. There was a little light from the moon shining through the clouds. The frost gripped everything. He felt for the front door key and spent some time hitting it with a stone as it was frozen solid underneath the mat where it was hidden.

Inside, the deserted house was calm, ghostly and cold. He went straight up to the bedroom and ignoring the icy sheets climbed into bed and went straight off to sleep, his coat thrown over his legs, his discarded shoes thawing by the door.

'You must write to me,' said Ibrahim emerging into his dream out of the obscure roar of the sand storm. 'I would like to hear from you your impressions of England now you are returning to it. It must be cold and damp and the sky must be clouded. I would like to hear about it before, as will surely happen, I will visit you in your English house and examine for myself the country that has lost so much power so quickly.'

Outside the snow began to fall, the wind rose and blew the snow flakes against the house. Soon the windows rattled with the force of the blizzard.

20

Annual Leave

It was summer, besieged by visitors. The sky was pale-blue, the leaves were rich green, the streams flowed bubbling over their black undercurrents.

The visitors dipped their feet in the English countryside; uncles, acquaintances, distant friends come by train, strangers visiting the wrong house. They delivered their quota of pain and anxiety and left. Violet felt sadness and a flickering resentment, a slight hardening of the eyes, whomsoever she welcomed at the door. This time it was her sister, Margaret, full of the minor crisis of travel, her eyes sizing up the house, dating the furniture, borrowing her lipstick. She talked constantly. She always did.

'I suppose you cry in your sleep when you are young and when you get old you cough and choke. When you are middle-aged, like us, you cry and choke at the same time. Harold just snores. Thank God he's still in Tunisia. Where is the artist, the brother-in-law? Is he working or is he sulking out the front of the house, pretending that I'm not here. Shouldn't he be out here helping you?'

Violet tried not to answer, not to get involved. She was getting on with little jobs out the back of the house; sweeping, picking up leaves. Margaret sat in a deckchair, watching her, trying to catch her off-guard. It was a pastime of hers. She seemed to find it soothing while she soaked up the sun and drank another cup of tea.

'Well, that doesn't look like light work to me. I wouldn't take it on. But then you were always stronger. I was younger, but a bit fragile. I was the one with the overactive mind, the one that everyone told to shut up, keep quiet, let everyone else

132

get on with what they were doing. Whatever was it that was so important, what were they doing, what were you all doing that was so consuming that you couldn't even find time to talk to your sister?'

The principle seemed to be, thought Violet, that the less energy she put into the situation the less likely it would be that they would finally have a row. Violet did not want a row. She was not going to have a row. She was not even going to answer. But she knew that Margaret would probe until she found her weak spot. She was off again, tipping her sunglasses to the end of her nose, looking up at Violet with an infuriatingly coy expression.

'The sun feels warm on my face. I like the English summer, don't you? Those rich green leaves and trees. Gentle breezes. So different to the awful tropics where you stay indoors and go yellow from the air-conditioning, if you've got it. What did you have in Khartoum? Mud roofs! These other countries are primitive, uncomfortable, and all the rest of it. But they have their advantages. This country is hopeless. It's a disaster. It's a place to come back to for the summer, and only in the country where there are green leaves.'

Here it comes, thought Violet. She could tell by the momentarily vicious down-turn of Margaret's lips, just at the corners. And she was shifting in the deckchair getting ready for an attack.

'I'm not clear at the moment. Are you here for annual leave or have you, without telling anyone, moved back here for good? Are you going to pretend that you are still away earning money in Africa for nine months of the year? You'll have to hide all that time hoping that you don't bump into your friends or relations, won't you? Not that there are many of those left in this country. Relations I mean. We have spread out all over the world in the hunt for the big buck. Disgusting, isn't it? It's almost treacherous. Shouldn't we have stayed and put our husbands' shoulders to the grindstone and rebuilt post-war England in our own image!

'I rather liked spivs. I thought their shoulders were rather natty. They had style and not a bad attitude to money all things considered. I know they were bad, criminal I suppose, but at least they had a bit of enterprise when all the other men were off getting themselves shot, wounded or disabled in one way or another.'

That was a diversion, thought Violet, knowing that she would get back to her main theme immediately. Violet attempted to divert it by starting to shift some stones from the rockery. But she knew that Margaret had really got her teeth in and nothing would stop her.

'Are you back in England for good, or is this annual leave, really annual leave? Or are you not going to tell me? It doesn't matter if you are not, I'm used to people not telling me things. I'm used to working it out for myself. I wouldn't lift those stones if I were you. You'll put your back out. Whatever are men for? I suppose, if you stay in England he will teach. Everyone teaches. You would have thought that with all these teachers someone would learn something. Oh, not a bit of it, the more teachers there are, the less people learn. The growing and ignoble continent of ignorance.

'Nobody finds out things for themselves like we had to do. Nobody told us anything except Father and he was a special case. Nobody could have accused him of being a teacher. He talked about the lessons of life, do you remember? Have you worked out exactly what the lessons of life might be? It seems to me that by the time you have found out it's too late, the time has passed.

'Of course, we would like a house in England. Not that we are planning to come back. It would just be an idea to have a base in a civilized country, if it remains civilized. Then all in good time we could return and get bored with it like we did years ago. We could bring all our souvenirs back and stack them on the mantelpieces and bore all the neighbours with stories of the strange and wonderful world out there. But, of course, we don't have children so we don't have to come back. You can't leave Michael to muddle along on his own.

'What is he doing? You never tell me anything about him. Are you hiding him in the attic or something? It's very odd that I can't get to see him. Is there something wrong with

134

him? Has he turned into a frog or is he homosexual? You must admit that I have to work on very little information, we all live our lives in considerable obscurity, thousands of miles away from each other. Who knows what is really going on? We don't talk to each other, we only write letters when we are apart. Letters are suspicious objects, I hold them by the corners and hide them away in drawers, because you only write what you want the others to know. You don't send copies of your husband's salary cheque, or your son's school report or photos of his girlfriend, or boyfriend. Never the things you really want to know. I don't know why we bother. We have just grown apart.'

Violet had given up trying to move the rockery and sat exhausted with her eyes closed pretending to be asleep underneath her sunglasses. If she died there and then she doubted if it would make any difference to the inexhaustible flow of guilt-provoking and subtly insulting words that Margaret produced, seemingly without the slightest effort.

'Sunday lunch yesterday was delicious. Roast potatoes, roast beef! A real English Sunday lunch and a good chat afterwards. Were you expecting me to go yesterday? The artist was looking at train times. Is he expecting to go anywhere? He is always finding a reason to get out of the room, even on Sundays when he can't possibly be doing any work.

'As I said yesterday I do like the house. It's smaller than I thought it was going to be. But then appearances are deceptive. But it would be nice to have some grounds. A little more privacy. The people over the road can look into your bedroom unless you draw the curtains all the time. Someone walking past can look into the living-room. It would be nice to have a drive and tall hedges. Then no one would be able to tell what was going on in there. If we get a house in England it would be a good idea to have a drive. We treasure our privacy. I don't think you are so bothered about it. But that sort of house does cost a lot of money.

'What a country this is. When you've got to choose between spivs or communists, I'll choose the spivs thank you very much. At least they were entertaining. Even if they did cultivate their own patch as enthusiastically as you do, they were not gardeners. Nothing as asphyxiatingly boring as that! Have you seen any spivs lately?

'You're going to tell me that you don't get them in the country lurking under the trees, avoiding the cow-pats, brushing the pollen off their jackets. Perhaps they are out of date now, I can't remember.'

Violet caught a glimpse of Thomas sidling around the corner of the building trying not to be seen. He was probably just checking on the current state of the war. On an impulse she launched herself back into the rockery wielding a trowel to divert any possible confrontation. But it was too late. Margaret was on the way to the kitchen.

'There you are, there's the artist. Thomas, could you, if you have a moment, have a go at mending this deckchair? It shouldn't be beyond your skills. I'll make a cup of tea. The sun has made me quite thirsty! That's the bit that's rotted just there. There, I think sitting up has broken it properly. It's got to be mended now.

'Stop gardening for a moment, sister of mine, playing around with that trowel. Come out of the garden for a bit, in the shade, and give me a hand with this cup of tea. I don't know where things are. You didn't give me a map of the place when I arrived, you know. Where is your tea caddy? Do you keep the milk in the fridge? Did you get these cups in England? They are nice in a rather arty kind of way! Is this a crack in this one?

'I've got this rather cloudy vision of all of us back in England. We could get houses close to each other so we could visit once in a while without having to make a special arrangement. I do like turning up out of the blue. This time you wouldn't even tell me where your house was until I told you when I was going to be in England. That's not fair, you know. I know where you are now. So whenever I'm in England I will know where to find you. Are you sure you are going back to Khartoum? This isn't an annual leave, is it? It just doesn't feel like it.'

They were, all three, sitting around the kitchen table

drinking tea. Thomas was flushed and angry but was saying nothing, not even under direct pressure. Violet sat, her eyes fixed on the surface of the table, wishing that silence would come.

'Why is it called "annual leave"? It sounds like the Civil Service. It's like school holidays with a more serious ring to it. Of course, they don't actually pay you to go to school like they do when you're abroad. Are you going to stay in England now?

'I must admit I do get lonely living out of England. All your friends seem a little, what shall I say, temporary. You feel that there is no point really getting into a friendship because sooner or later you will be off and back to England, I suppose we belong here, ratty old country, full of traitors and men on the make. You fall back on your family when all else falls away, even if they can't stand you. We always were a close family, all the sisters together, each one a little bit older or a little bit younger than the next. Each one a little bit prettier or brighter or with a sharper tongue than the next. Think how we fought over our husbands. Each one had to be more handsome, more exciting, more enterprising than the next. How is it that we finished up with all these dead ducks?

'Well I know that's not all of it! There is a lot to be said for all of them. They all have virtues. But when you think of what we had in mind. What we really wanted! It doesn't really repay close investigation.' This was all too much for Thomas so he grunted and walked out the door. Violet had had enough too and put her foot down. That immediately caused Margaret to burst into tears.

'I know I'm always dissatisfied. One is only really satisfied when one is dead! Dissatisfaction is a sign of life! I feel the baby crying inside me. I was telling you, the baby and the old woman at the point of death. Don't you listen to the slightest thing I say? You know I don't want babies. I really don't want to talk about it. It's much too late and there is nothing selfish about it. I'm sorry I broke the cup. I'll certainly go tomorrow. There is a plane I can catch if the artist will get me to the station in time.'

Margaret calmed down a little and was talking softly in a hurt voice that implied untold suffering, dark and everlasting secrets. It was a clear sign that she was now going to play the victim. Violet had her arm round her in a comforting position but found this stage of the proceedings rather more upsetting than Margaret's more aggressive mode. Violet found that her eyes were full of tears. They burnt as they ran down her cheek. They were, more than anything else, tears of resentment.

'Now the sun's gone in and we won't be able to have tea outside, even if the artist has mended the deckchair. We'll have to have it inside. We can carry on talking here. After all, we don't see much of each other.

'I don't know what got into us, travelling all over the world like this. Here we are homesick and with nowhere to go. Well I'm not getting on very well with him. But I will have to go back soon, otherwise he will get sulky and that's the one thing that I can't take. I just don't know what to do about it. I feel like locking myself in the bedroom and crying. Sometimes I think it would be better if I were dead.

'It's not greed on my part. I think it's reasonable to expect a certain standard of living. We did go through it in the war. There must be a certain recompense for all that suffering. I know I didn't do anything in the war, but there was all that suffering all around. It didn't do anything for us all. It's right to expect a reasonable life. I only wish that I knew what a reasonable life might be. Nobody told us anything!

'It's no use acting like this. It's no use getting upset. I know it's me getting upset, but it's a situation that affects both of us. I know you've got a house in England now but all the same our situation is desperate. We don't know what we are doing or what we have done to ourselves. We should have stayed in England.

'It's all right I feel perfectly calm now. It's just the shock of seeing you after all this time and your changed circumstances, your new house. It's not jealousy. I'm glad that you have somewhere to live here. I only wish I was living close by my elder sister. I always relied on you for advice, even if you didn't give it and told me to talk to the older ones. But they aren't here, spread all round the world, in Australia and California. So I came to see you with hopes, I might say, of a sympathetic hearing.

'No, I don't intend to talk about my husband. He is fine, there is no trouble except we can't agree about sorting things out. What do I mean? Well I'm not absolutely sure and that's something of the problem. Sorting out, settling down, something like that! He says that we have to keep on moving around to keep the money coming in. If we stop we can't pay for staying in one place, England in particular. I don't think he wants to come to England. But I do, or I think I do. I don't want to run out of money. Do you see what I mean? We can't find the solution. Having left the country we can't get back in the style that we want. Do you want to come back to England poverty stricken? I don't!

'It's so dark in the country. Of course, there are no street lights. The sky looks absolutely black when you draw the curtains. Angels with black wings are passing.' (In the sky an angel of foreboding aspect, silver flecks in amongst its black wings, stared down at the house, back-lit by the summer moon. Then in an agony of beating wings it vanished as it was only a childhood nightmare, resurrected for the moment by the passing anguish of an adult.)

She left in the morning, smiling and kissing, giving back the lipstick she had borrowed, throwing her head back to the morning sun in an exaggerated masquerade of gaiety, taking the wistful last breath of the country air into her lungs, waving through the window of the car with a last bitter and seductive smile as though she were a child defeated in all her wiles by the power of an absent parent who had, mysteriously, withheld her rightful inheritance.

Violet went back into the house, momentarily triumphant that she had successfully defended her territory. She was sad that the trivialities of childhood had lasted into her middle age.

21
Giant

But all the family were, in one way or another, coming home. All were damaged, somehow incomplete, on the defensive, finding it difficult to work out where they fitted in. Gerald was one of them. His wife, he thought, had insisted on a return to England, it had something to do with her sisters. Irene insisted on things in a way that he still had not deciphered. He just found himself doing what she wanted. Often this was not enough.

He stooped slightly as if carrying an invisible weight of unknown dimensions on the back of his neck. He was bent as if by a constant gale. He leant slightly to one side, buffeted by anxiety. Unobserved he would sometimes straighten up, square his shoulders and smile to himself. But within a few minutes the pressure would bear down again, his shoulders would sag, his legs crack and bend. Then his face would develop an expression of concern and foreboding, a face with an oddly wistful air.

He used this air of oppression, though it was genuine enough, as a way of putting others at a disadvantage. It went with his other habits, exasperated sighs and sad shakings of the head that occurred spontaneously without immediate or obvious justification. It went with his responsibilities and acumen, his known capacity for hard work. His stooping and lop-sided posture was, however, entirely involuntary and he imagined himself as an upright figure with an almost military bearing. This was how he looked when standing in front of the mirror in the bathroom.

It was his long experience in opposition to the relentless and irresponsible carelessness of the world, as demonstrated most clearly in the behaviour of his wife, that gave him a firm base to confront the crushing nature of his responsibilities, a solid foundation in his quest to hold back the tide of negligence.

He was cleaning the car on the gravel path outside the house. He straightened up, uttered an exclamation, not far short of a cry of agony, that had no obvious cause but was clearly directed at the windows of the house nearby where his wife might be watching. Then he got back to work again. The sound he made would have been right for someone who had slipped a disc or suddenly put his back out.

As he worked he spoke in a quiet but firm tone, admonishing himself and the car again and again as he found yet another defect in the paintwork, another recalcitrant spot of oil. He rubbed anxiously with a chamois leather, stood back and examined his handiwork and returned to his quest for perfection. His feet scrunched on the gravel.

The car was already gleaming in the pale autumn sunlight but he had not finished and had no intention of finishing until the light began to go. His daily life, composed of such trivial events, had an ulterior motive; it was all a play in a clever game. He did not worry at all about spending more and more of his time in these demonstrations of his true worth. It seemed necessary and he was certainly not going to give up now he was back in England. It was even more essential that he kept a firm grasp on things now that circumstances had changed and Irene and, apparently, all her sisters and their husbands had decided that they really had to be back in England. Iran, Kuwait, California now seemed distant indeed and he brushed them out of his memory like a speck of dust off the car.

There was something greatly satisfying to him about the complex nature of his activity. He was cleaning the car and simultaneously demonstrating the indolence of his wife and the irresponsibility of his son. His son was not in the house, away somewhere with his girlfriend, but it was evident that he should have cleaned the car before he left and should not have allowed his father to take on such work. The conscious nature of his thoughts on this situation, all within his control, pleased him. He was in his element.

He noticed that Irene was standing in the window looking out over the landscape, with a far-away look in her eye. He recognized this look. It was usually the precursor of a move to another house or another country, a look that indicated dissatisfaction with the weather, the servants, the furniture, the nature of the local tradesmen, or any number of other irregularities over which he had no control. He moved to one side to see the direction of her gaze.

Beyond the wooded autumn valley was a steep hillside with a giant figure carved into it. It was a crude representation of a man flaunting a huge and erect penis, the Giant of Cerne Abbas. He moved back again to decipher the nature of her immediate attention. She was not looking at it. Her eyes had the staring almost glazed inattention that he knew so well. She was not seeing anything. Probably she was only standing there to have an effect on him, to dramatize his neglect of her.

He watched her slight figure through the glass, undecided if it required action of any kind. He decided it did not and continued with a comprehensive and triumphant inspection of the car. He bent low to look under the wheel arches and took the opportunity to steal a glance back at the window to see if she was looking at him. She was, but quickly looked away with a reproachful shrug of her shoulders. When he glanced again, she had gone. He sighed deeply and started on a further, perhaps final, polish of the whole surface of the car. The light was beginning to go.

He opened the bonnet of the car and looked down at the engine. He pulled out the oil gauge and inspected the marks at the end of it. Then he cleaned it with a cloth and reinserted it. When he withdrew it again he noticed that the oil was below the low mark. This had a peculiar effect on him. He could feel himself suddenly become unsteady. He put the oil gauge back and slammed the bonnet down, too hard. His wife re-emerged hearing the sound and watched him for a moment before disappearing again, allowing herself a minute reproof about his disruption of the evening calm in the form of a particular and irritating angle of her shoulders as she turned.

He found it difficult to work out his sudden feeling of insecurity, or even panic. In a way he felt that there might have been a slight earth tremor but was unable to place the feeling exactly either inside or outside himself. For a few moments he wandered around the forecourt looking up at the darkening trees as if he might find evidence there of his, or the world's, sudden condition.

The trees whispered in the evening breeze, moving the weight of their branches above him. He found them soothing and listened quietly for several moments. Then he went inside and locked himself in the bedroom.

Irene had been wandering up and down the living-room in a state of unease. She jumped at the sound of the bedroom lock and sat down suddenly in a large chair covered by a sheet. At one side of the room there was a pile of packing cases with their tops ripped off but nothing removed. They had not been in residence long. She sniffed, perhaps the preliminary to a good cry.

In her hand she was holding a few sheets of paper. They had been delivered to her by a messenger from the village earlier that day. She had been trying to get around to speaking to her husband about them but somehow had not yet managed it. She looked at them again for the hundredth time, an expression of utter disbelief on her face. Then she stood up, placed the papers on the chair, and walked over once more to the window. Outside it was nearly dark. With a series of firm movements she drew the curtains. She was not going to be able to talk to him now, not for some time. When he locked himself in the bedroom there was not much that she could do about it.

She wandered around the room with a duster, arbitrarily polishing table tops and the wooden backs of chairs. She had no idea what to do. Somehow she had beached herself. All the excitement of the move was over. They had moved in, made a few excursions into the neighbourhood and, suddenly, there did not seem to be anything to do. She was pleased to see the dawn, found it difficult to sustain herself through the day and found the nights intolerable. There was nothing to do. She could have unpacked more of the cases but she did not feel like it. She had already begun to feel angry that morning, even before the sullen person from the village delivered those papers. Her mouth tightened, the sign of an impending storm. Her eyes filled with tears.

The few sheets of paper on the chair were a series of cartoons, duplicated and folded in half. They were the cause of her distress. They had been pushed through letter boxes in the village, apparently by her husband. She looked at them again, turning the pages as though they were legal documents or letters from the bank. She had no idea her husband could draw. He had shown no signs of it in the past and she could not understand how it was that he had taken it up at this point in his life.

The cartoons were all obscene. One represented a doctor's full waiting-room. In the centre there was a notice that said 'No Smoking'. Underneath a man was sitting masturbating. She could not work out the significance of it. She could not see the connection between this work and what she knew of her husband. Indeed it was the opposite of what she knew of him; it was the devil inside him, the other face of his predictability.

She made up her mind that he was going mad. Then very quickly afterwards she changed her mind and decided that there was reason and rationale to this event. He was making it impossible for her to stay in England. Delivering messages of this type to the few houses in the village made it too embarrassing for her to be seen outside her house; it was a public humiliation from which she could not recover. His actions were inexplicable in any other way. She went into the bathroom to think. She smoothed the lines under her eyes, filled the sink with water and emptied it again and then flushed the lavatory. She would have to act. She would have to do something about it. She would have to take charge in some way. She wanted to stay in England however dreadful the weather might be at some times of the year.

Her difficulty was that she was not in any sense used to acting on her own behalf. Normally her actions were confined to her effect on her husband, her manipulation of him. Her complement of skills in this direction were hostile silences, sour mouths, sidelong glances and a battery of sharp retorts and innuendoes of which she was no longer fully conscious. When confronted by a situation that, in some sense, required practical moves, she was baffled. Without the presence of her husband all her wiles and manipulations were without effect. The walls would not move for her.

Her one area of expertise, apart from letter writing, was the telephone. She dealt with the outside world this way; it transmitted her desires and troubles to those whose job it was, in her view, to allay her pangs, of guilt, of hunger, of apprehension, of discomfort.

Irene thought, because of the extreme nature of her present needs, of God. She decided to ring the local vicar and engage him in her predicament.

She drew the curtain slightly and looked out at the darkening sky attempting to work out her relationship to God in case it came up in the conversation with the vicar. She found it difficult to immediately crystallize her feelings in that direction. For her, God was intimately involved only in the question of her own death. God was a sentimental fiction that she used to distance any thought of personal annihilation. She could not be at all sure if she believed in Him, she just believed that it would be nice if He existed in order to prevent any thoughts of a morbid or unreasonably terrifying nature. She was not sure, she thought, almost at the point of giggling, that this constituted a proper belief in the sense that might be required to call upon the services of His servants on Earth.

She made sure that she had sufficient sherry to offer him a drink. She did her hair and sat down to telephone, glad that she was capable, when it came to it, of being decisive. While the phone rang the other end she poured herself a small glass of the sherry she had set ready.

In the bedroom her husband was sitting on the edge of the dressing-table stool facing away from the mirror which was now scrawled with indecipherable marks in lipstick. He heard the telephone click and picked up the phone to over-hear the conversation between his wife, the vicar's wife, and eventually the vicar who had, it seemed, been unwilling initially to come to the phone. When the conversation was finished he put down the phone and went to check that the door of the bedroom was indeed locked. Then he went to lie down on the bed and attempt once again to decipher the change that had come over him.

Outwardly he was calm. He closed his eyes and attempted to sleep a little, thinking that the night might well require reserves of energy and unbounded initiative. At the moment he was exhausted, evacuated and unable to make energetic decisions of any kind. He drifted away into a network of resentful dream-thoughts where his wife chattered at him in variously blank rooms full of gifts from airport shops, blue fluffy chickens, glass animals, bright orange kangaroos and pink candy-floss flamingoes. All around him he heard the roar of air-conditioning units, the delicate electric fluttering of fans, the muffled reports of distant gunfire and the Arabic chatter of a few characters in the street outside. He was woken by the bang of the door-knocker; the arrival of spiritual comfort in the form of the vicar.

He woke in a feverish and uncomfortable sweat and rolled over on the white embroidered counterpane. The pattern of the counterpane was impressed on his face. He crept over to the door and listened. There was the clink of sherry glasses. Slowly he unlocked the door and went in to join them, his face wistful and apologetic.

This expression put the vicar off his guard and he approached the cause of all the trouble with his most articulated and pastoral smile only to be thrown back by a severe blow in the stomach from the object of his concerned attention. He staggered back, suffering a multitude of confused and unfamiliar pains and an immediate perception, a parable of himself as an old man attacked by thieves. Recovering quickly, he moved cautiously round the edge of the room in the direction of the door still grasping his, now empty, sherry glass. Without a word he slipped out of the door into the hall, put his sherry glass on the hall stand and, in a final act of evangelical defiance, slammed the door after him. The wheels of his car spun in the gravel of the drive as he hastened to get back to the vicarage and recover his dignity in the sympathetic company of his wife.

Without a word the defiant husband had locked himself back into the bedroom leaving his wife grasping her third glass of sherry and beginning to tip over into a state of hysteria.

The doctor, when he came, was met in the hall and ejected forcibly, his head ringing from a blow from a volume of Dickens that happened to be at hand in a small decorative bookcase inside the front door. The bedroom door locked once more.

Irene, now beyond any rational action, locked herself in the bathroom and ran the taps so that she could hear as little as possible of further events.

The policeman, when he arrived, stood awkwardly in the centre of the room. He could hear the sound of water in the bathroom and, just distinguishable, a soft weeping. He was about to approach the bathroom when the bedroom door opened and a man ran past him, through the drawn curtains and, with an appalling noise, through the closed windows. The glass shattered and he fell bleeding into a flower-bed. Picking himself up he was escorted back into the house by the alarmed policeman, the blood running down his face. His wife emerged from the bathroom in time to see her husband throwing himself at the officer and battering him over the head with another leather-bound volume, this time a copy of Herman Melville's *Moby Dick*.

In the car on the way to the hospital, handcuffs round his wrists and the blood beginning to thicken on his face, he succumbed to melancholia. The headlights of the car swept past the dim hedges, the field gates of the countryside that he had had little time to investigate. In any case winter was approaching, the leaves would soon be gone and they would have to be thinking about the heating of the house. His wife was susceptible to both cold and heat so the temperature

147

would have to be controlled most exactly. He had already organized electric blankets for the beds and had begun to get his head around the habits of the boiler that heated the radiators. He hoped that would be sufficient, but in small moments of despair as they drove through the night he knew that it would not. The other occupants of the car met his every question with a sullen silence and kept their eyes on the road. He had no idea where they were going.

After only a few minutes in the hospital he somehow managed to leap through another window on to the grass below and ran off into the darkness with more cuts and fragments of glass on his face and hands. He wandered through the night staggering a little, blinking in the darkness at the lit windows of houses and moving on before he was noticed.

He found a late-night garage open. There was a taxi filling up with petrol. Despite his appearance, his torn clothes, the blood on his face, he managed to get the driver to take him as a passenger. But this was, in the end, at the cost of his gold watch and a few Saudi Arabian *riyals* that he still had in his pocket.

In the car the driver and he managed to sustain a reasonable conversation that touched on the price of oil and petrol, the advantages of working abroad and the desperate inconsistencies of foreigners when looked at from the viewpoint of an Englishman. The conversation was beginning to become quite animated about the lack of a clear foreign policy by the British Government when they arrived and he was deposited into the darkness. The taxi drove away with a little too much speed, inconsistent with the friendly conversation they had been having just a moment before.

The night enveloped him and the cold air began to sting the wounds on his face. The house in front of him was in darkness. He had not expected that. Perhaps they were away. He rattled the front door hopelessly but it was locked. Then he moved uncertainly round to the side of the house. There he broke a glass panel and opened the door from the outside. It seemed to make a loud noise but he was past caring.

He felt around in the darkness trying to find a firm footing.

He kicked into metal tools that bounced across the floor making more noise and metallic clinking. His hands ran into a confusion of wire. Further down he felt the flat surface of a platform. Awkwardly he sank on to it and managed to find a surface upon which he could sit, just for the moment.

Then the lights went on, all around him. He was dazzled and looked up at the huge metal object above him. It was a sculpture of a horse. Deposited at the base, as he was, he appeared to be a discarded rider who had slipped off its back and was now lying there injured, bloodied by his rejection. The lights blinded him so he could only just see the figure of a man approaching him, holding, rather self-consciously, a poker.

'I thought you had gone away,' he said staring into the lights to see his brother-in-law, Thomas, more clearly. 'Things seem to have been getting a bit much for me.'

22
Paradise

He arrived in Accra at night having watched the sun set over the Sahara. Africa had not changed. It was still a mirage, a huge continent that was both permanent and transitory, ungraspable, unstoppable. It was a continent that swallowed dreams and played them back glimmering on the horizon, always out of reach.

Looking down at the desert there were no boundaries, no frontiers, no straight lines, but an immense solidity that defied comprehension. It accentuated the fragility of the plane, caught in the hard rays of the sun, in a paradoxical whirring time zone of its own (watches and timetables, minute clicking urgencies and fleeting desires) rather than the monumental and irreversible bass whisper of geological time that seemed to be in process underneath it. There had not been a cloud in the sky.

The first bounce of the wheels on landing produced a detectable shudder in Michael's body. His face was hot, he was breathing sharply, unable to focus his eyes. The waft of African air through the opening aircraft door swept over him, still cinnamon, still heavy with the smell of charcoal stoves and warm bodies, hot as the air from an opening oven door. It reversed dream and reality, shot away his memories and turned them into raw physical experience.

The taxi ride was a blur of lights, glimpses of the night markets, acrid sandy streets and tumbledown houses; then acacia trees and lit verandas, swinging single bulbs in passing rooms, hooting brightly painted lorries. It was almost familiar, almost his own.

Yellowing air-conditioned white faces smiled at him, they shook hands, their wives glistened with greetings, juggling the fact of an unattached man just arrived. He sat on strange furniture, sipped from strange coffee cups, proffered strange politenesses and received them in return. He glanced around rooms he had not seen before, checking on the books in the few bookcases he could find, the African mementos ready to go back to England, the outdated record-players playing 'Strawberry Fields' for his benefit. He ate grey imported food, imparted what he could remember of England, offered to help with the washing-up forgetting the servants at the back of the house.

He was caught by husbands in odd hand squeezings with their wives, forgetting himself in the liberties that the air itself seemed to offer. Once it was a kiss grazing his cheek on the way to his lips before it was diverted by others arriving in the room. He took it all for granted and was easy prey for invitations to see distant rooms, the flowers at the ends of gardens, to help in mysterious liftings and movings and mendings that evaporated as soon as there was a little privacy.

But he was flustered by so much secret touching, so many unfamiliar scents and smells, the close proximity of so many different and aroused female bodies, the cooling and cynical glances of the men. The women seemed to have caught his sexual expectation from the surface of his skin. But perhaps he was only the carrier of the smell of England, to be flirted with, to act as a part-player in an endless power game between husbands and wives, the means of resurrecting desire and a kind of distant passion before it was air-conditioned out of existence.

Nevertheless he was flattered and spent some time trying to get to sleep, disconnecting himself from so many hinted and explicit sexual offers, so many glimpses of soft flesh, arched necks and eyes full of apparent desire. He discovered that when he responded and touched them out of his own desire, they withdrew and were even repelled by his advances. Desire belonged to them, not to him. He was breaking the rules.

They had found him a place to sleep in a rest-house that

151

was at present empty apart from himself. He went to sleep with the reflected night fires of the servant's compound outside flickering on his ceiling, a sheet over him, his body melting into the bed expecting to be joined by a warm and unidentifiable female body in a moment or two. But the wives had subsided and were elsewhere, having recovered from the passing novelty of his appearance and having gained momentary advantage in their quest to outline the causes of their dissatisfactions with their husbands.

He had arrived in Africa by a ruse, arising out of a casual conversation. A friend had a father who worked here. They were to discuss the problem of the exporting of excess profits which could not, in the ordinary way, leave West Africa. He was the advance guard of a project to translate the money into commodity of a different sort, a commodity that was not subject to exchange control. They were to make a film; a film of, as yet, uncertain subject. But this was not really his interest. He wanted to return to Africa. It was still, in complex, diffuse yet passion-filled ways, home. It was still, in every important way, alien. They went together.

He was living in a web of passionate impracticality. That was where his intense and unpredictable opportunism arose. He was not in control of it or of himself. He was in love, not with any person but with the condition itself. Emotions of empathy and nakedness were brimming, all on their own, awaiting a human object on which to crystallize. He was capable, in the absence of a human being, of falling in love with the African dawn as it assailed him with the smell of cooking from outside, the warm clear light through the trees, the wonderfully unfamiliar and musical clicking of African birds outside.

He had formed himself in a spinning fragment of accidental, incidental, post-war optimism when, for a moment, for an instant, hatred was past, forever consumed, burnt off, in an apparently terminal festival of death, suffering, evil and malevolence. The horror of it had raised the safety curtain, just a fraction. He had slipped through on to the stage, a dangerous innocent, not having been corroded, or civilized, by hate or boredom.

He was standing in the middle of Black Star Square, dowsed with sweat, attempting to convince a Ghanaian cameraman to lower the camera to foot height so he could take a dramatic shot of the feet of passing soldiers. The cameraman, not having seen *Battleship Potemkin*, was uneasy about reducing the height of the tripod which had never been moved from its just below head height position. From his point of view, the camera was most convenient from that height as it did not require him to grovel on the ground. They argued for some time, the troops stamping past them oblivious to the aesthetics of camera position and the theoretical statements of Pudovkin or Eisenstein. Then in a ferocious attack of perspective Michael burst into uncontrollable laughter whereupon the cameraman immediately lowered the camera to the required height, frightened by this inappropriate and obscurely insulting outburst.

Michael had suddenly seen himself objectively, in his soaked tropical suit, a suit he had only just purchased to meet the Ashantehene, the King of the Ashantis, standing holding a discussion of film aesthetics in the midst of a demonstration of the might of the military Government of Ghana. His suit was soaked, sweat running down the arms, changing its colour from light to dark grey. The heat beat back from the concrete surface of the square as he laughed. The soldiers were away in the distance as were the thousands congregated in the stands to witness the glorious power of the military State. There was not a trace of a breeze, the air was absolutely still and shimmering with heat.

For some time afterwards his laughter brimmed just below the surface. He enjoyed its ironic edge. For some reason it set him free, it made him feel unfettered. It unlatched his emotions and did away, temporarily, with his habitual sense of dread and foreboding. He spent less time saddened by mysterious guilt and slept, for all he knew, without dreaming.

He read avidly, in the evenings, about the ancient empires of Africa as though he had, illogically, found an ancestry, his own trace in the past. He identified with them, with Kanem Bornu, with ancient Ghana, only because they had been unknown to him before. They were distant, exotic, redolent of human motivations that were, by definition, unable to be deciphered through sheer lack of detail. They corresponded exactly to his own knowledge of himself.

He travelled, in a battered car hired at great expense, to meet the Ashantehene and found that they had nothing whatever to say to each other. He had watched the small wizened man dressed in gold, red and green, expecting wisdom, expecting him to say something. Instead they sat in polite silence for a few minutes until they both discovered, simultaneously and with mutual relief, important engagements elsewhere.

The inconsequential nature of the interview failed to dent his euphoria. He drove back to Accra smelling the hand that had touched the King of the Ashantis. He found a trace of grey ash on his sleeve, perhaps from the scatterings of a fetish priest. His eyes were full of tropical green and his mouth full of the hot taste of the giant cooked roadside prawns that he had stopped and bought wrapped, like fish and chips, in newspaper.

He was sitting by a swimming pool at night, the lights reflecting on the smooth unpuckered surface of the water. He disturbed the reflection with his foot. There was a gap in the conversation. He looked abstractedly around the concrete shapes of the newly constructed flats round the pool and the dark sky beyond them, waiting for something to happen. He had been told that they were for diplomatic or commercial use. At the moment only one of them was occupied, by the girl he was with, a secretary at the Embassy. He had the suspicion that some, if not all, of the men passing through Ghana, finished up dabbling their feet in this pool, accompanied by this same girl. Perhaps it was to divert them away from the wives, who might, despite the appalling consequences, seduce them. On the other hand she might have been checking them out, their real or assumed need to be in Ghana.

He had, a few moments earlier, accused her of being a spy. It was an incitement, an attempt to dent her impermeable surface, her finishing school veneer. It was also a clumsy attempt at verbal seduction for he was quite aware of the potential sexual *frisson* that could be aroused by conspiratorial games of this kind, magnified as they were by the balmy African night and the stars reflected in the surface of the pool. However she had seized upon it immediately and had given him to understand that she was indeed engaged on activities of this nature. He had let her go on in this manner and now she had run out and had herself begun to be a little awkward.

He kicked the water again, all conversation dying before it could come to his lips. He could not understand how someone who was so beautiful was, as far as he could find out, so hollow. It emptied out his desire for her. Nevertheless he placed his hand gently on her thigh feeling that it was what was expected of him. She removed his hand and put it against her cheek. He thought, for some reason, of her parents, took his hand away and with an unaccustomedly athletic leap jumped into the pool. He hit the water and also the edge of the pool cutting a deep gash in his forehead. The blood swirled in the water and then disappeared.

She fluttered round him in Korle Bu Hospital as they bound up his wound. Then she vanished. He concluded bitterly that her romantic feelings must be confined to swimming pools in tropical nights.

The bandage left one ear open to the air through which he could hear the wailing of the families of the hospital patients who were encamped along the fluorescent-lit balconies, cooking at their stoves, swaying backwards and forwards. They sounded to him to be in early mourning for the sick members of their family, propped up as they were in gleaming new metal beds in brand new wards in a hospital that was still in construction.

He staggered out of the hospital and took a taxi back to the rest-house. On the way he noticed a sign that pointed to 'Paradise'. The taxi was moving too quickly to catch a glimpse of where it led. Turning his head so suddenly displaced the bandage and a trickle of blood ran down the side of his nose. But his equanimity was undisturbed.

He padded around on the tiles of his room for a few

minutes and then went to bed. The blood slowly soaked into the pillow.

The wound was not so bad. He replaced the bandage in the morning with a plaster and walked around the empty house not sure what to do. He went outside, screwing up his eyes in the morning sun, looking up at the trees trying to trace the bird sounds he could hear. He looked through the hedge at the bicycles going by and then returned to his room to find a resentful servant stripping his bed, glancing at him meaningfully and then silently carrying the blood-stained pillow case away with its stain pointing towards him. He could hear the servant swearing in the bathroom as he struggled to remove it.

Later the pillow and the sheet were hanging out on the line amongst the trees and the bird-song and the sound of bicycles passing. He stood at the window watching it sway in the breeze.

'Don't mistake me,' said the economist looming out of the night, 'it's no good looking at statistics when you want to discover the economic condition of an African country. All you have to do, it's what I do, is to go down to the beach, undress, put your clothes in a pile leaving your watch on the top of the pile. Then go into the sea, swim, splash around, avoid the sea urchins, and have a good time. When you return you will find that your watch and probably all your clothes have been stolen. Now, this is the important point. The time it takes for your watch to be stolen is an important economic index. The quicker it goes the worse things are. Fear of being caught on one side, hunger and desperation on the other. The balance between the two is an exact reflection of the state of the economy at its sharp end, well before any statisticians get moving on figures that are already out of date and probably fabrications anyway.

'They are coming out of the villages and working in the cities or near the cities. If there is work they live, no work they starve. The Kaiser Aluminium Corporation has it worked out. It's so clever! They put part of their business here, just the smelting, fuelled by electricity from the Volta Dam. The aluminium comes from elsewhere, Jamaica or somewhere. All the parts of the business are in different countries. No point nationalizing an industrial plant that depends on other plants spread all over the world, out of your control, is there? Cheap labour that can be taken up or dropped just as you please, that's the nature of it.'

The sea whispered in the background. The economist toyed with his drink, banging it for emphasis on the tin table. His head leaned confidentially, the eyes piercing but blurred, the finger pointed round one side of his glass. The angle of his head was mimicking, if you allow for a lack of synchronization, the movements of a sharp mind, a rapid incisive intelligence.

The economist sat back in his chair, tired by his own efforts, nodding to himself in agreement with his own drunken analysis. The night closed round him and he hardly noticed when Michael stood up and walked over to look at the sea. The palm trees were waving gently, the high-life band was playing *Baby Pan-cake*. The metal tables were in the gloom away from the light of the dance floor. The breakers were white on the dark sea. There was a fire further along the beach where the thieves were resting from the dangers of the daytime. He could hear their chatter. He walked along the white sand towards them, stopped, and walked back. There was little he could say to them.

The economist had subsided and was snoring busily. Opposite him was a black girl with bright eyes and a mouth curled with amusement at the snoring opposite her. He knew her. They had met before at a party. Their eyes had caught.

They shared a taxi, jokingly sharing the responsibility to take the economist home to his wife. They sat together in the back while the drunken economist snored in the front, immune to the taxi-driver's backchat, lolling further into the seat with each movement of the car. They slipped too close as the taxi swerved round a corner. The touch made them kiss deeply and hold each other closely. Accra flashed past them unseen.

The taxi parked outside the rest-house. There was something he had to get before delivering the economist back home. He could not remember what it was. She came too, keeping him company, keeping him close, looking at him with eyes that were half sad and glad, too.

They went into the bedroom and he unwound her headdress, laughing; then her dress, which was wound round her, one piece of material. He unwound her until she was naked. They were lying on the bed in the darkness, he absorbed in her blackness, she in his whiteness. He looked at the palms of her hands, the pink softness between her legs. She watched his face, his body moving between her legs, looking over his shoulder, absorbing his difference. He looked into the black haze of her eyes astonished at her perfection, the textured absolute of her skin, her firmness and the taste of cinnamon between her teeth. She laughed and absorbed him completely in the joy of their difference, shivering.

He stared at the ceiling and then at her. He thought he could hear the chatter of the thieves along the beach, but they had left the beach behind. There was the flicker of another fire on the ceiling, the call of still strange birds, the sound of bicycle tyres on tarmac, the roar of distant lorries, the movement of underground slipping rocks, the sound of the heat working on the sand. He looked at her sleeping, incredulous, not believing she could be so beautiful. She woke and laughed at him as though she were a girl smeared with mud years ago in the Nuba Mountains in another part of Africa.

Outside the taxi was still there. The economist and the driver were asleep, both snoring, sprawled over the front seats of the car. They had been waiting all night. Michael left them sleeping, in the rising heat of the dawn, and went back to bed, not wanting to explain his absence, not wanting to leave her. They slept together, wrapped up in each other.

They woke and the bed was full of blood. Her menstruation had started while she slept and had stained the white sheets of the bed. She was ashamed and hung her head while she dressed. He said he did not mind and held her tight, not wanting her to go. She did not believe him and left, leaving him staring at the blood-stains on the sheet. He heard the taxi driving away and went down to see if he could catch it, knowing he would be too late.

While he was away the servant assumed he had left the house and went to strip the bed. Michael found him in the bathroom scrubbing the sheet, holding the stain up for him to see, facing him with a look of unmediated hate. The red of the blood stuck in his eyes and in his mind. It was a bright living red.

23
Spivs

Violet was not a sentimentalist. She would not allow herself. But despite herself she had arrived at the funeral of her long-lost brother, Tom, knowing that the event was bound to provoke in her feelings for which she had no use. It was such a long time since she had seen him. She was the only one of all the sisters that had bothered to come. It was bound to be interesting. He had the same name as her husband.

The coffin was made of a light-coloured wood. It could have been pine, but as far as she was concerned, it would more likely be veneer. It would for him! A plastic-covered coffin disappearing down a shute! If you could see the gas jets flaring, burning his remains, it would be some kind of justice. Or did they remove the corpse behind the scenes and re-use the coffin. Perhaps that was why that part was out of sight. She shifted in her seat to get a better look but there were plastic flowers in the way.

She felt irritable, put upon. She should not, for a start, have come wearing this particular dress, a dress designed for mourning only in the sense that it was black. It was uncomfortable. It had something wrong with the lining that made it difficult to sit still without stopping the blood to her legs. That inconsequential music was playing. It was meant to induce a reverent sorrow. It did nothing of the kind for her.

She was surrounded, not surprisingly, by people she did not know. She had not seen him for years, that dead body in the coffin. How many years? She tried unsuccessfully to count them, she tried to imagine his face, that youthful face now much older, with what kind of expression? Was it fear? In any case it was before the war or just afterwards. All these people knew him in another life, one she knew nothing whatever about. They were his post-war accomplices.

Did they care for him? She found it difficult to imagine care being felt for him, who cared for no one but himself, his profits, his schemes. She could not imagine why she had come, on her own, without her husband or any of her sisters. She had travelled by bus, another indignity. Nevertheless to her shame and chagrin she discovered that she was crying, a large tear was falling down her cheek. She put it down to the atmosphere of the chapel. Perhaps, on the other hand, she was feeling sorry for herself. It was a funeral. People cried at funerals. It was natural, normal and to the point and even a kind of celebration that one was still alive and not subject to whatever kind of final judgement there might be. She might have been thinking of the death of her father. There were all kinds of possible reasons. But she was sure that she was not crying for him.

She looked around and discovered that none of the others was crying. Not that she could see. They all, instead, were looking stern, disapproving, and there was one who appeared visibly to be grinding his teeth. As the coffin disappeared there was a chorus of light coughing from the company and a shuffling in the pews. None of them was crying.

She had arrived first and had, automatically, sat in the front as she used to do at school. Because of this she had not had a chance to look at the rest of the people who had arrived after her, except out of the corner of her eye. The woman next to her was wearing a chiffon scarf and horn-rimmed spectacles and throughout the short service constantly clicked, opening and closing her handbag as though she were about to get out her purse, extract a few coppers, and throw them on the coffin. As she did so the corners of her mouth turned down in what could only be called a pout. She looked like a spinster, a secretary perhaps, who had missed the opportunity to find a husband. She was not crying. She and all the others were inspecting Violet with interest and some concentrated curiosity. They were trying to place her, discover her relationship to the body in the coffin, the nature of the tear on her cheek.

Violet turned away, feeling vulnerable. She would not have minded knowing who they were, what relationship they had with her brother, what brought them along to his funeral. She felt defensive, picking up a feeling from the others in the chapel that seemed mysteriously hostile. She could feel it on the back of her neck as a slight warmth that could have been a blush. She was flustered and made a move to leave. She grasped her handbag and stood up. She turned towards the door, blanked out the curious faces looking at her. For a terrible moment she thought she might have come to the wrong funeral, and she had been crying over the wrong corpse. But that could not have happened. She had checked and checked as though it were the departure of an aircraft or a train.

Outside it was bright sunlight, a raw and aggressive spring. There was the pink of the blossom of an almond tree in front of her. The grass was sunlit, a violent green. There were the first daffodils pushing up, too yellow for her eyes. She sat in a seat and allowed herself to get cold in the sharp wind. It was a peculiar kind of penance. Possibly she would get pneumonia. She settled her hat in a firmer position on her head so the wind could not move it. Her husband should have brought her. Why was it inconvenient? Couldn't British Oxygen deliver the cylinders another day? Why couldn't he delay the welding?

The sun was too bright for her eyes so she put her hands over them and disappeared into a red glow behind them. Her eyeshadow had probably started to run. Was she crying again?

First there had been the chocolates. It was his shop. Her brother's. He had taken on the lease. It had every prospect of success. There was nothing wrong with the idea of a sweetshop. People didn't have many sweets during the war. They were luxuries, like bananas and pineapples and oranges. People were going to want sweets; they were going to have a higher standard of living. There was nothing wrong with the idea.

Her husband had spent hours, days, arranging the chocolates in the window. There were circles and swathes of chocolates; elegant pyramids with coloured summits, squares with intersecting triangles, a rhapsody to basic design. It looked wonderful. Then just when it was perfect and the shop was ready to open two men arrived, pretended to be perfectly friendly and then destroyed the design by taking all the chocolates away. Her brother had failed to pay for them, or had tried to pass off a cheque in someone else's name, or something of the sort. She had never been able to get to the bottom of it. Her husband had tried to blame her for the fiasco but she wouldn't have it. How could she be responsible for her brother? He was older than she was. He was her elder brother, so she naturally had expectations of him. She was sure he was going to be a great success.

But even before that there had been trouble. It was on the last day of the war when he had nearly been killed. It was nearly a tragedy, it was nearly the end of him. But it finished with the bullet bouncing around in the car and finally hitting his foot, smashing his big toe. They had all tried to treat it as a war wound and for a few days he was a hero, if only of a minor kind. Then, partly because of the nature of his wound, and even more because of the circumstances of it, this feeling began to die away to be replaced by a feeling of uncertainty, perhaps it was shock, as the whole story came out.

He had been shot by someone on his own side. It was a guard at the base in Germany. He had been hailed going through the gates, had not given the right password and the guard had attempted to shoot him. What was worse, what was difficult to accept within the family, was the fact, established in the end in court, that the car had been full of contraband watches and other items of the same kind. Her brother had been involved in the black market. Again there was a feeling at the end of it all that the guard knew very well who was driving the car and was using the premature levity of the last few days of the war to settle a few scores. Nobody in the family could be sure what those scores might have been.

She opened her eyes and blinked at the clusters of people outside the chapel. They had gathered in groups and were talking quietly. Some were clearly talking about her. Beyond them were serried ranks of graves.

What were they mourning? She was thinking about the holes that he had drilled and chipped through the wall to connect up his electricity supply to the mains next door many, many years ago. That was criminal. Then there was the Rolls-Royce that turned up at the door with him at the wheel, smiling brashly in a new suit. It was removed a few hours later and the suit had to go back too. That was fraud. But he never doubted himself, he always had an explanation! His fundamental mistake, he used to say, boiled down to a question of timing, the unwise use of future income. He was always learning; he used to say that, too.

His problem of timing had landed him in jail and now, to be grim about it, in a coffin. Now he had stopped learning; there would be no future income to draw upon. She thought of the damaged big toe on his dead body.

Some of the guests were leaving. They all seemed to have large cars and expensive shoes. She caught herself hoping that they might give her a lift. The wind blew at her hat and rustled the daffodils behind her. She knew she would have to leave soon, the clouds were coming over.

The woman who had sat next to her in the chapel was advancing towards her, clipping her handbag in a determined manner as she walked. Was she going to hand over some money? She looked away, juggling her emotions in the wind, frightened to speak to her. She didn't want to speak to her. But there she was, standing looking down, her lips ready to talk, still with that strange pout at the corner. It occurred to her out of the blue that this was really a secretary, his secretary.

'I don't like the ashes, I don't like the idea of them, stupid pots full of ashes that were once men. He wouldn't have liked it. He wasn't dust, he was substantial, he had weight and firmness. He was rich, generous and without bitterness.' This was not his secretary. This was his wife. That made it all even more frightening.

'You are his sister. I know you are. I recognize the face. He

164

talked of you many times.' But she was only one of his sisters. Hadn't he talked of the other six? She was a little panicky. Would she give away too much if she opened her mouth? Now she was sitting down carefully next to her on the seat with the slow and calculated movements of those mourners who had to take especial care of their own bodies in the presence of the dead.

She, his sister, was not going to be able to get away easily. She looked away across the graveyard with an expression that implied, she hoped, acquiescence and a kind of humble sorrow. Her mouth twitched ironically with the weight of repressed knowledge. He was a criminal. He had let the family down. They had rejected him when he went to prison. They didn't like him, he was unpleasant, a liar, he was a traitor.

'He always spoke of you with affection. He said he depended on his family. They were the source of his good luck, his will to succeed. He was sorry he had little contact with you. But I think you were abroad weren't you? He never left the country. A real Englishman making his money back home.' She was inspecting her with an unpleasant concentration, as though she were attempting to decode the expression on her face, the angle of her head. Who was lying to whom?

'He was a generous man. He looked after his nearest and dearest. We are well looked after, he made sure of that.' From the expression on her face it seemed more likely that it was she who had made sure that she was well looked after.

'It's been delightful talking to you. I hope we will meet again and under less depressing circumstances. Goodbye!' She walked away throwing a grim smile over her shoulder. Then she climbed into a car and was gone.

Violet watched the car moving away and caught a glimmer of a smile in the corner of his wife's mouth where there should have been a pout. She was kissing the hand of the man with her. She could see her leaning towards him through the back window. Her brother had fallen among thieves!

The light from the sky went suddenly and she looked up to see a huge black umbrella being held over her. It was being

165

held by a sallow, silver-bearded man who leant over her in an ingratiating manner. She was not sure if he had been in the chapel. The rain began to spatter on the surface of the umbrella. He leaned forward further as if he were trying to hear her speaking.

'I must interrupt you,' he said with some courtesy but little volume. His voice was faint and somehow originated in the back of his throat. He produced an envelope and handed it to her. It was a summons addressed to her brother. She inspected it and handed it back to him.

'This is nothing to do with me.'

'You are his wife?'

'No, I am not! You have just missed her.' She pointed vaguely after the missing car.

'She informed me that you were his wife.'

'I am not.'

'Then I have more work to do.'

With that the umbrella was removed, the rain began to fall on her head, and he was gone. She sheltered in the door of the chapel. A few people had arrived for the next funeral. She was shivering a little, the wind had dropped but the air was damp. She was fearful of the experience she was having. She did not know where it would lead. Automatically she followed the new mourners into the chapel. She sat right at the back away from the others.

She was afraid that if she was honest with herself, which was not often, she would have to admit that she had hero-worshipped her brother. Only, of course, when she was much younger and could admire his style and panache, the fact that he was handsome and at least looked successful. She thought that he must have had an influence, must have determined in some way what all the sisters wanted of their husbands. They all wanted excitement and daring without the dull ache of failure. They all wanted to be carried along in a magic world without hard responsibilities, somehow without effort, without any voice of realism talking in their ear. They wanted to be free, to be able to give vent to their desires, without having to be too specific about what those desires might be. They wanted money, but not only money. They wanted property without effort, beauty without time, desires without commitment. They wanted to float in a paradisaical world without frowns, rages and recrimination, without injury, pain and death. But, at least, they had all reacted to a different life without too much resentment, perhaps with too sharp a tongue, perhaps with not enough work, perhaps with too little generosity. But they all still had a touch of magic because they were not quite of this world and only touched it in places, a foot down from time to time but only to take off again. They were all like their brother when he was young. Now he was old. The coffin contained a fat, indulgent corpse, overfull of office air, plump lunches and the fawning of accomplices. Soon he would be ashes.

Despite herself, she was crying again and this time with abandon, the mascara running down her face, making an audible sobbing from the back of the chapel. She sniffed and blew her nose and watched as far as she could, from her position, another unknown corpse pass through doors into oblivion. Again the mourners looked back at her wondering who it was who was so affected by the service.

The mourners passed by her on the way out, watching her curiously. She stayed in the pew until they were all gone, and until the priest arrived to minister to this weeping woman, to fulfil his function. He had not realized that she had somehow been to two funerals. He was affected by such a response to his conventional words and his choice of reverent music.

'It is God's will that our brothers and sisters are taken from us. We are left with the good that they have done in their lives and the love that we have had, and still have, for them. It is God's will. Take comfort.'

He repressed a note of irritation as she did not seem to want to move. He wanted to go home and it was raining outside. He thought he had heard thunder but it really was the wrong time of year.

24
Hell

On the way from Accra to Kumasi the car slid carelessly off the road and came to rest with its bumpers against a tree. It fulfilled Michael's prophecies of doom. He had to get out of Accra but had expected a disaster, something waiting for him as a punishment, an expiation of guilt. She did not know where he was. He was leaving her.

He was impatient with the owner of the car-hire company who had refused categorically, and at length, to hire his last available car without driving it himself, insisting it was both convenient and safer, and the car itself was much too valuable to be entrusted to a stranger. The owner, with much self-congratulation, bombast and time wasting, described the important business he had in Kumasi. He would reduce the charge correspondingly, of course, of course. Michael had agreed in the end, but only after a prolonged argument over two bottles of Fanta.

He wanted to be on his own, he wanted to give himself up to his isolation, the certain knowledge set in the pit of his stomach that something was going to go wrong. He did not want a witness.

He had flopped into the back seat, putting on an expression of outward calm, but distracted by the rapid accumulation of near misses with errant lorries and wandering bicycles. He attempted to join in, nervously ingratiating, with the boastful talk that streamed out of the driver, but he was terrified by these supposedly trivial and commonplace dangers of the road. He dissolved into frightened silence. The owner of the car-hire company was a man of property and influence. This apparently protected him from all kinds of catastrophe.

It had started to rain and the road, already covered with a thin sheet of red mud, became impassable in a matter of seconds. The slide across the road happened surprisingly gently in an accidental moment of silence when the rain had stopped battering on the roof; he could even hear the cries of birds deep in the forest and the squeak of the driver's hands as he wrestled with the wheel.

It was all less dramatic than he had feared and, in a way, wanted. He required a dramatic up-turn or down-turn in his fortunes. A full stop. They rustled through some undergrowth and came to rest with a slight jolt. The driver swore to himself quietly; the dripping silence of the forest enveloped them. Neither said a word. Michael breathed easily for the first time in the journey. Here, nestled in the forest, there was little chance of further alarms. Then the rain started again. It exploded out of the dark sky that burst, suddenly perforated.

The sudden noise of water hammering on the roof was so unexpectedly loud that his instinctive impulse was to duck low into the back of the car. The rain hit them and the road, bounced back with sheer energy and volume and created a dense haze of water and steam. The stream of water flooded the red-stained road, apparently with volumes of blood. Then it flushed off the surface and became so deep that the car shifted like a boat in a red sea and threatened, so he felt, to float away.

The sky was dark violet blue, it was pierced with lightning, it reverberated with thunder; it was immanent with obscure threats to his person. Through the haze and the soaked purple green of the waving forest foliage burst a huge yellow roaring truck, its wheels spinning waves of red water. Behind the high windows, behind the hopeless thrashing of windscreen wipers, could just be seen the mad, gesticulating figure of the driver, his truck out of control, slipping on the same corner.

The truck swerved off the road and thundered towards them along its own path, searching for equilibrium. The back swung, hit the car with a crunch, and threw them further into the forest.

The affronted owner of the damaged hire-car, his immunity from catastrophe dented, leapt out of the front seat in a fury and waded through the rising water waving a stick, after revenge. Through the window he could be seen hitting the underside of the upturned truck. His mouth opened and closed. Nothing could be heard of his voice. It was overwhelmed by the roar of uncontrolled and satanic water.

Then, as suddenly as it had begun, the rain stopped. It left a hush broken by dripping water, the sound of distant waterfalls, and the swirl of the blood-red flood around the crashed vehicles.

Michael stayed in the back of the car unable to think of an appropriate move. The darkness, the rain, the storm, the truck flying out of the gloom, the distant rumble of the thunder, were what he expected. The indigo sky, the dark green of the forest, the blood red of the mud and soil, the hard yellow of the truck, they became the colour of his closeness to death. He was frozen into the back of the car waiting for something else to happen. He could hear the thwacking of the driver's stick hitting, uselessly hitting, the truck.

He was eaten up by thoughts of her. They had seen each other again and again. They locked themselves in her room, limb to limb, with the danger of her father finding them. They had consumed each other over and over again, swinging in her hammock, in his bed. They had held each other in public and private, whenever the opportunity arose. A moment away from each other and their mutual desire rose to intolerable proportions. It was not going to last. It was stifling them.

The leaves spattered drops and slight streams of water on to the roof of the car. The sound, the coda to the drama not a minute before, relaxed him and he sat up in the seat trying to see the driver. He caught a glimpse of him disappearing up the road, kicking the red mud, looking ahead and behind. He vanished in the steam coming off the road, an angry spectre on a quest of his own, shaking his wet trousers as he walked. The road was silent, snaking away after him, the red mud congealing and clotting on its surface, the rain evaporating into white drifts of vapour.

Michael sank into the back of the car in a fury of introspection, reminding himself of her, drawing her in imagination, counting each second that they had together. Then he forgot her. He had made up his mind. Michael, a new man, climbed out of the car and started to walk, dragging his suitcase. After an hour he was picked up by a lorry and bounced all the way to Kumasi squashed in with singing Ghanaians. The sun steamed the road in front of them. His skin was hot and wet and he was bruised from the sudden movements of the crash and the upheaval in his emotions. He had forgotten about the truck driver who was hanging upside down in the front seat of the truck, dead.

The hotel was in the centre of Kumasi. It was a skyscraper with some three hundred and forty bedrooms. It had been built by Nkrumah in the expectation of a stream of international visitors who had not materialized. It was built, so he had been told, to buy off the antagonisms of the Ashanti. It was an international hotel soaring over the town, surrounded by gardens. It was also, as far as Michael could see, absolutely empty. There seemed to be no residents whatever. There were numerous staff hanging around the corridors, cleaning the floors, polishing the glasses in the numerous bars, and stacking clean, untouched sheets in cupboards. The hotel was glistening. There was not a speck of dust anywhere. He stood awkwardly in the foyer aware of the mud on his clothes.

He was greeted with apprehension, as if, at his slightest whim or discomfiture, he would leave immediately and the hotel would be empty once more. His case was taken softly from his hand before he had time to place it on the floor. Simultaneously, he was offered drinks by two different waiters, one on either side. He wrestled himself away from the surfeit of attention in the foyer and went to his room. He could hear an argument outside his door. But nothing could prevent him from going to sleep.

The subject of their disputes slipped easily into unconsciousness on the top of his bed, his suitcase still closed, his shoes flung across the floor. He dreamt of a dead man hanging upside down. He did not notice a tap at the door and the surreptitious entry of a member of the staff with a master key who removed his shoes, cleaned them and replaced them, all without the knowledge of their owner.

He woke to the outraged tones of an Englishman shouting and hammering on his door. He listened quietly until it subsided. He could not make out a word. The voice was that of a drunk. He was in no mood to open the door. He felt bruised and sick, a physical feeling of exile. The last person he wanted to see was another Englishman suffering bouts of resentful homesickness, accentuated by alcohol. He would not know what to say to him. But he was hungry and had to go down to dinner.

He walked along the corridor towards the lift, inspecting each numbered door. Some were open, revealing a room exactly like his own. The floors gleamed. Through the windows could be seen the yellow lights of Kumasi flickering behind distant trees. But he could hear nothing of it, smell nothing of it. The air-conditioning erased everything. The lift hummed on the way down. In the corner of the lift, on the floor, was an alarm clock. Its glass face was splintered and its hands bent.

The dining-room was an expanse of glittering cutlery, white tablecloths and plastic flowers. In the distance he could see what must be the drunken Englishman busy with his main course, his eyes down. Michael also kept away from any eye contact. He read the menu several times, unfolded and folded his napkin and rearranged the wine glasses in front of him, nervous at the cluster of waiters around him. Then a voice rang over the dining-room.

'Hell is what you expect!' said the voice. 'What you most fear always happens.' Michael made no response to this disturbing comment but a bruise on his leg immediately started to ache. Was it addressed to him? The waiters who were blocking his view parted for a moment to satisfy their curiosity and he could see the distant figure still eating, still with his eyes down, giving no sign that he might attempt to start a conversation. The waiters melted away with Michael's order and he was left confronting the expanse of dining-room between him and the conversationalist over there in the distance who was, maybe, brooding over his own mordant sense of humour, muttering to himself.

They both ate in silence for some time, pretending that the other did not exist. The waiters drifted between them in silence calculating the odds of a tip from either or both of them. Then the other diner heaved himself out of his chair and made for the door. They did not even exchange glances. Just before the doors swung back after his departing body, he spoke into the air. 'See you in the bar!' he ordered and vanished.

Michael toured several of the bars, all of which were empty, before coming upon the largest of them. In contrast it seemed to be full. The Englishman was there, leaning on one end of a long curving counter, perched unsteadily on a stool, smiling at him. On the other side of the room were eight black girls, their hair brushed up into fancy shapes, their flowered dresses pulled in with belts, their high-heeled shoes polished and brightly coloured. They wore heavy make-up, blue eye-shadow and touches of rouge on their cheeks. They were chattering nervously but stopped when he came in. He could feel them inspecting him. He turned his back and wandered along to the white man at the other end of the bar, taking in the sardonic face watching him as he approached, his small blue eyes juggling as if he were about to produce a witticism, his mouth curled down holding it back for the moment. Michael could see the girls reflected in the glass behind the bar. They had started to chatter again.

'It's the Devil or the deep blue sea,' said his new companion loudly. 'You have the choice of an enlightened conversation with a drunk or the sexual favours of any one or two of those, in any order, in any combination. They are very poor despite their apparent skin-deep sophistication so you will be able to afford them no matter how broke you feel at the moment.'

One of the girls was leaning further down the bar trying to catch his eye, trying to get him to buy her a drink, flashing her eyes in a hectic parody of flirtatiousness. The Englishman laughed bitterly to himself at Michael's discomfiture.

'Hell is what you expect. Hell is what you get. It's not, friend, as we thought, our deeds that must be punished, but our lack of faith, our dishonesty. In other words, it's our bloody repression. That's where we get this pervasive bloody awful feeling of dread or guilt. There, does that comfort anyone here, serried ranks of Freudians, where is your lack of faith?' He stared across the room and addressed the girls rhetorically. They stared back at him. He shouted at them.

'What the hell are you doing here? This is a bloody military dictatorship, don't you know that, a tag-end of imperialism! It's no place for tourists, of whatever kind. Everyone of any moral stature is in prison.' He turned towards Michael, looking up at him in mock humility.

'I'll tell you something very interesting. My thoughts on imperialism. No, please don't stop me, I don't often get the opportunity to come out with it. It's better than screwing these ladies any day. And you won't get the clap. It puts the venereologists out of business.

'It goes like this. Imperialism gave us all great and wonderful aspirations. We could all have servants, that goes without saying. We knew there was an everlasting supply of riches, if we dug deep enough out there in the world. We could, given a little bit of luck, live in large houses, free from woodworm, from which we could survey the world with some detachment and serenity and occasionally ride horses.' He surveyed the bar as if it were the world. The girls looked up at him expectantly.

'The aspirations were always too much, irrelevant or just unhealthy, but they hung there in the air, a Victorian ectoplasm. It was what people aspired to, it was what they really wanted. Then after hundreds of years it all went. Snuffed out by the World War. England was crippled by the debts of the war. India went, Africa went. Out of the war crept the Spivs, whose aspirations went as far as money and no further. Out of the war crept the Sentimentalists, who said this will never happen again. Out of the war crept the War Socialists, who saw their opportunity to fight their way to the White House Lawn.

'Now it's the pursuit of money that has won out. The Imperial Aspiration has shrunk back to its nasty little core. The Spivs have it. Now everyone wants to be a Spiv, though the name has gone out of fashion. I'm a Spiv, you're a Spiv! We'll set up a shop together and sell the people mementoes of British India or African souvenirs. Or we could get into fashion and design clothes with cheaper or less material in them. Perhaps we could get into property and make a killing there! All the glory has gone.'

This speech was interspersed by delicate sips of his drink, a Martini, and much doleful shaking of the head. But his eyes remained hard and ironic. Then he subsided and became distantly ingratiating.

'Now I have a request to make as you are a white man. I seem, for the moment, to have run out of money. I could do with something of a loan. Just until tomorrow. I'm kept here until I get some expenses from my paper. I'm a prisoner, you understand, until the bloody money comes.'

Michael handed over some one hundred *cedi* notes, and then a few more in response to the disappointment on his face. The journalist lurched out of his seat, waved the girls after him and left the bar, swearing gently to himself. The girls followed him. There was one left. She sat looking over towards Michael. The journalist, if that's what he was, had left one for him. In sorrow, rather than lust, he bought her a drink. They inevitably found their way to her house later in the night.

Her children were sleeping behind bead curtains. She went in to see them, came back and watched him for a moment. Then she took off her clothes and lay on a wooden bed. She asked him if he wanted her to wear wooden beads around her waist. She said it would increase his pleasure. He could not see how. He lay next to her stroking her pale-brown skin and then made love to her, bitterly as if his life depended on it. There was something perverse about the act, it included a break with his past, a gentle shattering of the place of Africa in his imagination, a dark and growing resentment of the recalcitrance of the world.

He left the rest of his money by her bedside and walked out into the warm early-morning air.

He sat in his room in the hotel fingering a scar on his leg. He had been struck by a bullet as they had driven a month ago through Nigeria. They had turned a corner driving fast at night, had broken through a road block, and had been fired at out of the darkness by the army or the police. He had not known that the Biafran war was about to start. He had not known that he had been struck by the bullet until the morning after when he had found the wound.

On the way back to Accra he stopped at the site of the crash. Both car and truck were still there but someone had removed the corpse of the truck driver. The mud around the vehicles had dried and had started to crack. He had forgotten to get back his money from the journalist.

25

Basic Design

It was the need for order that drove Thomas on, though he no longer expected his life to pass evenly or rationally from event to event. Each day contained its own disruption, its own turbulence, which then set the tone and atmosphere for the remaining hours. At worst it spread overnight, corroded his sleep with nightmares and he would wake with the taste of the day before in his mouth. Then he would have to struggle to put back the pieces, to insist on the integrity of this moment, this decision, this act. If he failed he would disappear into a black and unapproachable gloom. He would sit, without moving, for hours at a time, staring into space.

When in this condition he would be afraid to move. Any action on his part might precipitate a crisis, an irreversible slide into oblivion. So he froze into one position, his awareness concentrated on the fluttering of the air around him, the weak sunlight coming through the top window of the studio, the curl of ivy that had intruded in a gap in the wooden beam above the door, the silent pieces of metal scattered around the floor and the incomplete form of the riderless horse that rose into the rafters above him. Then he would snap out of it and busy himself with simple tasks, clearing debris, washing out a mug, picking up discarded pieces of emery cloth, splashing his face with cold water, washing his hands with a sliver of soap that had minute fragments of metal embedded in it. He would look preoccupied while he was doing these things as though they involved his whole consciousness.

Once, his bank manager had visited him during one of these periods of intense concentration, and had failed to elicit a single word. The bank manager was left mouthing inane and, in retrospect, even insane platitudes about the rearing horse in front of him, before retreating back to his office and its regular routine. His Head Office had asked their managers to visit customers with outstanding loans and he was merely following orders.

The horse would not allow itself to be represented, it was fugitive, riderless, an image of chaos. As soon as the sculpture took on reality, it became domesticated and no longer appropriate to his inspiration. More than once he had to dismantle it with an oxy-acetylene torch before it became too familiar and overbearing. Then the work had to begin again and his hands would accumulate further abrasions and small burns, minute metal splinters and tiny cuts.

Normally he would not work like this. He would progress easily from the initial sketches to the solving of the technical problems of execution, problems of materials and construction. When the work was done, the work was done and he had few doubts about it afterwards. This was different. For the first time anger intruded into his work and disrupted its even flow. For the first time his subject matter eluded him and denied his skill, humiliating him.

He was working without precedent. Sculptures and paintings he knew expressed a solid interaction between man and the animal beneath him, either in action or in repose. Men and horses fought together, hunted together, stood in repose together. Always the animal was beaten, it had no volition of its own. It was directed energy. He was after something different; the impossibility of the rider remaining seated, tragically incompatible with the energy of the animal. He wanted the rider to be projected diagonally away from the body of the horse, suspended in mid-air, tangled in his own flailing limbs, about to hit a hard and unresponsive ground. He wanted the horse to be an expression of sheer energy and without the solid and comforting outline that reasserted itself from time to time in his own work of construction without him recognizing it.

He dreamt of equestrian statues that during the night threw off their celebrated bronze riders and emerged in the day, coldly spattered with condensation and dew on the patina of their bronze surfaces, only horses. He wanted to catch that elusive moment, the rider thrown, irrecoverably leaving his seat and poised about to descend, a secret moment. He was trying to reassert order by representing the point where chaos intervened, where history bubbled up, where a riderless landscape emerged. The fragments of metal horse spread over the floor were evidence of his failure to convince the material of his anger.

The trouble with his work, he realized in a moment of lucidity, was that the dismounted rider flying through the air disconnected from the horse was irresistibly comic. Standing back a little one was forced to admit that a dismounted rider caused inward laughter; there was not much that was tragic about it. Tragedy for the rider appeared as comedy for the onlooker. The dismounted rider inevitably appeared as a clown engaged in a circus trick ready to be greeted by applause, by laughter, certainly not by tears or a tragic catharsis. Sculpture, after all, was a solemn form; it was not in its nature to deal with outbursts of giggles or secret jokes. He felt deflated.

His wife was away at a funeral and seeing her sisters. He made himself endless cups of tea, always in the same cracked mug to save washing up. His subject was slipping away but he continued to work, hoping that the sculpture would solve its own problem by default.

He bent metal and battered it into shape in sandbags, the noise carrying on deep into the night and sometimes into the early morning. The spatter of welding in the night gave the impression in the village houses nearby that the work inside was infernal, the work of the Devil. They were a little superstitious and affected by their immediate perception of the welding, by what they thought were the violent spitting conversations of demons accompanied by diabolic lightning.

But he was sufficiently absorbed by the bubbling of metal, the fusing of shapes, the tracery of his metal lines and arcs, to ignore momentarily the overall significance of his work. But when he stood back, gripping the welding arc in his hand, he was overwhelmed by the absurdity of what he had done, the irredeemable daftness of the figures he was creating. He had put in passion and thought and what he understood as significance; what emerged was an irrelevant and fanciful jest, a circus act in metal, a looping idiot falling from a resentful barrage of thin wire, a transient shape descending in a whirl of steel watched by an inconsequentially wild metal animal.

He could not convince himself of the authenticity of his own work. Consequently he set to work and destroyed it once again, furious at its banality. He had the strange feeling as he cut through a metal leg that he was really cutting through flesh. It seemed, when he was close to the work, that it took on life, was palpable, breathing, thrumming with the circulation of blood. When he stood back it reverted to cold metal. He walked backwards and forwards testing out this perception holding the oxy-acetylene torch like an instrument of surgery. He was unable to experience this feeling again. The metal was metal and only metal. He toppled the structure from its perch. He stood back and watched it fall, its legs bend, its haunches collapse. Then, deep in the night, he regarded the pile of twisted metal in front of him with something like equanimity.

But that did not last long. The arbitrary coils of the metal itself generated further constructions, further elaborations of horse and man, further welding and brazing, further bending and twisting, further misrecognitions of metal and flesh, further metallic horse breath. He left it half-reconstructed and went to bed, his hands hot, perhaps burning.

He slept the sleep of the dead, his hands grimy, clutching at invisible metal shapes, leaving hand-prints on the white sheets, minute metal shards curled on the pillow.

It was afternoon before he woke again. He washed slowly taking care to remove all evidence of the work from his hands. He inspected them again and rubbed harder to take away each spot of grime. When he had finished his hands were pink and spotless, a little swollen. The nicks and blisters made them appear vulnerable and raw. He looked at them as though they were from a different body, one that was responsible for his anger, his will to represent horses and men, power overwhelmed.

He responded automatically to a ring at the doorbell and let into the house a brisk encyclopaedia salesman who was touring the village. He made tea for them both and listened with a vague detachment to his patter. It seemed to come from a great distance. As he made no response to the keen questions about the education of his children and his own prospects of advancement, the tone of the salesman began to falter.

He took a glossily printed folder automatically out of the salesman's hands and leafed through it. On the second page was a photograph of a falling equestrian statue in a section that dealt with history. It was from Iran or India or even Russia, he could not be sure and was not really interested. What had engaged his attention were the ropes or wires pulling the statue down. They radiated out from the head, were connected to the body of the rider and even to his head. He walked out of the room leaving the salesman in mid-sentence, holding the photograph by his side. The salesman, losing courage, waited for a minute or two and then let himself out of the front door.

In the studio he started to draw in pencil a new version of the dismounted rider and horse. This time the horse and rider were falling together pulled by a thick tracery of wires. The legs of the horse were already broken, the body of the rider was decapitated. The head fell tangled in the wires. All the wires were from one side, straining at the weight of the statue.

He covered page after page with drawings, whirls of stretched lines, falling heads, cracked limbs and distorted necks at the point of rupture. Then he pinned them on the wall and looked at them intensely for some moments.

He had made the statue lean away from the pressure of the wires so it seemed to be resisting their strength, pulling away from them. The horse had its own volition, its own life, it was resisting its collapse. But the head of the man had been pulled away and was flying away with a noose around it leaving an absurd decapitated body stiffly upright on the cracking horse. The point where the rider was fixed to the horse was the most solid of all, the greatest weight. Even if the top of the body was pulled off, his legs would remain firm straddling the body of the horse. The legs of the horse, however, would crack first; they would crack and bend and the statue itself would finally collapse.

He cleared the studio methodically, piling the twisted fragments of metal in one corner, arranging his tools on the bench. Then he swept the cement floor carefully, emptying the dust he had produced into a plastic sack.

He started to bend thick metal wire into sometimes sharp, sometimes wide curves. He laid them on the floor in some kind of order, apparent to himself. Then he pulled out into the middle of the studio the heavy metal base he had used before. He levered it on to some blocks of wood to make it the right height for working and began to weld the metal wire on to it. The rusted black metal looped up into the air, welded at one end, loose and shaking at the other.

He had a break and sat looking intensely at the tangle of flying and gently vibrating metal that he had produced so far. Each of the four sections grew from what was to be a hoof of the horse and wavered in the air ready to be bent into shape to complete the animal.

He went off and made some tea, checking to make sure that the salesman had indeed gone. He opened the front door and looked down the street to see if he was still in the area. The road was deserted. He closed the door after him and went back to the studio at the other end of the house. He padded through the house quietly as though he were a stranger in it, unwilling to disturb its shadows or any other possible guests.

It was to be a statue of a living horse and rider; it was being pulled down, uprooted, as though it were a statue in life. It was contradictory. The wires pulled at a living horse and rider that had the breaking points of a real statue. That was what he was representing. The complexity of the metaphor appealed to him.

He leaned the horse more to one side making it resist further the forces that were trying to overturn it. He could feel the muscles in the horse's legs straining under the skin. He could feel the straddling legs of the rider gripping harder, pressing into the body of the horse. He felt that the structure was rising out of his physical connection with the stresses of the shattered and collapsing horse and man he was struggling to portray. He was destroying it and creating it simultaneously.

Staring out into the garden at the back of the house he was aware of the presence of the missing Minister, the murdered Minister of the Interior. He could feel his bulk and breath close to him, demanding in one way or another a facsimile of the mounted Lord Kitchener, a statue for himself. He spoke, phantom-like, in tangential cheating words that were hard to follow. Thomas turned round quickly in case he were really there. The studio was silent, the spring chaffinches were singing outside, a little sun splashed on to the studio floor crisscrossed with the shadows of branches outside. There was no one there.

He came out of his self-imposed mental exile and began to take in his surroundings; to accept them. It was as though a severe pain that had been endured for years had suddenly moderated making a lightness in the limbs, a bubble of thoughts in the brain, a slow relaxing of his scalp.

He left the studio and began carefully to strip the old wallpaper from the hallway. He worked consistently without stopping until the work was done. Then he began to patch the cracked plaster underneath meticulously. Soon it was a smooth surface ready to be repapered. He left it and went back to the studio.

He worked slowly and methodically, bending, welding, brazing. The horse was a war-horse, sliced through by history. The rider was anonymous, a headless body welded to the horse. The head itself was trapped in the wires as if in a web. It had no expression as it was a merely formal construction, the head of anyone.

In the middle of the night he walked away from it, disentangled himself from his position inside its structure and looked at his work from the furthest position in the studio. He had the taste of sand in his mouth, the taste of death. Perhaps it was the taste of himself. He could feel the heat of the desert on his hands. He wanted to hang them out in the cool air like the Sudanese did from their car windows.

He plunged his hands into cold water and held them there. The studio was silent. The horse and rider quivered, not quite stable, perhaps at the point of collapse.

He slept again, his mind full of the angles of long black limbs, the screaming of kites overhead, the waves of heat over the desert, the cool green glasses of lime juice a third full of sugar, the hard sparkle of tropical stars and the sound of the bullet entering Mapplebeck's brain.

He went out to the village shop and bought a couple of large padlocks. Returning, he closed all the doors of the studio and locked them. The two with no locks were fixed up with the two padlocks and locked as well. Then he left the horse and rider still quivering, still at the point of collapse, and closed the last door.

A bluebottle settled on the neck of the horse waiting for the flesh to decay.

26
Traitor

Michael was happy enough when responsibility was taken off his shoulders, by snow, by flood, by thunderstorms, by an international crisis or an election. Then his anxieties were neatly materialized outside himself and he could watch the progress of the crisis knowing that he could not be held responsible for any of it. The rest of the time he remained in deep gloom, jingling a few coins in his pocket, sunk into intense reveries in launderettes.

He would watch the desperate shovelling of snow, the steaming blinded cars creeping up the road, the tripping women with shopping bags, watching their feet as they stumbled past his basement window, with a light but perverse depression, likening the snow to his own emotional coldness.

He would lie in bed during thunderstorms, seeking to analyse the next burst of violent sound, watching for the flashing of lightning on the wall opposite with its instantaneous pattern, the shadow of closed blinds. The more cataclysmic the thunder, or the rain, or the proximity of universal destruction, the more secure he felt. He would read avidly about wars and famines, not in any sense of enjoyment or misanthropy, but in the belief that somehow his fate was being juggled, rearticulated in these often distant places. From that he took pleasure.

He justified himself by pleading ignorance. He just did not know enough, he explained to himself, to be able to make rational decisions, to do anything about his own condition, his own dullness, his own lack of conviction. He was not yet an adult, not in his own reckoning.

In a flood, a thunderstorm, or a crisis of war or politics, the madness would start. The adults would scatter; they would turn aggressive, allocate blame, suddenly generate spurts of unreasonable confidence while the world, like a tin globe, span under their fingers, knowable, banal, ridiculous, and set on a path to destruction.

He just did not know. He was an agnostic, for the moment. It was not God (He did not arise as a problem) that activated his scepticism. It was quite clear that there was no evidence on which to base any practical decision to do one thing rather than the other; to think one thing rather than another. He could not do anything about his current poverty, the cracking of the damp plaster on the bedroom wall, the wild garden that the landlord had arranged to be sprayed with poison as he, the tenant, had not kept it neat in the terms of his lease. He could do nothing about the broken window in the front room that had been kicked in by someone from upstairs in a rage or, maybe, in sheer joy, he did not know.

He had a recurring aim, a distant and vague prospect of reorganizing the garden with diamond-shaped beds, hedges and flowering shrubs. He opted not to do it, with a bitter laugh each time. He spent a great deal of time in bed, hoping in this way to make the time pass unconsciously and speedily, to get as far away from childhood as possible.

Metaphysical wisdom did not interest him but he was pursued by it. He despised Buddhism, Hinduism, Tao and any form of Christianity, all of which at one time or other had arrived at his door and got him out of bed with pamphlets and collecting boxes and enquiries as to his spiritual health. But they could get nowhere. They all had that glassy look of conviction in their eyes. He was not going to join anything.

In any case, he was surrounded by tragedies. Everyone he knew or had heard about seemed to be immersed in an intolerable and tragic situation that was caused, in his view, by a firm commitment on their behalf to change their lives. The slightest move to contradict one's fate seemed to result in appalling catastrophe. Better to rest things as they were and attempt some kind of stasis, hoping by inactivity that things would get no worse.

There was the man, an acquaintance only, who was a rotund figure and a quizzical character, who determined to change his attitude to life and lose a great deal of weight, become a new and dynamic character, a centre of demonic energy. He vanished for several months and re-emerged transformed and invisible. No one recognized him as he had changed so much.

He was a physical type whose size and shape of personality derived from the shape of his body and the owl-like aspect of his face. He implied wisdom and wit and a sophisticated knowingness. It made him many friends. They relied on his detached and ironical attitudes, they found them soothing. But in his new form he appeared shrunken, wizened, a ghost of his former self. His face had become apologetic. Perhaps this was connected to his friends failing to recognize him in the street or it may have been an effect of his sheer loss of facial padding. It was hard to tell. Over a few months he turned yellow and sad and was seen in the street less and less often until he was not seen again. No one knew where he had gone or if, indeed, he was really still there but in some totally changed form.

Again, there was a literate, novel-writing young woman, who determined to herself that her first baby was not to take up too much of her time. A degree of civilized neglect seemed to her to be the appropriate behaviour for someone in her condition. She grew to despise the other young mothers who dressed their babies in purest white, who drove elaborate prams, who leaned constantly towards their babies and talked to them in nonsensical tones. She dressed her baby in dark, rough brown. She did not worry too much about the cold, she did not fuss, she did not bother with bonnets or prams or disposable nappies.

But after a few months, her baby became ill and soon, under obscure circumstances, it died. She divorced her husband and married again. She changed her personality entirely, she dressed in the smartest clothes, she drove a smart little car, she stopped writing. She was brisk and efficient and brittle, as was her new husband. Then she killed herself with an overdose. Her husband went to London and after a few months, married again.

Michael enjoyed these highly selective choices of, to him, highly symptomatic events, they became his alibi for total inertia. He treated each day with intense suspicion as though it contained hidden events that would spring out at him without warning and throw him into new and desperate circumstances.

In the meantime he became obsessed with his plans for the garden. Perhaps he was pricked into activity by the attempt at intimidation by the landlord, the sudden arrival of two hefty men with heavy eyebrows and small eyes who had sprayed the garden, killing everything in it. They had left with his wheelbarrow and the rest of the few garden tools he had accumulated over time, leaving him in no position to complain to the landlord as he had not paid the rent for six months.

He compensated by developing elaborate plans for the dead and dying wilderness. He drew complex plans on squared paper with neat circles and squares for permanent plants. The month of flowering was inserted in each shape so it would be possible to plan for flower and colour throughout the year.

He discovered what he thought was the ultimate small tree. It was a species of Myrtle which was evergreen, which had white flowers in the summer and edible fruits in the autumn. It had a decorative peeling bark and was, if the description he had was right, also fragrant. He placed it in the centre of his plan and worried a great deal if it would in the end be hardy enough for the somewhat windswept area at the back of the house. He was concerned a little that he had not seen a tree of this type and was not, therefore, in a position to make proper judgements about its suitability.

The plans were never to work themselves out in practice. It was rare for him to venture out into the garden. He would, when he was feeling confident, pace out the length and width. But he would hastily return inside after a few general glances at the proportions of the garden and a guess at the length of the shadow from the house in the summer. He preferred to be working inside where he could perfect his plan without the necessity to plant a foot on the soil itself.

All this activity was, no doubt, compensatory. He was driven to it by a mental obligation, a nagging source of energy that had no proper outlet. There was something he had to do. But he had no idea what it was.

The mystery was about his lack of ambition. Where was it? Was it an absent or vestigial impulse? Ambition came with a pre-existent path to follow, a line to traverse, a tangent to inscribe, even a yellow brick road to dance along. The apparent absence of all possible trajectories left him with bottled-up energy, bitten nails and a mad and searching stare.

His wife and child watched him with awe and fear as if they were spectators at the falling of icebergs into the sea; he was outside their control. It was well past the time for recriminations and analysis. Now it seemed all to be part of a natural process, an inexorable deterioration, a breaking-up, a crumbling away. For the moment he had stopped talking to them, stopped staring down into his son's blue eyes trying to work out how it was that he looked untroubled.

The sky was covered with white uniform cloud, the sun was hazy. It was humid, sticky, but not really warm, and a kind of quiet had fallen over the town. People were walking in the streets but they seemed silent, self-absorbed, their eyes blank and inward-looking.

The nearby hostel for the mentally disturbed had, as if in sympathy, turned out its inmates. Those who were not so categorized had to turn on a blank persona, a convenient piece of self-hypnosis, so they should not see or feel too much or appear in any way to be disturbed themselves. The inmates were not allowed in the hostel during the day on Tuesdays and Thursdays. They spent those days wandering in the area, rain or shine, some begging, some silent and absorbed in compelling internal struggles that cut them off from the world. It was something to do with cutting staffing costs but it had an unplanned satirical effect on the neighbourhood. It threw into self-conscious relief the to and fro of normality.

Michael encountered a naked man, shouting and frothing at the mouth, sat on the stone wall outside his flat. They ignored each other, each pretending that the other did not exist, valuing their own delirium. This small event, working underground, threw Michael into a hail of activity, a demonstration of his own sanity. He was going to redecorate the flat, he was going to start reorganizing the garden, he was going to the court to have a judgement made on their rising debts. He was going to do this, he was going to do that!

He was interrupted in his burst of activity by a series of visits, one after the other, that sent him off on a different path. He had managed to pull out a metal ladder from one of the garden sheds, and was inspecting the caved-in ceiling of the lavatory which had been subject to a leak from above at some time in the past. The plaster had fallen and was continuing to fall. He peered up into the darkness attempting to identify the source of the leak. He was not going to attempt to mend it if it was going to fall again when it next rained.

There was a banging at the door. On the doorstep was a young and bespectacled man holding a brief-case. He was from the bank and was enquiring about the outstanding overdraft. He was invited in but stood at the door of the sitting-room passing his eye over the torn and filthy furniture, the rumpled carpet, the swinging naked light bulb, the cat with her six kittens on the sofa, the pile of torn newspapers in the corner, the pail of wet nappies, the chipped plaster by the window with its broken pane, the television on the floor. Then he kicked over a saucer of milk just inside the room and was full of absurd apologies. He did not mention the overdraft again and beat a hasty retreat, smiling hopelessly, stepping gingerly over the loose plaster in the hall, stiffly walking past the naked man at the gate as though this crazed person were yet another symptom of total dilapidation.

Michael watched him through the broken pane of glass with a curious feeling of pleasure, as though he had discovered an important truth. He went back to work on the lavatory ceiling with the strange feeling that this event had happened to someone else.

Then there were two bailiffs at the door who had come to take away his furniture and effects. But they looked round the flat and could not find anything that was worth taking. They stayed for a cup of tea and stumbled up the drive making ribald remarks to the naked guardian at the gate-post. Soon the police came and took him away. He went quietly, seeming to be almost relieved.

Michael was taken away from his work in the lavatory by the noise of the washing machine. It had started to leak. None of the switches would work so it had to be switched off by pulling the plug out of the wall. It continued to leak afterwards and the hall flooded with soapy water mixing unpleasantly with the residue of the fallen plaster from the lavatory. They pushed at it with brooms hoping to sweep the water out the front door. There they met one of his aunts, just back from the Middle East, who was about to press the doorbell not knowing that it did not work. She was invited in, with family smiles and conventional greetings, and she stepped without flinching through the water and the plaster slurry, only a little concerned with the state of her high-heeled shoes.

Sitting on the arm of one of the chairs, the seat of which had obviously protruding springs, she accepted a cup of tea and sat there chatting in an animated manner with her eyes flickering and making notes on the exact state of the flat, the exact number of present and future cats, and the lack of normal facilities. She insisted very soon on a tour of inspection, the bedroom, the kitchen, and afterwards was interested in Michael's plans for the garden. She found it a little difficult to understand why the garden had to be poisoned and why everything in it was dead. As intimidating landlords were outside her experience she remained puzzled by that particular aspect of her nephew's life. She expected to see them again soon as they were now returning to settle in England.

Michael carried on working and by the time it was dark he had temporarily patched up the ceiling. Then he sat in the semi-darkness talking to his wife. The events of the day had released some of his energy. He talked on and on as though nothing would stop him. At half-past three in the morning he looked up at the window, which had been left open a little at the bottom, to the street. Perhaps he had heard a slight noise. There were two feet standing on the window sill, clad in rough boots. The body was hidden by the closed blinds. Michael stopped talking, hesitated, and ran out to find out who it was who was spying on him.

Outside he could see a crouched figure of a man running away, his pale face looking apprehensively over his shoulder, lit by a street lamp. The man scuttled away as Michael chased him. He jumped with some agility over garden walls and hid in shadows only to move off again realizing that he could still be seen. But he was not moving fast. He was like a small jumping animal, agile over short distances but lacking stamina. Michael caught him, shivering with fright in the doorway of a church. He stood with his back to the studded door looking up at his pursuer with a pale worn shabby face and black frightened nocturnal eyes.

Having caught him, Michael was unable to work out what to do next. The man talked at him in a falsetto voice, pushing himself back against the door, raising his arm to protect himself against blows that never came, his body cramping in pain at the imaginary punches.

'No, no, no,' said the man, 'I will not betray you. Your secrets are safe with me, I have sealed lips, stuck together, they never say a word, never, never, never. I will never betray you. Walls have ears. I am the ear, but I stay silent.' He was shaking his head desperately at each phrase. Then he pulled himself together having received no blows and, standing to his full height, walked calmly away without a backward glance.

Curled up in bed after these accumulated events Michael lurched uncertainly towards sleep, wondering what secrets of his had been overheard, overseen. He was trying to reconstruct the conversation of that early morning and could not work out what it could be that he had said that could possibly be taken as any kind of secret. He disappeared into unconsciousness with that question in his mind. What secrets?

He woke with a feeling of certainty, a rounded, pleasurable sense of achievement. Somehow, in the night, his questions had been resolved. It took him some time to reconstruct the nature of his new certainty, turning it over in his mind.

It was to do with the aspirations of others, not his own. He was responding to ambitions that he had overheard, assimilated by osmosis, smelt in the night. They were not his ambitions. He rejected them because they were confused, amorphous, lacking structure and direction, and application to himself. They had little to do with him. But he was still held in their grasp. They were the expectations of his family; the guilty, but less than sinful, dreams of other histories than his; the hopes of other bodies, other desires that had been written confusingly into his actions and drives and had pretended to be his own. The night had separated them out, spinning centrifugally, and they were now distinct, separate, and not to do with him. That was the answer to it. He was grown up. He was himself.

He went back to sleep and smelt in his dreams the doubtful fragrance of the Myrtle tree; he gazed on its cinnamon-coloured bark, edible fruits and evergreen leaves. He worried still if it was sufficiently hardy to survive his windswept thoughts and the frost of his emotions.

27

Empire

Michael flung his arm out of the bedclothes (red blankets, coarse sheets) in a sudden violent movement, a reflex action half in sleep, responding to subterranean tremors, uncertain fears and prophecies. There, at the outer edge of his universe, torn and fragmented by the onslaught of his constant need to recollect them, were a thousand miles of parched and blackened desert. It seemed to lie burning under his outstretched arm. There, at the furthest tips of his fingers just out of his grasp, threatening to crush him, were giant bluish-black granite boulders towering in careless piles under a scorching blue sky.

They were heating up in a raw morning sun, their surfaces glittering and blistering, spangled with metallic traces. Growing out of dark cool crevices between the rocks were small trees with wide silvery boles, festooned with a few pink flowers but harbouring scorpions. A black cocktail dress hung incongruously between two trees, gently swaying.

The rocks were black, sinister and motionless but seemed to be slightly unstable, poised, as though they might fall accidentally, at any moment, if he moved a fraction of an inch. Squatting in the higher reaches of the *jebel* were a few baboons, lined up, scuffling and arguing or staring out on to the flat desert beyond. There was silence around the rocks apart from their chattering momentary angers, sneers and protests.

The heat was causing the wind to stir, he could feel it brushing over the palm of his spread and outstretched hand. The volume of air round the rocks buffeted, spiralled round itself in sudden gusts, then fell still, only to start again in a few seconds.

The baboons picked at themselves, their tufted hair blown and released by the hot air, shaking their heads in the blown grains of sand. The air was rippling, breaking solid identifiable outlines into bright air-washed phantoms, uncertain realities, slipping identities, mirages. He clenched his hand trying to grasp them. They evaporated, visions slipping through his fingers.

Michael was dreaming he was dreaming (wanting to live at his imaginary centre). The dark beams above him (in the first dream) that supported the high dormitory roof seemed like the arched cage of his own ribs flying over him as he lay in his black metal bed. They moved as if he were breathing. He was living inside himself, tucked into his own heart, attempting to recollect the substance of his own experience, to make it real.

His arm was feeling the warmth from the radiator next to his bed. The rising heat was transformed into desert air. He seemed to be lying on his back, his arm touching the hot sand. He looked up into the darkness, deciphering the shadows that were thrown by the street lights outside the school, diagonal patterns across the angled ceiling.

He crept through his intersecting dreams searching for certain pleasures, gliding over black smooth skin, arching round her breasts, sliding between her thighs, touching her lips, gazing on her smile. But her skin turned into desert sand before he could touch her or even elevate her into something more than a series of erotic fragments.

Then he was enveloped in a cold black sea, his skin puckered with the icy water, his head underneath the surface, his hair waving in hard currents, his underwater limbs banging against rusted metal stanchions as though he were a floating submerged corpse, an arriving scandal to be beached next day, dead limbs stirred by moving shingle, body ready to be wrapped in plastic and removed.

He was numbed by the cold, curled round the bole of a tree with the sound of night birds in his head, a frosted night landscape around him that was unfamiliar, untouched, barricaded with barbed wire and high gates, private fields laid bare in the moonlight, the tufted grass white-frosted. In the distance was the sound of Duke Ellington. Then there were the staring eyes of a dead cat.

He picked through this receding sequence of images as a desolate beggar searching for scraps of enlightenment. He ploughed through the black soot falling from the sky, the staircase open to the air, and climbed into the Anderson shelter and began to eat the chocolate biscuits in the Libby's milk tin. His life began with a war, a flying bomb next door extinguishing the neighbours, a shatter of glass that wiped out his mother's face and thereby changed the world.

'Vicious little prig!' came a voice out of the darkness. It was a white-haired priest, breathing alcohol and spite, limping a little as though he was crippled by arthritis. He wheezed, waving his stick, gathering his breath for a sermon, caring not at all whether it was the appropriate time or the right place, but determined to take his opportunity. He spoke with an emotional grate in his voice that came from either illness or irony. He flapped his white robes around him as though they were just further irritations, something in the way of his direct speech, his last chance to get on record some words that he had missed out in the past for reasons that he could not remember.

He organized his face into something of a snarl and began.

'Life is full of opportunities, you little bastards! You sweet young crocuses thrusting up into the sky, damn you all! It all appears so urgent to you now, now, now, does it not? Full of sap, bursting with venom, ready to pass out into the world and make it in your own image, your own object.'

As he spoke he banged his stick on the ground to emphasize his points. When he was silent he banged the stick, emphasizing the voices in his head that had not yet reached the condition of speech, or, perhaps, had got beyond it. While he was doing this he was looking down at the ground with only the white top of his head visible, seeming to be inspecting his feet in hatred and disbelief, hammering his unsaid words into the ground. Having been through this process, he calmed himself, raised his head and spoke softly as though his previous words came from another being that spoke through him but for whom he was not responsible.

'The world is not to be taken so easily. It gets away from you, it is not to be had, do you understand me? The empire of things that you want to possess (I assume that in deep humility) does not belong to you and you will not have it.' He stopped and held his face out as if to be patted, adored. He seemed to be waiting for a response.

'The original sin is only the belief that you own the world, your mother's body, that you can truly possess it! It is a belief, in the end, that is only nonsense. What a relief!' He sat down on a chair and subsided into a thoughtful pose as though there was indeed more to say but, just for the moment, it had escaped him. He seemed to remember an appointment, rose, and shuffled off down the dormitory continuing his monologue, banging his stick for emphasis.

'Nonsense,' he said, 'not on any terms, not on any terms!' Then he went through the door, holding it open irritably with his stick. His voice could be heard outside, arguing with an invisible antagonist.

His stick banged on the floor outside and then he was gone, perhaps to continue his enigmatic disputation in other men's dreams, to finish his sermon with a more responsive audience. He left a deep silence behind him. The shadows thrown by the street lights outside flickered on the ceiling. The curved black metal at the end of the bed glittered, his feet were trapped in the tight red blanket as Michael turned over on to his back.

He was attempting to wake, to come back to consciousness. But he was waking in the empty dormitory of his school, absurdly sitting up, an adult, in what was only a translated, worked-up memory, a blurred and distant trace with areas of acute clarity. There were stairs somewhere to a washroom. There was a door and a corridor behind it that led to a grey fug, a mist of misremembered lop-sided rooms and further doors, windows, more doors, more windows. There was the feeling of clenched teeth, the taste of a mouth; his own. There was the dormitory captain's cubicle in the far corner of the room.

From inside came a gentle noise; the dormitory captain was humming to himself. His curtain flew open and he walked over to the bed with the saunter, the casual stroll he put on to emphasize his status as a premature adult.

'Squirt!' he said, 'that's enough of your stories. We don't want to hear them.' He produced a cut-out picture of Brigitte Bardot leaning against a wall, clad in black-net stockings, her arm behind her head, smiling guilelessly out at the world. He waved it meaningfully and retreated to his cubicle to engage in mysterious creakings and gasps of imaginative passion.

Michael unwillingly lived his own fiction, turning over awkwardly in his school bed, aware of being adult and fully clothed and acting as though he had slipped into bed to avoid a confrontation, pretending he was asleep. He found himself stepping out of bed and quietly tip-toeing past the cubicle on the way to the door, blocking his ears (his hearing seemed to be acute), staring deeply into the dark, wanting to leave.

Outside, the first rays of morning sun were visible as they came through the high windows and lit the dusty floor. Down some stairs he could dimly see the tarmac surface of the playground, some dustbins and the chain that hung from the school bell.

He was afraid of the floorboards creaking and walked slowly and with great deliberation looking carefully about him. In a little time day would come and he would be involved once again in the edgy painful routine of the school. He would have to explain himself. He would have to explain his inappropriate adulthood, why it was he had not yet left school, why it was he was still there. His adulthood was a humiliation, an empty alibi, a hollow attempt at special status. He stood at the top of the stairs rooted to the spot, great charges of fear coursing through his body, fear that had no immediate object or application. He was afraid that the bell might ring, he was afraid that he might be recognized, he was afraid that he would be carried away into a running urgent mass of boys intent on mysteries to which he no longer belonged and did not wish to return.

The fear turned into anger. It overcame him in a torrent of

words that emerged from within as though it were a wave breaking inside him, out of control, seeming not to be part of his consciousness. It was addressed to the face in front of him, the red angry bare bespectacled face of his Headmaster. He looked into the eyes of this man and saw them shifting, the pupils contracting, the red blood vessels pulsating uncertainly. As he spoke, he watched with pleasure and seemed to see inside this man, this epitome of authority. He saw him as a small ugly child screaming for its mother, beating its hands and arms in an inconsolable frenzy as the world did not arrange itself satisfactorily within his grasp.

He wandered down a dusty corridor stepping superstitiously over broken parquet blocks on the floor. He pushed a door at the end of the corridor and went outside into a small courtyard. It was an area of the school that was out of bounds and he had not been there before. But there was enough of his anger left to ignore it. He moved on, exploring, pushing doors open ahead of him. They squeaked closed behind him. There was a confusion of rooms and a narrow staircase leading steeply upwards. He went up it in a mood of defiance. At the top was what seemed like a hatch. He pulled it open and could see nothing much beyond. He climbed in, closed the hatch behind him carefully and was swallowed up in the darkness. Under his feet seemed to be piles of sacking. They tangled round his feet so he found it difficult to move and to feel his way around. He stretched out his hands to feel in front of him. He found another wall and set into it another hatch. He opened it and climbed through.

So intense was his concentration on his own thoughts that the room in front of him became dim. He could still smell the sacking, the smell of old wood with a residue of creosote, the aroma of dampness, but he saw the smooth surface of a map, the turned-over page of a coloured atlas with tiny sharp words printed on it, the colours of high ground, the wriggling blue lines of the Nile, the expanse of the Red Sea organized neatly with figures for its depth at particular points. He searched the surface of the map for evidence, something more than a blank representation of the desert. The same names came out at him, Kassala, El Obeid, Omdurman. They were still emotional, still afire with implication, still signalling absence, a disconnected continent represented by abstractions.

28

The Defence of the West

The phone was ringing but Thomas was damned if he was going to answer it. Instead he sat tight and looked at a small black cloud on the horizon that he could see through the window. He invested it, grimly playful, with dark forebodings. He imagined it expanding, blotting out the sky, raining radioactive debris, blowing out the windows.

He gripped the arms of the chair. Nothing would make him move at this moment, not even the telephone. He was totally involved in the attempt to paralyse himself, to take himself out of the action. He was old enough for it to be taken as a symptom of illness. It might even, quite reasonably, create sympathy. With a bit of luck, when they came they would ignore him and carry on their guerrilla wars, sniping over the Christmas table, the conversations peppered with shot, without involving him. He would have his Christmas dinner sat down, on his lap. They could treat him as though he were ill, it did not matter to him. He was giving up.

He stared at the cloud, willing it to expand, making it his final justification for total silence and inaction. There was nothing he could do about it. It was fate, disaster, death rolled into one. How could he be expected to respond to his brothers-in-law who all bore the same responsibility, the same weight, as himself? He could not bear the apologetics, the faint jokes about manhood, the men washing up in the kitchen while the women chattered over the relative merits of the presents they had given each other. He would take no part in it. They had all, in one way or another, failed.

It was not only the lack of earning power, although that was bad enough. There was something else. They had failed on a grander scale.

He staggered mentally even though he was encased in his chair. He put out a foot to support himself. He could not place quite what it was that had not been done. He still could not place it, even after all these years. It was as though there were, somewhere, an alternative group of men, alternative husbands, to whom they were being constantly compared and, inevitably, found wanting. These men were shadowy images, misty piratical figures with boundless and imperial confidence, stern authoritarian faces. They had smiles at the corners of their mouths as though they had certain and incontrovertible knowledge of the world and were used to acting on it. They were farcical, out of time, out of date. He was damned if he was going to answer the phone.

On the other hand, he was not entirely complacent about the passage of his own life. He was bewildered by it. It was full of knots, splices and frayed ends. Nothing ever came to a resolute conclusion. Episodes in his life merely petered out leaving new areas of uncertainty, new moods of disenchantment. He was looking for a strategy, a certain way of dramatizing his condition. It needed an ironic, if not tragic edge, a flourish, strong and imperative punctuation. For the moment he had opted for a minimal response, shrunk into his chair, his hands gripping his knees, his shoulders slumped, his eyes clouded over, the telephone ringing remorselessly in his ears.

He walked slowly past the laid table with its crackers, gleaming silver cutlery, red napkins and mats, all ready for the Christmas dinner. He had decided to answer the phone, to put the sound out of his mind. He could not remain for ever in his chair. It stopped ringing as soon as he put his hand out towards it. His hand hovered over it indecisively as though it might ring again in the next second.

He went back to his chair. There was nothing more to do. His wife was dressing, making up, making her peace with herself, constructing her defences into what would be a temporary whirl of gaiety, hugs and kisses, ohs and aahs. Everything was spotless, ready for inspection by the family, the result of more than a week's work. He had planted some early flowers outside that they could admire if it were not raining, he had arranged on the coffee table a few items from Africa, a few reminders, a drawing or two, as though it were work in progress. He had done this and that, quelling anxiety, hiding the presents from the year before that were untouched, still wrapped. He had polished the silver, mended the Christmas tree lights, wrapped the presents and labelled them with love and kisses. Now there was nothing more to do but wait.

Then, seemingly without an interval, they were all there, car doors slamming, Christmas smiles ready, all commenting on everyone else's gain or loss in weight, their agelessness, their appalling problems in dealing with England but, on the other hand, their inability to deal any longer with the cruel and unpredictable nature of the rest of the world.

En masse, they merged into a collective organism, shuffling themselves between table and chairs. The food went, the crackers were pulled it seemed almost before anyone had arrived. He was experiencing an acceleration of time. They were talking as if silence were death itself and their collective blood would fail to circulate if it were not lubricated by further words, squeals, exclamations and frivolous jokes. Again it seemed to him that if a silence did emerge then it would be murderous, pregnant with things unsaid. Silence would make them kill each other. He felt that is what they really wanted to do. All their resentments were played out, covered up within the family. It was the family that had failed. Unless the talk covered it, diverted it, they would fall upon each other, taking the nearest weapons, stabbing and murdering, each blaming the other for hurts, insults and wounds that, until that time, had remained hidden but for casual parting jests at the door about the breaking of family ties, the lack of letters, the need to meet again very soon.

He was sure they loved each other too. He turned awkwardly in the room unsure for a moment who all these people were, what his relationship was to them. He was talking to someone, looking intently at his face, but he had, just for the moment, forgotten who he was. Nevertheless he managed to answer, the words spilling out of his lips without his command or control. As he spoke he recognized the man whom he had found on the floor in the middle of the night grasping on to his sculpture. How could he have, even momentarily, forgotten. He was the fallen rider, covered in blood and apologies. He was a brother-in-law.

Thomas remembered, from a distant and past conversation, that he had something to do with the aiming of missiles. Did he work for the Americans? Or did he design the nose-cones of missiles, the sharp end? He could not remember. They were talking about terrorists and bombs in Kuwait. There was something about the printing presses of the Palestine Liberation Organization, he did not really catch it. They appeared to be talking about the threat of Islam to Western civilization. They appeared to be in agreement.

Trouble seemed to have followed him around. He arrived somewhere at the behest of mysterious employers. Soon afterwards there was a coup, a bomb outrage, or an assassination. Was this bad luck, or was he working for the CIA? The face in front of him was still full of squashed cuckolded apologies, a face carrying on a sensible family conversation under the impress of the family curse, the intimidation of the group of phantom husbands that oppressed them all. The strain of having a manly conversation was oppressing them both, the conversation was stuttering to a halt, they were drinking too much, they were thinking of other things. How could he possibly be involved in international conspiracies?

Violet was laughing and, at the same time, watching him. He caught her cold glance as she was bent almost double in a paroxysm of laughter at what was meant to be a shared joke with one of her sisters. He was aware of her glance but could not determine the nature of it. Was he doing something wrong? Perhaps he and his brother-in-law were talking too loudly. The others were watching, trying to divert them by talking more loudly themselves, perhaps in an attempt to drown them out, make them part of a more appropriate tone of conversation, to stop the possibility of a scene. They were still pulling crackers.

He could not think what was the matter. As far as he was concerned they were having a perfectly normal and reasonable conversation. What was it about? It was about America. It was about the Americans doing their damned coach tours of Europe, doing the sights, catching up with the culture they were missing at home. He found it bloody humorous that their idea of England still consisted of the Tower of London, the Beefeaters and other oddments of the tourist trade. He was not exactly angry, he was inquisitive, questioning. He was not insulting or aggressive, he was querying the sense of it.

He was especially demanding about the extraordinary fact of a British citizen touring his own country as though he were, for all the world, an American. How could this be? What mental blank could produce such a charade? All talk of cheap fares and coach tours passed him by. He could and would not understand. But, despite the incitement, he was quite calm, he was not angry, he was not attempting to cause any kind of problem. He merely thought that these visits, now deep in the past, were, if one thought about it at all, ridiculous, obviously ridiculous.

Everyone was acting as though they were about to have a fight, as though they had indeed already put up their fists, squared up, glared at each other and started to swing absurdly in the air. But none of that was happening. There they were, holding a reasonable conversation, in a reasonable English Christmas. It was a discourse entirely appropriate to the occasion. The lights were flickering on the Christmas tree. Perhaps one of the bulbs needed changing.

He swallowed heavily, too full of turkey and alcohol. He was watching the face of the man opposite him. It was sweating. It was flushed and red. He could see the blood vessels in his eyes, he could see the pupils contracting. He was confronting an angry man and he could not see why his partner in conversation should be undergoing these physiological changes. He, himself, a British citizen, was being entirely reasonable. He had done more than his fair share of the Christmas organization. Now he was going to say what he wanted. Any reasonable man would have done the same.

He swayed backwards just missing what appeared to be a blow aimed at his face. He could not entirely work out where this blow had come from. It appeared as a red blur passing his eyes. Somehow he had responded quickly enough not to allow it to hit him. Then there was a darker blur which he thought was his reply to the attack. It was, he thought, the blur of his jacket as his arm swung out. It was a response to this absurd and uncalled-for attack.

There did seem to be a mess on the floor. It was his plate. The one he had on his lap. His Christmas dinner. He bent down to pick it up, to have a go at clearing up the mess. There was a whole number of distant sounds, the clatter of cutlery, the breaking of plates and a high-pitched buzz of conversation which was not quite at the pitch of a scream, it was more at the level of a series of shouted orders. It came from some distance away. That was clear enough. It seemed to be coming from the sisters, who had clustered around them, their eyes wide with complicated, even ambiguous, expressions as if he were fighting for their honour, for their place in the world. But he might have got it wrong. Perhaps they were angry, perhaps they were offended. He could not tell.

He was at the centre of some kind of drama. Perhaps this was the resolution he was looking for. Maybe this was dramatic punctuation. Perhaps this was a turn, a twist, an ironic end. Perhaps it was the ironic end for which he was searching.

He was splashing his face in the bathroom. He was looking at himself in the mirror. Automatically he picked up his shaving brush and lathered his face. Then he shaved. He felt a great deal better and began to worry about how much he had had to drink. The events of the last few minutes, or maybe the last hour, seemed confused. It was all indistinct as though it had happened a long time ago, was regrettable but inevitable, part of the passage of life, the warp and weft of human nature. He shaved happily, enclosed in a temporary web of intuitions and vague philosophical justifications. But underneath there was a residue of anxiety, a tremor of distaste, a marginal feeling that he had somehow tipped over some invisible precipice, touched some raw nerve, dropped into deep waters where he was, for the moment, out of his depth. But these things never clarified themselves. He had noticed it before. They merely petered out.

He resented the American Empire. The Americans were always there before he was, taking all the prizes, queering the pitch, holding on to their contacts, keeping off the others. Wherever it was they kept their standard of living. Everywhere became an extension of America. The world was a network of air routes carrying thick steaks and bottles of Bourbon whisky to the deprived expatriates. He thought, with a whiff of irony, of the war, of good old Joe Stalin coming to Britain's rescue, his impassive and indecipherable face, his immovable eyes. He would have sorted them out. But then, strangely enough, considering the strength of resentment he had for them, he had never really been confronted with a problem with an American. They were always there in the background, always an object of resentment amongst his friends, but never in the foreground, never a direct obstacle. They were only a distant affront, operating indeterminate power in the background, getting up everybody's nose with their loud voices and hectoring manners. Perhaps the problem was that he felt as though he was inhabiting their universe, tolerated perhaps, but not quite in control of his own destiny, his own order of things. That made him, amongst other things, ill-at-ease, unsure of his place, irritable and somehow recalcitrant, throwing off offers of help or sympathy as though they would demean him, undermine his essential dignity. In any case, he did not need any help. He could deal with any financial problems. Nothing was as bad as it seemed. But he wished they had not spent quite so much on Christmas.

When he came back into the front room, freshly shaved, they were all sitting around with cups of tea on their laps and balancing plates with crumbled slices of iced Christmas cake. He sat down deep into his armchair. No one had taken that over in his absence. It was his centre. He could see the whole room from there without turning his head. No one was paying any attention to him. That was a relief!

One of them, whom at that moment he did not recognize,

was talking rather loudly, with a peculiar kind of anger. He knew the face and the way he leaned forward in an intense way staring into people's faces and then getting his gaze fixed elsewhere, at the bottom of a chair, the edge of a table, somewhere like that, so that his audience were disconcerted, wondering why he was addressing this inconsequential detail with such intensity.

At the moment he did not want to hear any angry talk so he closed his eyes diplomatically, pretending to have an after-dinner snooze, his arms placed neatly on the arms of his chair. The voice irritated him. It used unfamiliar words and had an unpleasant air of certainty about it as though the author were not subject to doubt and uncertainty, worry and pain. The words came out of a boundless but somehow limited confidence. They came only from anger, a mysterious and deep-seated bitterness. That was what he thought about it.

Out of the corner of his eye he could see the distant black cloud through the window. It had not moved. It was poised over the horizon as though it had been nailed to the sky, a permanent fixture. He closed his eyes again and tried not to listen to the voice from the other side of the room. He looked at the red glow behind his eyelids. Shadows flickered over it, mysterious bar lines and passages of print as though there was a book attempting to emerge surreptitiously behind his closed eyes, an after-image. He could not read any of it. None of it would stay in focus. The voice went on without answer or contradiction as though the audience for this exercise in jejune knowingness was either cowed or embarrassed into silence.

The voice faded as he became lost in his own thoughts. They scurried through his head like wind-blown clouds racing from horizon to horizon, casting shadows, bringing sun and rain, populating the imaginary sky inside his head. Then they evaporated, boiled away, leaving a blank blue space in which black kites wheeled, their wings fixed. He could hear their distant cries and feel the heat beating on his head.

'This family is tied up with guilt, don't you see that? I have the guilt of my parents. It's no good to me. There is nothing I can do with it. It is not my guilt. It does not appertain to me, it is not part of me. It's a bloody lemon.'

Another voice spoke. A woman.

'I really don't see what you mean. I don't see why you are saying it now.'

'Guilt is like having lost something. A penknife . . . You don't really know what it is, you only know that something has gone and in some way you were responsible for it. Because you can't sort it out, you can't identify it, you pass on the responsibility to someone else by induction, you induce guilt in your closest family. They don't know what is going on either. But they are nevertheless resentful. Why are they feeling like this? What are they guilty and apprehensive about? It pursues them through their lives. They dream about it, they think they have perpetrated a crime, they are consumed with anxiety. They resent the rest of the family, they stop seeing them, they lose touch. They remain incapable of deciphering what it is that has gone wrong. Really nothing whatever has gone wrong. They are just ignoring their own history, thinking the world is their family, that there are no other motives, no other desires, no other drives apart from what has been inherited, what has been induced out of incomprehension. If all of you thought for a moment what you could have done, if you were not enmeshed in family plots, family conspiracies, family intentions, family mysteries, family motives, all of which are inexplicit and indecipherable. If you had thought what you want to do, what your skills are, where your desires lie, then . . . it would be different. There would not be fights.'

Another voice.

'Why would it be different? I can't see how it would be different! I don't think you understand a thing of what we have had to put up with. You are living in a different age. We need to defend ourselves against our enemies, not yours.'

He woke some time later, erasing the desert from inside his head, and realized that he had not recognized his son, his characteristic tone of voice. It was some time since he had seen him. It had probably been him on the phone a long time ago before all the guests had come.

29
Theft

Violet sat still, leant forward in her red chair. She looked out at the dark room in front of her, listening intently. She was wearing a pink dressing-gown and blue fluffy slippers, costumed for midnight confrontations, panics and escapades. She had thought of getting dressed properly in her outdoor clothes, but had decided against it. It was the middle of the night, time had passed, and it seemed no longer appropriate. She was immersed deeply in the dim yellow glow from the gilt lamp in the corner and the deep blue-black midwinter night edged in white that she could see through the drawn curtains. Her fingers moved slightly, agitated, as though under the influence of a dream. But she was not dreaming, she was wide awake, every sense stretched and tensed. She was waiting for the slightest noise, the tremble and stir of a dead leaf outside, the lost notes of a midnight bird, the crack of a contracting floorboard somewhere in the huge crumbling house that she could feel intensely around her, the overwhelming psychic weight of glimpsed empty cold rooms, broken hinges and splintered doors. If she heard even the slightest sound she leant forward a fraction as if to move closer to it, check its direction and origin. If there was nothing, she leant back, also fractionally, ready for the next stir, the next symptom of the frost eating into the stonework, the crack of ice expanding in the fissures of the yew trees outside, the distant sound of a stranger's car rasping along the icy road over the hill beyond the silted-up and frozen lake. It was what she was waiting for. She did not want anything unexpected. She had something to do that required the absence of the unexpected.

Thomas was sleeping, as he always was these days and nights, fighting his own wars, on his own, in dreams. Sometimes she heard him grunt. There was an unwashed tea-cup and saucer on the draining board. She had left it there earlier when she had been sitting in the kitchen, making up her mind. She was not going to wash it up now although in some ways she wanted to move, go out into the kitchen, make a loud noise in the sink and get it out of the way, and then go to bed. Destroy the silence. She did not like leaving washing-up. She did not like listening so intently. It made her feel cold and alone.

The black Alsatian dog that was tied up to the front door had been silent for hours. It was either asleep or frozen to death. They wanted them out, the new landowners. Violet agreed with them, she wanted to go. There was intimidation with dogs and noise and bad temper and unreasonable behaviour. Everyone else had left because their roof leaked or the floorboards were rotten and dangerous, or, mostly, because the new landlords were unbalanced. They were left. Why could not she leave as well? No one could tell what would happen next. The old man had been eccentric but, in terms of personal relations, fairly sane. He had died suddenly leaving the land to his sons. It had created an immediate and then a developing crisis. The sons had left the cows to starve in the fields until their ribs stuck out as though it were Africa in a famine year or a drought. The cows dropped in the fields and were hauled away by tractor, a heap of bones. The sons were not farmers. They only knew how to spend money, crash fast and expensive cars and fight amongst themselves. In addition, they were in league with criminals. She knew it! They wanted to sell the house and the land and split the money between them. Of course they did, money was money! The tenants had to get out, whoever they were. The dog stopped them using the front door, that was the point. It barked and barked most of the day because the owners did not always bother to give it food. That was the way of it! Violet wanted to go but Thomas had, at last and too late, found something irreconcilable in his nature. He was not going to go at the behest of manifestly unstable and irregular thieves. They were going to sit it out. Violet shivered suddenly as if she had been struck by a cold draught, a premonition. She leant back and wrapped her dressing-gown closer round her body and retied the cord. There was something defiant about her movements.

She crept towards the window in front of her in an exaggerated manner, quietly, as though she did not want to be heard by anyone; she crept as if she were playing a game which involved suspicion and intrigue, a burglary, a theft, a torrent of crimes. But when she opened the window and slipped out, leg out over the window sill, all pretence was bitten away by the icy cold. It ate into her skin, made her shut her eyes. There was a drone overhead. It was one of the heavily loaded cargo planes that she had heard overhead since the Falklands war. It had come every night since she could remember, a reminder of that belated revenge for the humiliation of Suez. It had come night after night as though the revenge itself were not enough, it had to be repeated in bass notes night after night everlastingly. She closed the window after her thinking to preserve the relative warmth inside.

She turned and looked away briefly from the house, down into the valley, to check that there was no one there, nothing stirring. Then she crunched across the gravel to her destination, her bony shoulders hunched in her dressing-gown. She walked as though she had made this trip before, as though it were a routine, almost a habit. Her blue fluffy slippers flapped away into the dark shadow of outbuildings. The drone of the passing plane faded to a distant throb. There was the distant metallic sound of a turning lock. Then a door scraping open.

Violet emerged out of the darkness in a hurry, as though she might be discovered. She was clutching a glittering object, a candlestick moulded with cherubs from which emerged fluted uprights. She put it on the window sill and with great care opened the window, making sure not to make any noise. She climbed in, retrieved the candlestick, and closed the window after her.

She placed the candlestick under the light and sat back in her chair to look at it. It glistened and took up the golden hue of the lampshade and its gilt stand. The cold air had made her eyes water. She half-closed them. The candlestick became a rich blur of light behind her lids. She looked at it with pleasure. For a few minutes she went into a warm trance, a half-sleep, giving herself time to get the chill out of her bones. Then she became alert, leaning forward, listening intently, a sparkle in her eye.

A deeper silence had fallen over the house. The cold had frozen all movement. The sound of the window opening was sharp. It echoed off the resonant surfaces of iced trees and vanished away towards the lake where it boomed over the tensioned frozen surface causing a minute crack where the roots of a tree went under the surface.

Violet knew the outbuilding in detail. She could move around it in the dark without knocking anything over, without causing an unnecessary sound. She knew the rough packing cases and tea chests where it had all been stored and hidden away. She could do nothing about the furniture. It was too heavy for her to lift. But she had cleared almost all the more portable items, the costume jewellery, the silver, the cameos. They were now all stored away in cupboards, wardrobes in the bedroom, even drawers in the kitchen. No one would know about it except when the thieves came to collect their goods. Then it would be too late. They could hardly go to the police.

The outbuilding was damp and smelt of moss. Amongst the loot there were rolls of wire netting, sheets of corrugated iron, boxes of rusting nails; the bits and pieces that were once needed for the estate farm that was now long fallen into disrepair and dissolution. She had found the key to the padlocked door by accident. It must have been a duplicate that had been dropped some time in the past. She had tried it one day, on a whim rather than with a conscious attempt to break in. It worked. From then on the outbuilding had become her night playground, a dimly-lit toy house full of treasure, an insomniac's palace. There was, adding up the pleasures, the private pleasure of an adult wilfulness, knowing that she was stealing from the thieves, taking the object of their greed and making it hers, secretly. Things had been taken from her. She was taking them back. It was a simple reorganization of loss and gain in the continuing and obsessional audit of her life. Somehow the process had become abstracted from reality. Her audit was an audit of memory, of crushed desires and sullied aspirations. She had been driven by an obscure resentment and had acted on it, without thinking. Each hidden object had become a fulfilment in itself, a replacement for something lost in the past. But she had forgotten exactly what it was she had lost. Maybe it was her son, wherever he was, perhaps it was the man she thought she had married. Again, it might have been herself she had lost, her own idea of herself, rightly and suitably confirmed by the world.

She felt around in the bottom of a tea chest. There was a wooden box. It had, she could just see, an inlaid gold plate that was covered in ornate engraving. She lifted it out. It was a box of cutlery, a wedding present to someone in the distant past. It was untouched, glistening. It was also heavy. She staggered out into the night, put it down for a moment, and locked the padlock after her. Then she picked it up again. It would be the last object she could take. Her slippers flapped back towards the house. The lights of a car momentarily lit the tops of the trees around the house.

She settled down with the box on her lap. She removed three place settings and put them on the floor next to her. She closed the box, took it out the back, and hid it away. Then, carefully, she laid the table, with napkins folded and the complete set of gold plated knives, forks and spoons glowing on the white tablecloth. She sat back in her chair and surveyed it all.

Perhaps because of relief, perhaps because she was tired, Violet dropped off to sleep, her attention lapsing. She did not hear the sound of people moving outside, the application of car hand-brakes, whispered voices, the sudden red blink of brake lights through the window. She ignored the tapping on

214

the window for some time until it became so insistent that her muddled dream thoughts could make no sense of it. She woke.

There was a figure outside, his face peering through the glass. It was a uniformed policeman. She wandered over to the window and, still half-asleep, opened it wide. She was used to letting in visitors through the window since the front door had been made unusable by the dog. She had no thought of danger or apprehension. He was tapping on the window wanting to come in. She had every faith in the police.

'We saw your light,' he said in a stage whisper, 'sorry to disturb you. We have an operation under way a few yards away. There is no need to be alarmed.'

'I wasn't,' said Violet. 'Don't stand around out there, come in, it's cold!'

He clambered in and stood holding his helmet, embarrassed by her dressing-gown and the peculiar awkwardness of climbing in through the window.

'We thought you should be informed,' he said looking around the room, 'we are recovering stolen goods. We did not want you to be alarmed at the noise.'

'I didn't hear a thing,' said Violet.

'Well done,' said the policeman as though deafness or sleep was a virtue. 'I think it would be best if you kept your curtains closed.'

'We don't usually have people outside at this time of night.'

'Of course not.'

She was beginning to stiffen, feeling that she was looking shifty.

'You are the only tenants left in the house?' he asked, still looking around the room with an investigative air.

'Yes,' she said, 'yes.'

'The . . . the . . . ' he was hesitating, 'the wire horses in the old library?'

'Those . . . oh, that's my husband. He's an artist.'

'I see . . . I see.' The policeman seemed to be hugely relieved as if the presence of an artist explained everything. 'And he will be asleep.'

'Yes, he's asleep. He's always asleep. I don't sleep these days.'

'Insomnia?' said the policeman with a fine attempt at sympathy, looking at the perfectly laid table out of the corner of his eye, putting it down to feminine hyperactivity.

'I suppose so.'

He climbed back out of the window.

'Close the curtains.'

She did so automatically having been told to do it. She sank with relief back into her chair. How could he not have seen the candlestick and the cutlery? Was he blind! But they could be perfectly legal objects to have around the home. People did have candlesticks and cutlery. If they had the money for that kind of object. She realized that she did not even like or want most of the things she had taken. They had only metaphorical value. They were compensation.

She stayed up and heard the arrival and departure of more vehicles. Then they went away. Presumably they had got what they wanted.

She smelt a strange smell and after some internal confusion she realized that in the tension of the moment she had broken wind. She felt alarmed that even the smell of her own body was no longer familiar to her. Even her own body had been stolen from her. What would she have to steal to get it back?

30
Optimism of the Will

Michael picked the apple out of the brown-paper bag and bit fiercely into it. It had been outside the shop on a stall, out in the frost. The juice had been frozen, concentrated into ice, waiting for him. It melted in his mouth and throat. Its taste flooded through him like the icy anaesthetic of an injection. It set off, without warning, the immediate conviction that he had lost control and was disappearing into unconsciousness, perhaps not to return. He put the bitten apple back into the bag and twisted the paper at the top so he could not see inside. The bag uncrinkled itself on the passenger seat next to him. The taste turned from sweet to bitter as it trickled through his mouth.

He absorbed himself, as he was driving, into a fictitious landscape, an occupied zone of arbitrary powers, denials and affirmations; his own forbidden territory. There were half-remembered, bare frost-whitened fields that extended off the road into shallow wooded hills and then up into a cold grey sky. Wire fences divided the fields. Along the road, from time to time, he passed red-lettered notices threatening prosecution. He passed them, driving too fast to read the smaller lettering underneath. The road wound in front of him, diving into dark wooded tunnels with high banks and streams running along the edge of the road. The tyres crunched in the wet gravel where springs had uprooted the tarmac.

He stopped at a turning where a muddy track led up to the rounded tree-topped hills of the Downs. He slammed the car door and started up the hill with a wild look in his eye, interrogating every detail around him as if his life depended on it. He was searching for familiarities, correspondences, connections. He was looking for a particular tree, an old tree that was hollowed out inside. It was where, if he remembered correctly, he had accidentally dropped a penknife deep into its dark centre, so far as to be irrecoverable. It had fallen out of his cold numb fingers when he was alone, guilty and afraid.

He walked up and down the path several times failing to distinguish the right tree from a multitude of possibilities. The tangled mess of 'old man's beard' was familiar enough, the delves and copses were in the right places, even the ploughed earth strewn with flints on the other side of the path was identical to his memory of it. The tree he was looking for had vanished. It had left no trace, no fallen trunk, no rotted carcass, no pile of wet fungal branches, not even a decaying decapitated stump. It had been erased, as he had, from the landscape. Nevertheless he persisted, mistrusting his memory, approaching his quest as though he were searching for an unexploded mine that would obliterate him instantly if he did not find it first.

He tried to retrace his path down the hill but lost all sense of direction and had to stumble across a field picking up sticky cold mud on his shoes and trousers. He stood at the bottom of the path, looking up at the hill, defeated.

He sat in the car, running the engine and heater, attempting to dry out and come to his senses. He had come, he thought, out of mild curiosity. If he had found the tree easily he would have been able to leave it at that, it would have been a casual visit and he would have forgotten about it instantly. It had suddenly become more serious.

Then he was overcome with laughter. The idea of an adult hunting for a penknife lost years ago when he was a child struck him as immensely comic. It was a hopeless attempt to retrieve other times, other panics, other landscapes, other fears. It was not to be. The tree had been eradicated by time. It was not to be disinterred. He could not get it back. It was gone.

He opened the paper bag and took another bite out of the apple. It was sour and floury. The frost had gone; the icy taste of the apple had melted away. He threw it out of the window and watched it bounce for a moment over the cold ploughed earth in the field. He was back as a passing motorist, someone who had stopped casually to break the monotony of the drive, to look at the winter scenery just for a moment, before continuing the rest of his life.

He drove away without looking back.

Several times he lost his way and found himself off his route in narrow roads that led nowhere or up to a farm building. He was finding it difficult to concentrate on the road. It was not that he was tired or liable to go off to sleep but his consciousness veered from one subject to the other. He incorporated what was in front of him into that vision and so failed to recognize it. He had a few narrow escapes so stopped by the roadside and closed his eyes to let his consciousness have its way without putting his life at risk. He was on the way back to his wife and family, a motorist like thousands of others, coinciding with the expectations of others, being on time, in the right place, a familiar outline to others if not to himself.

He was out of equilibrium, volatile, subject to chance rather than force of habit. He was waiting for something to happen to him, out of the blue, unconnected with his own history or memory, something that would disturb the gentle and inevitable fall of atoms, the legislations of fate. That was essential. He was exhausted by the momentum of his efforts at recollection; it had turned him into another being, someone he did not recognize. He was no longer part of his own fiction. He had stretched away from himself so far that he had parted almost physically with his own substance and inheritance. He wanted dreams and passion, turbulence and re-enchantment. He felt there was no place for him. The car was rocked by the wind from passing lorries. He fell asleep.

He dreamed an exact, instant and vivid dream. It came upon him immediately as though it had been lying in wait until he had slipped out of consciousness.

He was driving another car down a muddy path that was full of puddles and the deep ruts of tractor wheels. The bonnet of the car, an old scratched white Mercedes, became loose; it unlatched and bounced up and down in front of him so it was increasingly difficult to see where he was going. The path led into a wood of young willow trees where the light was hazy and dull, the sun hidden behind uniformly grey cloud. He stopped the car being unable to go on with the bonnet in front of him. He could not see ahead. He walked into the wood and left the car behind.

In a clearing in the wood was a gnarled tree, an old mulberry, that was twisted into bent shapes, branches like old arms reaching out over a patch of churned-up mud underneath. Round the tree were children, dressed in thick linen clothes, their faces muffled so they were anonymous, almost heraldic shapes. They were dancing a clumsy dance, stirring up the mud under their feet. Overlooking them were two old faces, their thin scrawny necks stretched towards the children, their eyes glistening with hope and parental aspiration. As he watched they turned their eyes towards him briefly and then back towards the children. The dance continued in silence with no music, the air hazy with catkins and floating pollen.

He woke with rain battering on the roof of the car wiping the white frost off the margins of the road. He watched it streaming over the car window distorting the world outside into liquid streaming shapes, cold slipping colours. He drove off into it, the windscreen wipers splashing.

By the side of the road he could see two soaked figures in leather jackets trying to hitch a lift. He stopped and they bundled into the back of the car, hair dye streaming down their faces, blue rivulets on the boy's face, red on the girl's. They settled into the back seat swearing quietly to each other. He passed back a box of paper handkerchiefs. They mopped each other filling the back of the car with soaked and multicoloured wedges of paper. Then they stared out of the windows as if the world moving outside had been transformed by their new position in it and had become an object of intense curiosity.

'Going somewhere?' said the boy.

'Where do you want to go?' he said.

'That's okay!' said the boy replying to an answer he had not had. 'Bloody raining, isn't it!'

They all settled into a period of intense silence juggling potential objects of conversation without much hope of success.

'Good car this!' said the boy, in a moment of activity, bouncing up and down on the seat. The girl gave him a withering glance and he shut up immediately, hanging his head in mock apology and then staring gloomily out of the window.

'I lost my penknife,' said Michael, 'so I came down to try and find it.'

The two in the back looked at each other suddenly alert, exchanging glances of joyful recognition at having found an unashamedly crazed adult.

'Penknife?' said the boy hopefully, thinking he might have misheard and that it might have been something less open to satirical comment.

'Yes. I couldn't find it. The tree that I dropped it in had vanished.'

'Vanishing tree!' said the boy unable to believe his luck. A penknife and a vanishing tree!

'It was years ago. When I was younger than you.'

'Years ago!' answered the boy savouring the absurdity of it all. ' "Younger than you?" ' He stared at the girl with an expression of exaggerated disbelief. She twisted her lips in disgust.

'Bugger me!' said the boy. 'That's it then.'

'That's it! I thought you'd like that.'

There was an immediate silence as the boy recognized from a multitude of similar conversations at school and at home that the stakes were now being raised, suddenly, as they always were and to his disadvantage. The girl curled up in the seat with an expression of exaggerated disdain, ignoring them both, putting up all the defences she could muster.

'That's it then,' said the boy gloomily seeing a possible area of entertainment vanish. He looked out of the window again, ignoring the surreptitious warning kicks the girl was giving him out of sight of the driving mirror.

'Schoolteacher then?' said the boy, testing out his worst

fears while still looking out of the window at the rain with an expression of unrelieved depression.

'No.'

'Fucking social worker!' said the boy with conviction.

'No.' The boy ran out of possible careers and worked his face up into an expression of mock and grotesque agony which he then directed at the driving mirror. He pulled his ears out and waggled them in the direction of the driver.

'I'm not a fucking social worker. I'm out of work.'

'That's it then!'

'No it isn't. That's just the beginning.'

'Oh.' The boy settled down to ignore what was going to come next. He had done enough hitching to know when the driver was about to exploit a temporary audience.

'Very interesting,' said the boy hoping to pre-empt whatever irrelevancies might come next by responding in advance. But there was silence from the front seat.

The radio was switched on. It was a Brahms quartet. Both of them shrank low in their seats to dodge the dose of cultural intimidation. They had a go at faking sleep but in the end they opted for the well-rehearsed fascinated stare out of the window, a stare so intense that it could not be interrupted. It was directed at passing hedgerows, lorries, corner shops, cows in fields, hoardings and country houses, all with a fine lack of discrimination.

But when the radio was suddenly switched off their heads snapped to attention to be ready, defences up, for the next sally against their dignity and understanding of the world.

'I think,' said Michael, ignoring the silently mimed and satirical conversation he could see in the mirror, 'that the English act like slaves.'

'Don't you know,' said the boy taking off his accent.

'Spartacus!' said the girl, unexpectedly.

'Not Spartacus!' said Michael. 'He led a revolt.'

'Oh sod!' said the girl as though she were taking part in a quiz and had got the wrong answer. She lit a cigarette as if to concentrate more deeply on the next question.

'I mean,' said Michael, 'that we are the last colony. The English colonize themselves.'

'Lord Mountbatten,' said the girl with bravado.

'No!'

'Oh sod! Try again!'

'The whole point of British politics since the war has been to keep up the imperial façade, including the international status of the pound.'

'Princess Margaret!' said the girl.

'Winston Churchill,' said the boy out of some mysterious depths.

'The colonies have gone, so there are only the English people left to exploit.'

'Elephants, no, baboons,' said the boy bouncing up and down, scratching under his arms.

'Niggers!' said the girl.

'An English people who think blacks are still servants and have no rights of their own.'

'It was niggers, I was right!' said the girl, triumphantly.

'Don't you say that,' said the boy, 'my father's black!'

'You've never seen him!'

'Doesn't matter. Don't say it!'

'All right, who cares?'

'I do!'

'Next question! Come on, next question. What was so great about this penknife. The one that you lost?' She asked with genuine curiosity.

'I was guilty about it.'

'Oh that! You said it was ages ago.'

'That made it worse.'

'Why?'

'Don't know.' Michael did not know.

'Next question.'

The boy was tapping on the car window as if he were trying to attract the attention of the outside world. It had stopped raining.

'Here we are,' he said, 'this is it!'

The car stopped and they scrambled out. Michael could see

223

them disappearing in the mirror as he drove away. She was bending down waggling her bum at him and laughing over her shoulder. The boy was watching her disapprovingly and as they vanished in the distance they were starting to argue, pushing each other this way and that in the middle of the road.

Children.